An American in Search of God

A Parable for Our Times

Other books by
ABIE ALEXANDER

CHASING THE WIND
SOMETIMES WHEN WE MEET
MEMORIES AND MIRAGES
THE MIGRANT AND THE MAVERICK
FOR THE LOVE OF ARMINE
OF MINGLED YARN

An American in Search of God

A Parable for Our Times

Abie Alexander

AA BOOKS

First published 2007 Infinity Publishing, PA, USA

AA Books ISBNs

Print	978-1-946593-38-2
EPUB	978-1-946593-00-9
AZW3	978-1-946593-01-6
MOBI	978-1-946593-02-3
PDF	978-1-946593-03-0

Published in the United States of America

This is a work of fiction. The characters, incidents, and locations described in this work (other than references to historical persons and events or actual places) are the products of the author's imagination and any resemblance to persons, living or dead, or real events or places is purely coincidental.

The opinions expressed by the characters of this work of fiction are not necessarily that of the author.

AA
BOOKS

7919 Mandan Road #103
Greenbelt, Maryland. USA 20770-2828
+1 (301) 335-5632
aa-books@outlook.com
www.abiealexander.com

To loved ones who have gone on before:

father, precise and logical;

mother, affectionate and generous;

and my wife who was all the world to me.

Contents

Chapter 1: Epiphany in the Skies

The epiphany came to John in the skies over Bangkok.

As the Boeing 747 lazily banked to the left, coming in for the landing, and the porthole fleetingly switched from the azure sky to the green paddy fields, John knew—just knew—that this trip was somehow going to change his life.

But scarce could he have surmised then, just how much.

Bangkok's Don Muang airport was much like any other international airport, with glittering duty-free shops and passengers of all hues milling about. The one jarring note, John realized soon enough, was the recurring leitmotif of gerontophilia—cherubic young Thai women, outlandishly dressed by oriental standards, clinging to the arms of wizened old Caucasian men old enough to be their fathers, if not grandfathers. "But then," he told himself, "decadence has always been passé in Bangkok." The Japanese seemed more discreet and circumspect; none of them seemed to have a hanger-on.

"Am I headed for a life of dissipation as the quintessential degenerate expatriate?" he wondered.

"No, that would be far too easy. And to what purpose?"

John again felt within him a strangely indubitable intuition that his life was going to be irrevocably altered in ways he could not then imagine possible.

Immigration was a breeze and he was soon at the curb waiting for the quaintly named 'taxi meter' to take him to the other airport. As the taxi driver spoke no English, John was left to his own devices reminiscing about the instant messaging chats that he had had with Mah Step over the Internet. It had been a little over six months since they had first bumped into each other in an Internet chat room discussion on comparative religion. After quickly exchanging email addresses they had moved out of the chat room to one-on-one instant messaging. From then on, they had kept in constant contact by emails almost daily and instant messaging on weekends. There was hardly a day that they had not been in touch with each other. The precarious dial-up connection at Mah Step's end limited their mode of exchange to the keyboard and not to the webcam or the microphone.

What initially sparked John's curiosity was Mah Step's comment that he belonged to an indigenously monotheistic tribe based not too far from Thailand. This was rather unique in a vast spread of polytheistic communities that spread across Southeast Asia and over into South Asia. Mah Step had gone on to state that his tribe had whole-heartedly embraced Christianity over a hundred and fifty years ago and was now predominantly Christian.

John soon learned that '*Mah'* was an honorific prefix that was invariably used for all men of the Sakhi tribe ("Much like the Japanese suffix *san* except in the Sakhi custom this was a prefix. And '*Ni'* was the prefix for women," Mah Step had explained.) and Step meant 'dawn' because he was born early in the morning just after daybreak.

In their exchanges, Mah Step had come across as an earnest and friendly person who seemed to think rationally and logically. John was constantly surprised by Mah Step's erudition and eclectic knowledge. In a single session, he had mentioned the story of Kekule's discovery of the molecular structure of benzene ("a snake biting its own tail"), Bertrand Russell's view of work and happiness and Noam Chomsky's theory of linguistics. John's amazement at Mah Step's grasp of so wide a range of subjects increased when he learned that the musty government library Mah Step had access to, was a far cry from the superbly maintained county library that he took so much for granted. If Mah Step had membership access to the library that he frequented in Greenbelt, Maryland, John thought, 'the walking encyclopedia' would have won *Jeopardy* hands down. But Mah step had only heard of—never seen—that TV show. He was more familiar with the BBC's *Brain of Britain.*

But the biggest surprise was Mah Step's mastery of the English language and the range of his vocabulary. He had a precision and exactness of expression that outshone a native speaker. This level of linguistic dexterity in a person who lived in a distant corner of the world where English was not spoken was quite astounding, to say the least. Curiously Joseph Conrad came to mind often in those early chats and John wasn't at all surprised to discover that *Lord Jim* was indeed one of Mah Step's favorite books.

In their online chats, Mah Step had consistently displayed the knack of coming up with the mot juste. "You know more words than I do!" John had exclaimed when Mah Step had shot back the meanings of the difficult words that John had thrown at him; *berceuse, consanguinity, limn, lugubrious, keloid, serigraph* ... he knew them all. The words on John's list were from a book he was reading then. He meant to look them up in a dictionary later but out of curiosity had popped them to Mah Step.

"I will be comparing your answers with the dictionary," John had playfully warned when the rapid-fire responses came back as soon as John had typed the words.

"I believe you will find all my meanings correct," Mah Step had affirmed modestly.

"I have no doubt I will. You must be getting them all correct on Reader's Digest's 'Word Power' then?"

"I haven't got any wrong in a long while. I think they have lowered the bar a little bit in recent years."

"Well ... I am truly surprised that your vocabulary is far superior to mine even though you are not from an English-speaking nation."

"My accent will probably compensate for that," was Mah Step's self-deprecating reply. "But to find that out you will need to come over for a visit!" Mah Step had added.

John's credulity took another beating when he discovered in a later chat that Mah Step was a practicing Christian with deep personal convictions and was not just a nominal Christian. Considering the fact that Mah Step lived so far removed from so-called civilization in a remote, inaccessible corner of a third-world country, that most Bible-thumping right-wingers from the heartland would label 'heathen' without missing a heartbeat, this was as incongruous as finding a dhoti-clad half-naked Asian at a Presidential reception in the White House. But to be fair to Mah Step, he never pushed his religion. His quiet faith seemed to John far closer to the true Christianity that the West had apparently meandered away from. Many were the chat sessions devoted to comparing notes on religion and to discussing diverse subjects and personalities: Kennedy and King; Thoreau and Emerson; Salinger and Fitzgerald; C. S. Lewis and Spurgeon; Pauling and Feynman; Donne and Larkin; and many others besides. It was in the middle of one of these sessions that Mah Step had come up with another bombshell.

"My tribe's traditional religion is the closest natural religion I know to Christianity. By natural I mean it is not a derivative of Christianity. There was so much pre-existing congruence of values that it was almost a logical transition for us to accept the Christianity of the Bible with open arms when the Welsh missionaries brought it to our land."

John found it so extremely curious that there would be such an indigenous religion that he just had to come and see it for himself. The best time for a long trip was between jobs and providentially his new boss was a tad too obnoxious, as bosses go, with a fake heartiness and a plastic smile that did not completely cover his meanness and manipulative inequity. What made it even more galling was that John himself had been a candidate for the position and there was not a day that had passed without John thinking how much better a job he could have done. If the honorable thing was to put in his papers, the leap of faith was to see this as perfect timing for a two-month break to go live with Mah Step's Sakhi tribe on the other side of the globe.

"You can live like a king here on five dollars a day," Mah Step had tempted him.

If that were true, the expenses for eight weeks plus the round-trip airfare would be less than the separation package he was due. The decision to travel was, therefore, quick and uncomplicated.

"An absolute no-brainer, if ever there was one!" he said to himself.

And here he was now just one short flight away from meeting Mah Step and his tribe for the very first time.

"What if your friend is nothing like what he says he is? It could be some kind of a trap. Next thing you know you could be an American hostage being held for a million-dollar ransom!" said Elaine shaking her beautiful blonde head over lunch at the Thunder Grill at Union Station.

"Oh, you get to know a person quite well after six months of emails and chats. We discussed almost everything under the sun. I have no doubt at all that he is what he presents himself to be," John replied.

Elaine still had her doubts. They had broken up nearly two years ago. John's idealism, utilitarianism, and an almost ascetic approach to life had finally got on her nerves. The parting was amicable. John was disappointed with the break but relieved to have all of his time to himself again. He resolved not to entertain any thoughts of romance till he attained his life's goal, though what *that* was he did not have the faintest idea then.

The domestic flight was an entirely different experience from the international flights that had brought him to Bangkok. At the check-in counter, he was the lone alien in a crowd of natives. Davie's poem 'Hearing Russian Spoken' came to mind as he listened to the gaggle of unintelligible voices, as did Prynne's poem 'Airport'. The flight was mercifully short. "Straight out of Graham Greene," he thought as he walked on the sizzling tarmac in the burning sun to the terminal and saw an armed guard in khaki uniform atop a rusted aircraft ladder that served as a makeshift watchtower, partly hidden in the tall, wild grass.

The immigration took forever. At least three officials probed him about the purpose of his visit. All of them seemed extremely suspicious of his intentions. Finally, they stamped his passport and let him out on the condition that he report to the 'foreigner's tribunal' (whatever that was!) once a month.

He was the last to exit the terminal into the sea of people restrained by metal barricades. On seeing a white-skinned foreigner shouts of "Taxi!" and "Hotel!" rang out and they jostled each other to grab a rich, generous and, hopefully, gullible prey.

"A bit like being thrown to the wolves," thought John as he gazed at the restive and noisy crowd.

'Where is Mah Step?' wondered John as he looked around at the sea of faces searching for his friend.

There was a light tap on his arm and as he turned to his left he saw a smiling Mah Step.

"Dr. Livingstone, I presume?" asked Mah Step.

"Then you must be Sir Henry Morton Stanley," countered John with a smile of relief.

"That's a reversal of roles!" laughed Mah Step.

John joined in. The easy laughter broke the ice, and each sized the other up.

"Pleased to meet you, Mah John," said Mah Step.

"Very pleased to meet you, Mah Step. You know, I've wanted to meet you for a long time now."

John wondered if he should give Mah Step a hug but decided against it and settled for a more formal handshake. According to oriental traditions, even a handshake was taboo in some societies, remembered John.

"Let me carry one of the bags," Mah Step offered and despite John's protestations the heavier bag quickly changed hands.

"You don't look very different from your picture," said Mah Step.

"I wouldn't have recognized you, though. In the scanned passport photo that you sent, you looked more like an axe-murderer," joked John.

Mah Step only laughed, pushing the bridge of his spectacles with his left index finger, a trademark gesture that John would see very often in the next eight weeks.

"But seriously, you look much younger than I expected. Had I not known I wouldn't have guessed you were a day above thirty," John said.

"Thanks," said Mah Step, "It is probably an Asian trait. I'm forty-two, remember?"

"Yes, of course. And I'm three years older than you," said John.

They were both in good shape physically. Mah Step looked strong and athletic with not an ounce of fat on his body. His close-cropped hair gave him an air of severity that tinged his demeanor of quiet assurance and self-respect. His eyes, bright and intelligent, looked out from behind the steel-rimmed glasses with expectancy and curiosity.

John's daily early morning jogs had kept him in good shape too. But he was lankier and, at six foot two, about five inches taller than Mah Step. He had the look of a philosopher and thinker and gave the impression of looking at the world from the outside. His L.L. Bean corduroy trousers, Adirondack jacket, and hiking shoes contrasted with Mah Step's polished black leather shoes, black trousers, and white full-sleeved shirt. And, of course, Mah Step's hair was jet black while John's wavy blond hair had streaks of gray.

"Is it going to be a long walk from here?" John asked. The sun was blindingly bright and the heat searing. The cacophony of people yelling and screaming added to John's disorientation.

"No, I have reserved a full taxi for us," Mah Step offered.

"What do you mean "full taxi"?" John asked.

"Taxis here are expensive by our standards. Instead of taking a taxi just for oneself, it is the practice to share it with others going in the same direction and split the fare as well," Mah Step explained.

"Oh, I see! I wouldn't have minded sharing a taxi actually."

"The wait can be long till there are enough passengers. After your long trans-continental journey, I thought it might be good to get home fast. Moreover, it is almost a four-hour drive from here. And I'd like us to get home before it is dark."

"OK! That makes sense! I need to catch up on my sleep after we get home. I'm sure glad you are here," John said as they pushed their way to the parking lot where cars were parked in random disarray. Their taxi was almost at the very end.

"I'll get the driver to open the boot for us," Mah Step said when they got close to what appeared to be a black post-war British car.

"You mean the trunk?" John smiled.

"I know that's what you call it in the US. We call it the boot after the English tradition. But I thought you told me you studied in England!" Mah Step asked slightly puzzled.

"So I did. That's why I knew right away what you meant. I lived in England for seven years."

The obsequious driver carefully loaded John's luggage into the trunk. The language Mah Step and the driver spoke sounded different from any he had heard before, including Thai. John made a mental note to ask Mah Step about it later. The driver bowed as he held the left rear door open for John and Mah Step got in from the right. The old car gave the impression of being as solidly built as an armored vehicle, but the seat was comfortable, and the inside was high and roomy.

Getting out of the airport proved more difficult than John could have imagined. All the drivers seemed to have their hands glued to their horns and each seemed bent upon cutting the other off. It was pure bedlam the likes of which John hadn't seen before. To top it all, the car had no air-conditioning. As sweat poured down his face and back in rivulets and the deafening noise battered his senses, John marveled at Mah Step's calm and stoic patience.

"You must be used to this," John remarked.

"Not really, but my getting worked up will not speed things up. Are you all right?"

"Under the circumstances. But I wouldn't want to stay here a minute longer than necessary!"

By mixing aggressive maneuvers with plaintive cries the driver was able to inch the taxi ahead of the competition. The drivers seemed to be trying to scare the pedestrians with insistent honking, but they might as well have been deaf.

"Vehicles seem to have right of way here," John could not help remarking.

"It's probably the pride of wealth and ownership. Less than one percent of the population here have cars," explained Mah Step.

Just when it looked like they had got clear of the crowd, they were stopped by a scruffy looking man wearing a dirty, grease-stained T-shirt and sandals. After a brief exchange, the driver paid him some money in return for a piece of paper and they were waved on through.

"Bribe?" asked John.

"No. Parking fees," replied Mah Step.

Soon they were out of the airport gates and speeding along a two-lane road that had no central divider. John's heart was in his mouth as the driver veered left and right, seemingly missing oncoming vehicles and pedestrians by mere inches.

"Did you say you drive on the left here?" John asked with a glint in his eye.

"Yes," replied Mah Step a little puzzled.

"How can you tell?" exclaimed John with a wicked laugh.

Mah step was a little late catching on but when he did he laughed good-naturedly.

"That's a good one! They seem to be going every which way, huh?"

The wind quickly evaporated the sweat, cooling the body in the process and making it a lot more bearable. Further down the road, they took a diversion circumventing the city. This road was less congested, and they headed straight for the distant hills, the farther ones of which looked blue and the nearer ones, green.

"How old is this car?" John asked when they were out of the two-way highway.

"I don't know. Must be about five years," Mah Step answered.

"I thought this one dated back to the '50s!" exclaimed John.

"The design is certainly from that period. I think this is based on the Morris Oxford III model that was manufactured in England after the war. They are sturdy and good for our rough roads, though more efficient Japanese and Korean cars are replacing them now. The reason I got this instead of a Suzuki or a Hyundai is that this is more comfortable for a tall person like you. I always get this for our foreign visitors. They can sit comfortably instead of having to crouch down on a low seat," Mah Step explained.

"I see. It *is* quite comfortable actually."

Overcome by the fatigue of the over forty-hour journey, John succumbed to the warm afternoon sun and the cool breeze and was soon fast asleep with his head lolling on the backrest of the seat as the car hurtled recklessly forward.

Chapter 2: Getting There

When John woke from his nap it felt much cooler. They had climbed to about two thousand feet leaving the muggy plains below. Instead of the ugly concrete buildings of the plains, they whizzed past bamboo and thatched huts; and it was green all over, mostly tropical trees, with a few pine trees here and there. The narrow two-way road continued to climb, hugging the low rolling hills. Strangely there were no people to be seen, in stark contrast to the madding crowd of the plains they had left behind.

John looked at his watch. They must have been driving for an hour and a half. Mah Step, awake, smiled at John.

"I guess I fell asleep," John said a trifle sheepishly. "I have a huge sleep debt to repay. Where are we?"

"We are about half-way there. We will stop for tea soon."

And sure enough, after another bend in the road the huts were more numerous and there were a few brick homes set amongst the thatched huts. There were people too; mostly red-cheeked children in tattered clothes and young girls carrying their baby siblings strapped to their backs. A little further on, a light green paddy field opened up on the right with a row of tin-roofed shops and houses on the left. The men were shabbily dressed in western style trousers and jackets, but the women wore clean red-white or blue-white checked aprons tied over one shoulder, reminiscent of the women of Cambodia. The taxi sped on till they reached a level plateau flanked by paddy fields on either side. A short climb from there and they reached a small town with shops on either side and buses and cars parked by the roadside.

"This small town, Dongpoh, is exactly half-way on our journey," Mah Step explained as they sauntered over to the row of tea-stalls, stretching their stiff legs. The ones farthest from the center were small sheds made of bamboo and had thatched roofs. The tea stalls clustered in the middle had tin roofs and whitewashed, plastered walls. By the side of the road there stretched a line of vendors and hawkers selling fruits, vegetables, honey, and other farm produce.

The restaurant they entered was the largest of the lot and was filled to capacity. The strong aroma of spices and herbs kindled John's hunger.

"The toilets are at the back," Mah Step said pointing to the wooden door with peeling blue paint. Seeing John's hesitation Mah Step added, "There are no roadside toilets after this till we reach home."

"In that case, I will risk it!" John said as he moved to the toilets. The room had a line of ten urinals against one wall and two washbasins to the left. While the walls were white-tiled the uneven, gray-cemented floor looked dirty with pools of spilled water here and there. At the center of the room was a wire-mesh covered hole that housed a noisy pump leading down into a bore-well. The two urinals at the extreme right were vacant and John chose the one at the very end. When John got to the washbasin he quickly gave up the idea of washing his face when he saw the sign in English that read: 'Danger: Water not good for drinking.' But the person next to him clearly had no qualms about rinsing his mouth with the same water. The tap did not work. Water had to be drawn with a discolored red mug from a large plastic drum next to the washbasin. After washing his hands John discovered there were no paper towels. Luckily, he located a paper napkin in the right pocket of his corduroy trousers.

Mah Step had already seated himself at a table and John joined him. A large family at the next table was busily engaged in tucking into the rice and an array of aromatic dishes.

"What would you prefer? A full meal of rice and curry or an omelet and toast or something local?" Mah Step asked.

"It's too late for breakfast and a little too early for dinner. I'd like to try something local, something light and not too heavy," said John.

"How about some flat bread and chickpeas?" asked Mah Step.

"Sounds good to me!" John responded.

As Mah Step tried to catch the eye of the waiter, their driver joined them. The food came to them after a very short wait, three large steaming plates skillfully balanced. Each shiny stainless-steel plate had two pieces of puffed, sizzling fried bread and a small stainless-steel bowl of chickpeas in thick brownish gravy. The chopped cabbage and onions on the side smelled slightly stale and rancid.

"Would you mind if I said grace?" asked Mah Step.

"No, not at all!" responded John.

Mah Step prayed: "Loving Almighty God, we thank thee for making this dream come true; for bringing John to my country; for journey mercies on the way and for keeping him out of all danger and the wiles of the devil. Lord, I pray that our friendship will be edifying to us and to the community. Lord, I pray that John will find meaning and purpose in life during his stay in the Sakhi Hills and that he would be able to use his knowledge and talents for helping us. We thank you for this food. Bless it, Lord, I pray, and strengthen our bodies with it. We remember the many who go hungry every day. Thank you, Lord. In Jesus' name ... Amen."

Instead of the perfunctory grace at meals that he was accustomed to when eating with Christians, this was more of a heartfelt prayer and John was moved enough to say 'Amen'.

The flat bread, made from wheat and fried to a golden crisp in an unidentifiable vegetable oil, was an absolute delight. The curried chickpeas provided the perfect counterpoint with the herbs and spices and just a faint touch of hot red pepper, which Mah Step referred to as 'chillies'. John tucked into the food with obvious relish and Mah Step was quick to order a second helping all round.

It was close to five o'clock when they got back to the taxi to resume their journey. The air cooled rapidly as they climbed steadily uphill. The sun went down in a little while, perceptibly lowering the temperature further, prompting John and Mah Step to roll up the car windows. The driver adroitly leaned across and rolled up the front passenger window with his left hand without reducing speed.

The falling dusk imbued everything with a dreamy, ethereal hue. An eerie quietness seemed to have descended along with the dusk. The huts they passed had either electric lights or hurricane lamps lit. There were even fewer people out than before and the oncoming traffic had also thinned out.

"Back in DC I'd be stuck in traffic and the evening would be just beginning," thought John. Aloud he said to Mah Step, "Looks like the day ends with the evening here."

"Yes, that's true," agreed Mah Step. "The life of the rural folk revolves around the sun and the seasons. As soon as it gets dark they have their supper and turn in for the night."

"Is that the same in the towns?" asked John.

"Till very recently, yes," Mah Step replied, "But satellite TV has changed our lifestyle irrevocably. American sitcoms are the rage now. They make our people feel rich and famous—and sophisticated," Mah Step added after a short pause.

"Do you also get channels like ABC, CBS, and NBC?" John asked.

"No, but we get CNN and BBC round-the-clock."

Just then a car passed them at break-neck speed, its tires squealing as it rounded the bend.

"He didn't have his lights on!" exclaimed John.

"Some drivers don't turn their headlights on till it is pitch dark," Mah Step replied.

"In the US, most cars have their lights on even in the daytime. In newer models, the headlights turn on automatically when the light falls. And if it is raining and you are using your wipers, you must have your headlights on."

"Here some drivers not only don't turn their lights on but also don't even use the wipers. They think they are saving their batteries."

"But the dynamo recharges the battery when the car is running!" exclaimed John.

"They don't seem to believe it. They think it's a waste of money," Mah Step smiled.

Another vehicle came up right behind them, its lights blinding them from the mirrors. The driver pulled the car slightly to the left edge of the road and simultaneously turned on the right turn indicators. John found this rather strange because to their right was only a deep gorge. But the moment the indicator was turned on, the car behind moved to the right and passed them.

"Was that a signal to pass?" John asked.

"Yes," Mah Step replied.

"And if you wanted to turn to the right what signal would you use?"

"The same," Mah Step replied.

"But isn't that confusing?" John asked.

"I see what you are getting at. Since we don't have multi-lane traffic and not too many intersections the same signal is used for both."

"I would hate to drive here! Driving on the left is confusing enough!"

"Don't worry. You will get the hang of it quickly enough. You will be driving like a native in no time at all."

"I doubt it," John said skeptically.

Just then it began to rain. The raindrops came down lightly at first but quickly increased to a pattering crescendo on the car roof that made conversation difficult. By now it had turned completely dark. They could hardly see each other except as ghostly apparitions in the reflected light from their own headlights or like startled deer when the headlights of oncoming traffic lit up the inside of the taxi.

"Can't we pull up to the side and wait for the rain to stop?" John asked not wanting to sound too anxious.

"If we do that we may have to wait till morning," responded Mah Step.

Seeing the disbelieving look on John's face, Mah Step added, "I'm serious. Sometimes it rains non-stop for days on end. I think we get almost as much rain as Cherrapunjee or Mt. Waialeale listed in the Encyclopedia Britannica."

"Really?" John asked.

"Yes, this is the monsoon capital of the world! But don't worry. This one won't last long."

The brakes of an over-laden truck made horrible grinding and screeching noises as it came down hill negotiating the sloping curve and the taxi had to pull over to the left shoulder to get out of its way.

The rain stopped as abruptly as it had started. The sudden drop in the noise level made the whine of the engine sound excessively loud as the driver increased the pace again.

"The road is dry here!" John said with disbelief.

"That happens quite often here. Probably has something to do with the hills. It rains heavily in one village but the neighboring village, a mile or two away, is bone dry," explained Mah Step.

"Are we there yet?" asked John.

"In another forty minutes, we should be home," Mah Step replied.

Soon they were driving by the edge of a lake. A thick mist hung low over the waters giving the scene a wraith-like appearance. The gradient of the road markedly increased after the lake causing the driver to shift to a lower gear further increasing the whine of the car's engine as it labored uphill. Just when it looked like it was going to be an easy drive the rest of the way home, a dense fog wafted across the ravine and descended on the road reducing visibility to only a few feet. The driver slowed down but, to John, he still seemed to be going faster than he ought. The yellow fog lights didn't improve matters much. The gray fog seemed to catch the light in its velvet glove and fling it back at them with an eerie delight. The driver kept peering towards the left to use that edge of the road as a guide to keep the car on the road. Though John could see neither side of the road, he knew one of them, judging by the gradient of the road, had to be steep gorge. John stole a glance at Mah Step in the light of an oncoming truck and was relieved to find no trace of anxiety or alarm on his face.

"I only hope it's not the famed oriental inscrutability," John thought.

At one point the driver had to stop and wait for the thick fog to thin a bit before moving again. The reflected light from the fog made it difficult to distinguish the headlights of oncoming vehicles from the reflected light of their own headlights. It seemed to take forever, much like turbulence when flying that seem to last longer than they actually do. After inching along interminably, the fog suddenly vanished magically when they turned the next bend in the road.

"We are on the other side of the hill now. The fog is hemmed in by the hills surrounding the lake," explained Mah Step.

"I couldn't see a thing. It was scary!" said John.

"There is Kyllang! We call it the Big Town," Mah Step said, as the car negotiated another curve, pointing at several peaks all lit up with lights that seemed to flow down their sides. The vaguely visible neighboring hills and the wan moonlight filtering down through the gray clouds accentuated the iridescence of the Big Town.

"It's beautiful!" said John reverently.

The drive from then on was uneventful except for the brief stop when two scruffy-looking youth ran out from a dilapidated roadside shed next to an upright long wooden pole with a large stone tied to the short end and collected the money that the driver handed over.

"What was that?" asked John.

"Oh, that's the government check-gate. They collect an entry tax from all vehicles," said Mah Step.

"They looked more like thugs than government employees!" John said.

"You are right. They really are not. At the beginning of the fiscal year the government auctions off these check-gates and other income generating licenses to private parties. It is a source of much corruption. The friends and relatives of the politicians are awarded these lucrative contracts for a pittance."

Soon they were driving past houses that had electric lights and then came the streetlights and houses more densely packed against each other. The sidewalks were filled with people hurrying in opposite directions. Buses and trucks and cars jammed the narrow road. At the junction ahead, the driver signaled a right turn and the policeman waved them on.

"There are no traffic lights!" John asked incredulously.

"You are right," Mah Step said softly. "We don't have any traffic lights in our town. Policemen are posted at busy intersections to direct traffic. Traffic lights would probably be more expensive here than policemen!"

Traffic was much thinner on the new road they had turned on to. After about a mile the taxi turned left onto a side road that climbed steeply uphill. At the top of the hill, they came upon a makeshift market by the side of the road. Men and women were selling vegetables and fish under the light of kerosene lamps. Opposite to the market place stood a beautiful church.

"That's my Presbyterian church," said Mah Step with obvious pride.

Mah Step's house lay by the side of a narrow one-way road that sloped away from the main road.

By the time John and Mah Step got out of the car the front door of the house had opened and three shadowy figures could be seen on the dimly lit porch. Mah Step paid off the driver thanking him profusely.

"You should let me pay the tip," John said reaching for his wallet.

"No, that's OK. We don't tip taxis here," Mah Step said. "In any case, I have given him a little extra for bringing us up to the house and not leaving us at the taxi stand in the middle of the town."

"In the US, it is practically mandatory to tip waiters and taxi drivers. Heaven help you if you don't!"

They climbed down a short flight of steps to reach the front gate. Mah Step's sister walked down quickly to the gate and held it open as John and Mah Step reached it.

"This is my sister Nora," Mah Step said.

John was struck by the beauty and innocence even in that dim light. The dark eyes in the fair oval face seemed to look into his soul. John raised his hands together in the traditional Asian gesture of greeting. He was surprised when Nora shyly held out her hand instead and said, "*Hooblei!*"

As John took Nora's hand he felt a strange sensation of being in the presence of genuine femininity, a feeling that he had lost in the asexual political correctness of the western world. Nora was grateful for the shadows that hid her blushes. Did he gently press her hand or was it her imagination, she wondered.

Pushing aside the tenderness he felt, John quickly recognized the greeting from his online chats with Mah Step. He remembered that it literally meant 'God bless you' and the same word was used for welcoming, for bidding farewell and for thanking someone. John reciprocated with "*Hooblei!*" much to the delight of Nora. Mah Step had told him that it was the most frequently used word in the Sakhi language. John remembered thinking how wonderful it is to bless one another while greeting and thanking each other.

"This is my father and my mother," Mah Step said as they climbed the two steps to the porch. (John learned later that Mah Step preferred to refer to it as the verandah.) John shook hands with the father and mother, respectfully wishing each of them *Hooblei*. John could not help noticing that Mah Step's mother was significantly taller than the father. John was led into a room about twelve feet by ten with white-washed walls and a naked electric bulb that hung under a white enamel shade in the center of the room. John made to remove his shoes, but Mah Step bade him keep them on.

"We keep our shoes on inside the house unlike other Asian societies, I think because of the cold. You won't feel it right now. You still have the heat of the plains in your blood. In about an hour it will wear off and you will begin to feel the cold," Mah Step explained.

By the time they settled down into the cushioned wooden sofa and the adjacent rattan settee, Nora was back in the room with a porcelain plate on which was a bunch of what appeared to be quartered nuts and a neatly arranged pile of folded green leaves to the side.

"This is our custom of welcoming a guest," Mah Step stood up and explained formally. "We call it *kwai.* The nut is incorrectly called betel nut, but the correct name is actually areca nut. Betel is, in fact, the name of the leaf. You don't have to eat it. It is an acquired taste. You can try it later if you like. Just accept a nut and betel leaf and keep it with you."

"Will it keep until tomorrow? I'd like to see what this tastes like."

"It will not spoil."

"What does the giving of *kwai* signify?" asked John.

"It is an age-old custom of our tribe, the Sakhi tribe. The offering of *kwai* to guests is a tradition common for the rich and the poor. *Kwai* is something even the very poor can afford to give their guests. They need not be ashamed if they cannot afford to give a meal or high tea to their guests. I'd say it is a kind of social leveler."

At that point, Nora entered the room with a plastic tray that held cups of tea and saucers. She was no longer shrouded in the thick blanket-like shawl, but she now had a red and white checked apron knotted over her left shoulder. She set the saucers down on the center table that Mah Step had moved to the middle of the room and then placed cups of tea on them. As she placed a cup of tea in front of John their eyes locked for the briefest instant, but she demurely looked down. After placing all the cups, she rushed back to the kitchen to come back with a salad plate piled with slices of brown cake, which she placed at the center of the table.

"Let us have some tea and cake first. We will have our dinner after you have had your bath. But let us first pray," Mah Step announced.

It was Mah Step's father who prayed this time. He moved forward in his sofa and bowed reverentially as he prayed. The 'Amen' signaled the end of the long prayer. As everybody leaned back in their seats and looked at each other, Mah Step's mother rose and gracefully lifted the cup of tea in front of John and handed it to him.

"Thank you," John said and then remembered to add, "*Hooblei!*"

Mah Step's mother held out the plate of cake to him and John took a slice. The others picked up a slice each as well. They drank the tea in silence. Nora did not sit down with them but stood in the doorway, her cup in one hand and a piece of cake in the other.

"My father thanked God for your safe journey and he prayed for a time of happiness for you and for us as you stay here with us for the next two months."

"That was very kind of him. Please tell him I appreciate it." John said guiltily remembering how he had taken the travel for granted. The thought of praying for safety had never once crossed his mind. His only concerns had been whether the flight was on time and how long the line was at the security check. He had cared about little else.

"I hope I don't outwear my welcome too soon. Eight weeks is a long time," John said smiling.

"I don't think that will ever happen," Mah Step responded seriously.

Tea was served pre-mixed with milk and sugar. John was soon to learn that when it came to most things there were few options or choices here. If you wanted tea, tea is what you got. You didn't have to agonize over green tea, red tea, English tea, lemon tea or a wide variety of herbal teas. Here tea was just tea. At best, it could be 'milk-tea' or 'red tea'; or, either with or without sugar. He learned later that it was the same with coffee. No one here had heard of decaf or regular, mocha or latte, much less Starbucks or any other brand.

"Was life simpler here because everyone had the same tastes?" John wondered.

"Some more tea?" asked Mah Step and Nora was quick with the white teapot as he proffered his cup. When their eyes met again briefly her hand wavered and she nearly missed the cup adding to her consternation.

When tea was done, Mah Step showed John to his room carrying his luggage for him. The room was about the same size as the sitting room, with a bed on one side and a desk and a chair on the other. On the colorful bedspread, near the foot of the bed, was a neat stack of folded blankets and duvets.

"Let me first show you the bathroom," Mah Step said, leading him with obvious pride to the wooden door at the far corner of the room. Inside was a bathroom that appeared to have been transplanted from a different world. There was a western style toilet (Mah Step called it a WC), a washbasin with hot and cold faucets, a regular bathtub and a shower area in the corner next to it. John was pleasantly surprised. The walls and the floor had color-coordinated tiles in different shades of blue.

"Wow! This is great! Fantastic!" gushed John. "The typical American response would have been 'Awesome!' but I don't like that word!"

"I'm glad you like it. I think the bathroom is the most important room in a house. It wasn't easy to make this one. I had to buy the bathtub and WC from a town in the plains over a hundred kilometers away. And then I had to hire special workers to install everything. When we get to the village you will have to make do with something much simpler."

"I think I'll be fine. I came prepared for rural living. This is a bonus!" said John.

"I hope it won't be too difficult for you. The geyser has been turned on and the water should be hot already. Because of your British connections, you know I'm referring to the water heater and not an old man! We will have dinner right after you've had your bath," Mah Step said stepping out.

It was sheer luxury to wash away, under the hot shower, the caked sweat and grime of forty hours of travel. For good measure, John also had a shave. "Must wash these clothes tomorrow," he said to himself as he bundled the soiled clothes into a plastic bag that he had carried in his duffel bag.

When he joined them in the sitting room again he looked so different that the family welcomed him with gasps and murmurs of appreciation. Nora's hand went to her mouth in stunned surprise.

"You look about ten years younger," Mah Step said laughing.

"Thank you. That was probably the most refreshing bath I ever had!" John responded. "I'm sure your American guests appreciated your bathroom."

"Oh, they all did. In fact, an American lady called me a 'civilized guy' after taking a look at the bathroom. I was actually offended. I was tempted to tell her civilization didn't depend on bathroom styles but didn't want to get into an argument with her. After all, she was my guest."

"I think you have a point there. Bathroom designs do differ from country to country. I wouldn't say a Japanese, Indian or Kenyan was uncivilized just because their bathrooms were different." John agreed.

At this point, Mah Step's mother said something, and Mah Step vigorously nodded in agreement.

"Mah John, let's have our dinner first. You must be hungry. We will have plenty of opportunities to talk later. Let me say again how happy I am that you are physically here. I almost cannot believe it!"

Nora and her mother led them to the next room, which turned out to be a very large kitchen with dining space. At the center of the room was a low square table around which were placed round cane stools. Mah Step's father waited on one side and gestured to John to take the middle seat, with Mah Step sitting opposite to his father. Nora and her mother did not join them at the table. Nora's mother sat down near the two open-coil electric stoves at the hearth and opened various vessels placed around them on the floor. Nora brought an aluminum bowl of hot water and the father gestured to her to start with John.

"What am I supposed to do?" John whispered sotto voce to Mah Step.

"The bowl is for washing your hand before you eat. Just dip your hand and rub the fingers together," suggested Mah Step gesturing helpfully with both hands.

John did as directed, looking to Nora for any additional instructions. He must have done it right because all he saw was a faint blush and a shy smile as she handed him a small white towel to dry his hands. She then took the bowl to her father and finally to Mah Step, both of whom washed their hands vigorously in the same water and dried their hands with the same small cloth towel.

Nora placed the bowl of water and the towel on the washboard next to the sink and joined her mother near the electric stoves. Then began the serving of the food with the mother passing the dishes on to Nora who first served steaming white rice on the porcelain plates set before the men, starting with John. Then her mother handed her a dish of curried chicken whose spicy aroma stirred acute pangs of hunger in John. Nora ladled the chicken and dark brown gravy over the steaming rice to one side of the plate. After the chicken came stir-fried vegetables and a thick lentil soup which she poured over the rice.

Nora brought around a spoon and fork and held them out shyly to John.

"Would you like to eat with your hands or use a spoon and fork?" Mah Step asked.

"I haven't eaten with my fingers before. I guess I'll use the fork today because I'm so hungry!" said John.

"When we get to the village you will have to start eating with your hand."

"I'll be more than happy to do that," John said smiling.

Then Mah Step gestured to his father who blessed the food in an earnest and suppliant tone.

The food was as delicious as he had hoped, and the watchful Nora was quick to rise from her stool near her mother and serve additional helpings of rice, chicken and vegetables as needed. One of the things that John learned right away was that it was the custom to eat silently. John suppressed his urge to chat and appreciate the food. Both Mah Step and his father were completely intent on the food on their plates. After dinner was over Nora brought around the bowl of water and the towel again for them to wash and dry their hands. John didn't have to use it since he had used the fork, but Mah Step and his father washed their hands in the same water and gently wiped their lips.

"An excellent dinner!" John said appreciatively.

Mah Step translated John's appreciation much to the delight of Nora and her mother.

"Was it too spicy?" asked Mah Step solicitously.

"No, it was not spicy hot, if you know what I mean. I enjoyed the flavor very much. So very different from the bland food I am used to every day."

"We are glad you like our style of cooking," Mah Step replied. "Let's go to the sitting room while the ladies have their dinner."

The satiety of the meal rapidly brought on a desire to turn in for the night, but John had one task left to do before he slept. When Nora and her mother joined them again, he went to his room and returned with the gifts he had brought for them. Never a good shopper, his difficulty had been compounded by the fact that almost everything was made in China. He didn't see any point in carrying Chinese-made presents to Asia. It was after much effort that he had bought these small gifts. Starting with the father, John handed out the gift-wrapped presents remembering to offer them with his right hand. Mah Step's mother received hers with a big smile and then it was Nora's turn. She blushed profusely and mumbled, "*Hooblei.* Thank you!" The last present was for Mah Step. John was a little surprised when they admired the wrapping and the bow but made no move to open the gifts.

"Aren't you going to open them?" John asked.

"In our custom, we do not open gifts in the presence of the giver. We open them later. But since you mention it, we will open them now," said Mah Step and spoke to his family.

Nora went to the kitchen and came back with a knife. Very carefully she helped her father, open his packet without damaging the gift-wrapping. Mah Step's father was delighted with the Swiss Army knife. He got up to shake John's hand in gratitude. Ma and Nora were happy with their gifts too—colorful Italian scarves. Nora playfully draped hers around her shoulders. Mah Step appeared stunned by his two gifts, a digital diary and an MP3 player. All of them shook John's hands again and thanked him for the presents.

This looked like an excellent time to beat a retreat.

"I think I'll call it a day, if you all don't mind," John announced. They were immediately concerned, and Mah Step led him to his bedroom saying, "Sleep well. You have had a very long journey. I'll see you in the morning," before withdrawing.

Sleepy as he was, John lay stretched on the bed for a few minutes gratefully savoring the events of a day that had exceeded his wildest expectations. He then changed into his pajamas and turned out the light.

Chapter 3: On the Town

John slept like a log within minutes of his head hitting the pillow. The cotton mattress on the wooden cot was much thinner than the thick pillow-top mattress he was used to but yet it felt surprisingly soft. Slipping between the fresh sheets and pulling a quilt and blanket over him, he remembered the drowsy numbness of Keats as jetlag and the warmly comforting bed conspired to pull him Lethe-wards into the deepest slumber. The dream-like state he had felt after dinner continued in his sleep as his mind conjured up images of green hills and blue mountains and an affectionate people. Past midnight the cold got through to him and he curled up into a fetal position and pulled the blanket and quilt over his head.

His sleep was suddenly broken by what sounded like galloping hooves and barking dogs right in his room. Startled, he wondered if he was having a nightmare, but it was all too real. For a moment, he feared something macabre was going to happen to him á la *The Hound of the Baskervilles,* but he soon realized that it was not inside his room but in the yard outside. As he listened intently he figured out that it was a pack of dogs that were chasing each other in frenetic pursuit and not someone on a foxhunt in the middle of the night. "How did they get over the walls?" he wondered. Then just as precipitately as they had come, their barking and yelping faded down the road into the distance. John listened acutely but the commotion did not appear to have woken the others and he fell back into the sleep he had just been rudely awakened from.

When he woke up again the room was bathed in the soft pre-dawn light that streamed through the glass ventilators above the two curtained windows facing him. The chirping of birds and the distant crowing of a rooster heralded the morning. As the skies through the ventilator visibly brightened, John got out of bed and moved to peer out of the window. The window itself was peculiarly constructed, he realized, with six-inch square glass planes on a latticed regular-size window and there were vertical iron bars on the window frame. He pushed the thick inner blind aside to find a gauzy, lace curtain. When he moved it aside, the view stunned him. To his right climbed the side of a verdant mountain with tin-roofed white houses perched on its side. Near the top of the mountain floated thin gray clouds of mist and fog. To the front and left he could see the red-painted tin roof of the neighboring house and above it the early rays of the morning sun tingeing the skies a bright pink. He could not admire the view much longer as the unheated room quickly robbed him of the warmth he had brought from the bed. John hastily retreated to the comfort of the bed and from there watched, through the ventilator, the pink sky gradually turn blue.

Comforting though it was, he could not lie there very long. He reached over the side of the bed to find his watch that he had left on the floor. It was a five thirty. "It must be too early for Mah Step and the family," John thought. But he soon heard surreptitious sounds coming from the kitchen and the other rooms. Realizing they were already awake John got out of bed, pulled on a sweater for warmth and moved to the bathroom. Thinking it would take time for the water heater to heat up, John completed the morning ablutions with witheringly cold water. Back in his bedroom he quickly changed into daytime clothes and pulled on the warmest pair of socks he had. For good measure, he put on his jacket as well on top of the woolen sweater. "What a difference central heating makes!" he marveled as he slipped on his shoes.

After gently knocking on the wooden door he entered the central room to find it unoccupied. The door to the kitchen was open and pushing the lace floor-length curtain aside he entered the kitchen. Nora, who was sitting on a short stool by the electric stove, quickly jumped up in confusion. She wasn't expecting him to be up this early, John realized.

"Good morning!" John greeted Nora in the friendliest and gentlest tone he could muster.

"Good morning, Sir" responded Nora in a shy, lilting tone blushing scarlet as she said it.

"Good morning, Nora. Just call me John."

"Yes, Mah John," she replied reflexively using the honorific Sakhi prefix.

"I think I will step outside for a minute," John said pointing to the door. "You carry on with whatever you were doing." The door creaked a bit as he opened it; stepping outside, he quickly shut it behind him.

Outside was a kind of cemented patio or deck overhung by the tin roof and set into the house like an alcove, but completely open on the outside. The cool freshness of the mountain air invigorated John. He looked up at the towering mist-covered peak in awe, overcome by the sheer beauty. The lyrics from Don McLean's "Castles in the Air" came to his mind from nowhere.

The house was very nearly at the foot of the mountain, with a jumble of haphazardly constructed cheek-by-jowl houses further below to his left. He wished he had the poetic faculties of Wordsworth as he took in the pine trees and the mountain and the wispy smoke that arose from the houses. On the nearest hill, he could see a road winding up amongst the pine trees. It was cold, he suddenly realized, and he thrust his hands deep into the front pockets of his jacket. He would have been lost in his reverie had not the door creaked open gently and Nora came out with a cane stool for him to sit on.

She went back inside leaving the door ajar but was quickly back with an open brazier of burning charcoal, which she carried with both hands. John could not hide his astonishment and stuttered his thanks, half rising from the stool. Nora smiled with happiness and retreated back into the kitchen. The brazier was delightful. John placed his feet on either side of it and rubbed his cold hands together above the glowing coals.

Don McLean was back in his head again.

The door opened a second time. This time it was Mah Step with a broad smile on his face and a cane stool in his hand.

"Good morning, Mah John!" Mah Step said cheerily, setting the stool down near the fire.

"'Morning Mah Step! How are you doing?" asked John.

"I am fine, thank you. Did you sleep well? How are you?"

"I am good! I slept like a baby till the barking dogs woke me up. What was that all about?" asked John.

"Oh, that. Those are pye-dogs. They do that every night," responded Mah Step.

"*Pie*-dogs?" John hadn't heard that term before.

"It is spelt p-y-e. They are street dogs, stray dogs, dogs of mixed breed. Not everybody keeps their dogs leashed here. And some who chain their dogs during the daytime let them out at night. All these dogs run around in packs at night creating a big ruckus. They are a nuisance, but we have got used to the noise, I suppose. I've got so used to it, it doesn't wake me up anymore."

"They scared the heck out of me," John said. "I thought we were being attacked or something."

"You know, in the neighboring province they do not have this problem," suggested Mah Step.

"Why is that?"

"The answer might come as a bit of a shock to you."

"Come on, tell me! What's the reason?" John could not restrain his curiosity.

"OK, here it comes. You asked for it. The Pangama tribe of that province considers dog meat a delicacy. It is the most expensive meat in that region and naturally there aren't any dogs to be found. They even make a special dog-meat soup for pregnant women. It's supposed to give them extra strength."

"Yuck! That is terrible! That would horrify most Americans. Dogs are a loved, and much-pampered, pet."

"I've heard that Americans spend a lot of money on their pets."

"That's true. It's big business. Does the dog-eating tribe love western food?" John asked with a glint in his eye.

"No, Why?"

"If they did, pye-dogs would be a perfect ingredient for pot pies—to say nothing of hot dogs!"

It took a moment to register before Mah Step laughed.

"You are funny," he said.

"I'm sorry, I simply cannot resist a pun," John replied sheepishly.

"On to more pleasant subjects. What would you like to do today? I thought I'd show you around the Big Town a little later," offered Mah Step.

"Oh, I'd love that. Is there anything special to see?"

Just then the door inched open and Nora brought out a small low table which she placed within arm's reach of both of them. She went in again to come back with a tray bearing two cups of tea and a salad plate of cookies.

"Please have the tea and biscuits. I mean, tea and cookies," Mah Step said catching himself.

"In England, they call them biscuits, so I'm familiar with that term," said John.

The tea was delightful. Mah Step dipped the 'Thin Arrowroot' cookie into the tea and brought it quickly to his mouth before the soggy edge fell off. John, on the other hand, enjoyed the crisp bites of the cookie between sips of tea.

"About the trip to the town. There's nothing spectacular to see, actually. But since this is your first trip here the whole place should be interesting!"

"Of course! I have no doubt of that."

"We could walk to the town center from here. It's only about a mile. From there we could go to the main market where the villagers bring their produce to sell."

"That should be interesting," John said. "But before that, I need to wash my clothes. I also need to check my email."

"Nora will take care of the washing. Just give her your dirty clothes. You can check your email in my study after we've finished our tea."

"I could wash them myself," said John.

But Mah Step was firm. "Nora takes care of the washing of the whole family. You don't need to worry about it."

Just then Mah Step's father appeared on the verandah. It took John a minute to realize that the dapper, well-dressed individual was the same shawl-covered person he had met the previous night. "Pa" stood about five foot four with a wiry frame to match. The snowy white hair was neatly combed, and he had had a shave. The black shoes were so immaculately polished the toes shone like mirrors. The gray tweed jacket, the white shirt and the dark trousers gave him a very distinguished air. In his left hand, he held a large umbrella, neatly folded and a woolen cap.

"Pa will go to the village today. He runs a small dispensary and there will be patients who need medicine."

Pa held out his hand and John rose to shake it.

"*Hooblei!*" said Pa.

"*Hooblei!*" responded John.

John walked Pa to the gate and returned.

"About my father and mother. Please feel free to address them as "Pa" and "Ma". It does not imply that you are calling them your *own* father and mother if you do that. You would be indirectly referring to them as my father and mother. Here people are known by their relationships. For example, a woman would be known as the mother of so and so or the daughter of so and so. Likewise, for males."

"That's interesting!"

"I mean, they are seldom called by their real first names. Everyone has two names; an official first name and a colloquial pet name which is more frequently used. That's why I suggested that you call my parents "Pa" and "Ma". You would actually be referring to them as my father and mother."

"That's not difficult," responded John. "In fact, it would make things a lot easier."

"I am glad. Would you like some more tea, or would you prefer to do email, Mah John?" he asked.

"I think I'll check my email first. I'm something of an email junkie, you know. But first here is some money to cover my expenses."

"Two hundred dollars! That's a lot of money! Why are you giving me so much?" Mah Step was surprised.

"This is an advance payment for all the expenses you will be incurring on my behalf. Just keep track of the payments you make and let me know when it needs topping up."

"This should last a long time," said Mah Step.

"Be sure to charge every expense, however small, to my account. Remember we discussed this before!" responded John,

"OK. Agreed! Let's go do email."

As they went through the kitchen, John's eyes locked briefly with Nora's and she blushed. She did not immediately seem to hear Mah Step reminding her to collect the cups from the verandah.

They went through the room where John had slept to a smaller room in the front of the house. The room had a small bay window jutting out, with the same small-paned windows as the bedroom. But what surprised John were the steel racks that ran to the ceiling on two walls. The shelves were packed with books of all kinds.

"Looks like you are quite a voracious reader!" John asked admiringly.

"I plead guilty to loving books. It goes back to my school days," Mah Step responded.

"Mind if I look around?"

"No, not at all. Go right ahead. And if you want to read any of them anytime, just help yourself. Only put it back in the exact same spot from where you took it. I hate having to search for things."

One whole row were the classic novelists of British literature—Dickens, Hardy, Trollope, Orwell, Huxley, Maugham, Woolf, Eliot, etc.—followed by the poetry of Donne, Marvell, Wordsworth, Keats, Shelley, Byron, Browning, Tennyson and others. American literature (Steinbeck, Faulkner, Hemingway, Fitzgerald, Cooper, Albee, Twain, Saroyan, Salinger, Williams, etc.) was on the other shelf. There was a shelf of reference books (including the complete works of Shakespeare) and a whole set of Bible translations and concordances. On a lower shelf, there were also language-learning books for German, French, and Russian, and an assortment of books on science, psychology, and Americana.

"I am quite impressed," John said turning around.

"Thank you, but it is nothing. I love books and I buy what I can afford. The prices of imported books have gone up so much that I haven't bought any books in two years."

"I should send you some books when I get back. We have books sales at the Greenbelt library once a year."

"No, you shouldn't trouble yourself. The postage would be too expensive. Anyway, let me get you connected to the Internet."

"It's an old Pentium II but it works," Mah Step said apologetically as he powered the computer on. It took forever to load and when he started the dial-up the modem made loud whining noises that John had nearly forgotten. But soon the connection was made, and they were online.

"She's all yours," Mah Step said as he got up. "Remember the connection may break sometimes and you will have to reconnect then."

"Many thanks, Mah Step. I recall our chats being frequently interrupted. I think I'll be done in about an hour."

The connection was very slow, but it worked. By opening two web pages and alternating between them he found he could save some time. Both his webmail accounts had over two hundred emails each, most of them junk. After deleting all the unwanted stuff, he was finally left with twenty-one emails that needed an answer. He had resisted the suggestion to start a blog for recording all his thoughts and experiences. As a matter of fact, he didn't like the word "blog" itself. Maybe he was being old-fashioned. He promised everyone he would send around an email newsletter whenever he could connect to the Net, but not oftener than weekly. He decided he would write the first email circular later. For now, he would just reply to emails to let them know he had arrived. He received some satisfaction in writing to Elaine and confirming that her fears were totally unfounded.

"Is everything OK? Is the connection giving you problems?" Mah Step asked when he returned to the room half an hour later.

"I'm nearly done. The connection has been good. No problems so far."

"That's good. Breakfast is ready. We can go to the town after that," Mah Step suggested.

"Perfect! By the way, did I tell you I brought a laptop with me?"

"No, you did not. What model is that?"

"It is not very new. It's an old IBM ThinkPad. A Pentium III. 256 MB. 30 GB hard disk."

"My desktop is a Pentium II. It has only 64 MB RAM. I can't get the right type of memory cards to upgrade. The new ones don't fit the old slots."

"You know what? I'll leave you the laptop when I go back. You think you'll have any use for it?"

"I will be thrilled to have a laptop. But are you sure?"

"If I can copy my data onto a CD, then you can have it. Remember it's not new."

"Many thanks in advance, Mah John. I'm grateful. How much would you charge for it?"

"I'll be more than happy to give it to you for free. You will make better use of it than me. Let's go have breakfast. I'm done," John said exiting from the Internet.

When they reached the kitchen, breakfast was already laid out. Nora stood up from the bamboo stool smoothing her blue checked apron and gestured them to their seats. For John, there was a pile of toasted white bread and two eggs fried sunny-side up. For Mah Step, it was rice and curry.

"You having an early lunch?" asked John with a smile.

"It is a force of habit really. I think it was Maugham who coined the term "brunch" after living in Burma. You see, the first meal of the day is a big meal for farmers because they have to be in the fields till evening. That habit has kind of stuck."

"Maybe I should try it too while I'm here."

Nora brought round the aluminum bowl of warm water to wash their hands and as usual Mah Step said grace before they started their meal. When they were nearly done, Nora brought cups of hot tea.

Sipping his tea, Mah Step asked, "Is there anything else you would like to do before we leave?"

"No, I'm ready. I only need to change my shirt."

Soon they were off. Instead of taking the lane that the taxi had brought them on the previous evening, they walked down a narrow footpath that meandered between the houses. In just a couple of minutes, they had reached the point where the lane and the road met that John had seen from the verandah earlier. Walking down was easy and pleasant and soon they reached an area with several small shops on either side, including three butchers' shops (beef, pork, and mutton) and a shop selling live chicken. Mah Step explained that the fish market opens only in the evening after the fish trucks arrive from the plains.

It was a motley crowd that milled around the street; smartly dressed men and women on their way to offices and rustics in stained shawls and aprons headed for manual labor. Some of the women laborers had conical bamboo baskets slung on their backs with the strap taut against their foreheads. The office-going men were dressed western-style and wore jackets or coats while the women were attired in the traditional dress. John thought this was quite symbolic, women upholding tradition and men looking out, a kind of marriage of the east and west. When asked about the dresses the women were wearing, Mah Step explained that the checked apron called *sainjyrshah* was informal and the *sainlem* worn by the office-goers was the dress for formal occasions.

"The *sainlem*, though formal, is in fact quite simple. It is just two pieces of rectangular cloth. The two pieces go under either arm and each is pinned together over the opposite shoulder. It is simplicity itself."

"Yet it looks so attractive and graceful," remarked John.

"For more formal occasions like weddings the women wear something called the *'khara'* which is made entirely of silk and is very expensive. It usually has golden embroidery along the edges but is generally of a single color, unlike the *sainlem* which comes in modern floral prints and other designs."

Just then a middle-aged man in an incongruous deerstalker hat accosted Mah Step. After exchanging pleasantries Mah Step introduced John to Mah Ap, the headman of the locality. Mah Ap had a huge toothless grin as he asked, "How many children do you have?"

The question caught John off guard and he could not hide his surprise, "I don't have any children." He was about to add, "And I don't plan to have any," but thought the better of it.

Which was just as well because Mah Ap's next question was, "Then why didn't you bring your wife?"

"Actually, I'm not married," John said a little stiffly.

But Mah Ap was impervious to John's discomfiture and continued, "But you *must* have a wife. Everyone has a wife. How old are you?"

John thought this had gone a little too far and asked a counter-question, "How old do you think I am?"

"Fifty-eight? Fifty-five?" asked Ma Ap.

At that point, Mah Step mercifully intervened and cut the discussion short.

As they walked on Mah Step said, "Don't be upset by the inquisitive personal questions. It is the practice here to inquire about marital status, age and number of offspring when meeting a stranger."

"No, I wasn't offended. I assumed it was a cultural thing. But my ego is a little bruised. Do I really look fifty-five?"

"No! Of course, you don't! It's just that they are not used to white folk. It's the same thing with Americans underestimating the age of Asians. Except in our case, it works to our advantage!"

"I'm not making the mistake of asking anyone here to guess my age again!" John said.

By now they had reached the main road, which was packed in either direction with cars, buses and trucks. Two policemen were waging a losing battle at the crossroads controlling traffic.

"Sometimes walking on foot is faster," said Mah Step as they crossed the road through the stalled traffic. "The roads were designed fifty years ago, when there were less than one percent of the vehicles there are now. Widening the roads is almost impossible with the houses and buildings on either side."

Walking briskly, they reached the government-run "Civil Hospital" and a little further on they reached the government-owned "State Central" library. From there it was only a short walk to the center of town called the Pulit Bazaar.

"Any idea why they call it that?" asked John.

"Pulit is the way "police" is spelt and pronounced in our language. The main police station in British days used to be close to the center of town. Somehow that name stuck. And "bazaar", as you surely know, means market in many languages, including English. There is a move to rename this spot with a local name but that hasn't picked up momentum yet because it is quite a tongue-twister for outsiders."

"Downtown" was a row of mostly single-story shops on either side of the road selling everything from readymade clothes, TVs and consumer electronics, to stationery, furniture and handicrafts. "City buses" stood unmoving while conductors yelled frantically for more passengers. Black and yellow taxis crammed with passengers stopped wherever they pleased to let out and take in passengers. Mah Step confirmed John's suspicions that this was the share taxi system in operation. Yet, in spite of all this, John realized that the cacophony here was way less than at the airport town in the plains.

"Do you want to see the main market?" asked Mah Step.

"Sure. Since we have come this far we might as well see it all. Is it any different?" responded John.

"It is totally different. This is the fashionable upscale market. The other one is the real market where agricultural produce is brought every day. Most villagers purchase everything they need from that market," explained Mah Step.

The descending road soon reached its nadir and slowly began ascending again. The number of pedestrians increased substantially. A little further on it became impossible to move forward without jostling others. By the time they neared the main market the road was packed with ancient-looking buses and ramshackle jeeps and the potholed road was strewn with decaying vegetables. The somewhat overpowering stench was exacerbated by the muddy filth they had to carefully navigate, picking drier ground to step on.

The market itself was thousands of tiny shops compacted into less than a square mile of area. Narrow alleys teeming with buyers and sellers wound between the haphazardly placed shops. Mah Step explained that there were distinct sections for different goods. The fish market was not difficult to locate. Almost all of the sellers here were women and they deftly skinned and sliced the fish for the customers. The butcher's market was all men. They had one whole section for beef, another for pork and a third for chicken. There was no refrigeration to be seen except ice-blocks in the fish section. Two men came towards them carrying a trussed up dead pig hanging upside down from bamboo poles and they had to step aside to let them pass.

"We will not go into that area," said Mah Step pointing to another section of the market. "That's where all the hooch joints are. Illegal gambling also goes on there. Let's take a different route back."

The footpaths were like a maze and John had lost all sense of direction. Mah Step knew his way, though, and they were quickly out on the main street again.

"Let's take a taxi back home," suggested John.

The ubiquitous black and yellow taxis were parked all over the street waiting for customers. Mah Step led them to the line that was headed for their part of town. The first taxi had two passengers in the front and only one in the back. John and Mah Step piled into the back. Any hopes of making a quick getaway vanished when Mah Step explained that they needed two more passengers for the back seat and one more for the front.

"Since it is morning there are more people coming into the market and town center than going the other way. So, we may have a bit of a wait," said Mah Step.

"How long?" asked John.

"Can't say. Maybe ten minutes, maybe fifteen. If he doesn't move in fifteen minutes, let's walk back."

"Good deal! I can wait fifteen minutes," said John.

John found it entertaining to watch the mass of pedestrians outside. Mah Step, on the other hand, fidgeted looking in both directions for any prospective passengers. Unfortunately, there were none.

"Mah Step, there's something I've been meaning to tell you. This might be as good a time as any," said John.

"What is it, John?" asked Mah Step, a trifle anxious.

"Remember our online chats on religion? I admired the fact that you never once tried to convert me or "save" me. You never pushed your faith. At the same time, you seemed to have a quiet assurance about what you believed in. One of the reasons I came to visit you is to talk to you more about your faith. Are you OK with my asking you a few questions now and then on the Bible and your faith?"

Mah Steps forehead that had furrowed with worry relaxed and a broad smile crossed his face.

"Absolutely no problem, Mah John. It will be a pleasure. If I may make a confession, I was hoping that during your stay here we would get a chance to discuss true Christianity. I see you are a seeker."

"That I most certainly am! Thank you for your willingness to discuss these complex issues. I appreciate it! But I must confess I am more attracted to the simplicity of oriental religions than the trappings of mainline Christianity."

"You are forgetting that Christianity is an Eastern religion too," Mah Step said with a smile.

A man carrying a cloth bag approached the car and the two already sitting in the front seat stepped out so the newcomer could get in. The front seat was now full and all that was needed were two passengers for the back.

"When do we go to the village?" John asked.

"I think we will stay one more day here and then move to the village the day after. How does that sound?"

"Will work for me! I have nothing on my calendar for the next eight weeks. Boy, is this pure heaven or what!"

It didn't take long for two women to come to the taxi overburdened with cloth bags filled to the brim with vegetables and other purchases. Mah Step moved closer to the passenger to his left and motioned for John to move closer, which John did. Nevertheless, the space left on the seat looked inadequate for the two women who were loading their heavy bags into the trunk. They came around to the door, peered in to find the white foreigner *sahep* and broke into uncontrollable giggles. After some cajoling by the driver, one of them pushed the other in first and climbed in after. There clearly wasn't enough space. Mah Step pushed himself out to the front edge of the seat and the lady next to John did likewise. By having three alternating passengers push themselves to the back of the seat and the two intermediate ones barely resting on the edge of the seat while clinging to the backrest of the front seat, the driver managed to slam the door closed. There wasn't enough space for him in the front seat either. He finally managed to sit squeezed against the door but the passenger next to him had to face the ignominy of straddling the floor-mounted stick shift between his legs.

With the overburdened engine screaming for relief, they were at last off. The traffic out of the city was thinner but as there were no lane dividers some of the cars coming into the city used the opposite lanes causing jams in both directions. John was surprised at the impunity with which traffic rules were violated here. There was no respect for personal space either. John tried to move away from the woman's body pressed to his right but that made him push against Mah Step to his left, which was even more uncomfortable. Caught in the middle John could only press his legs together, hunch his shoulders inwards and keep both hands in his lap.

The last thing he wanted was to be accused of being a groper in a foreign land.

The journey was mercifully short. When they reached the Presbyterian Church the two women got out. In another two minutes, John and Mah Step got out also, with Mah Step paying the fare.

“That was uncomfortable. Why do people have to travel like that? I can’t think of one good reason,” said John.

“It is the expense. For the two of us together it cost only fifteen cents. For poor people who live on a dollar or two each day that is a lot of money.”

“Is there no public transport like a bus service?” asked John.

“The government does not subsidize public transportation. The “city buses” you saw are privately owned. They ply only within the city but they don’t go to all localities. Some of the roads are too narrow. Those “city buses” are notoriously slow. As a matter of fact, I maintain I can prove Einstein’s Theory of Relativity with the way these slow city buses operate.”

John could not resist the mischievous glint in Mah Step’s eye.

“You have kindled my curiosity. How do you do that?”

“A city bus will wait at a stop till the next one comes along before it will move on to the next stop. The one that just arrived then waits till the next one comes along and so on. Here’s my proof. Imagine me waiting at a bus stop. There is a bus already waiting but I don’t board that. Not just yet. I wait till the next one comes. But instead of getting on the bus that has just arrived, I hop on, in the nick of time, to the bus that is leaving. At the next stop, I jump out of that bus and get on the one that is just leaving. And I repeat that at every stop till I reach my destination. Do you see it now?"

"No," said John puzzled, his brows creasing.

"Think through what I just said. If I switched buses at every stop, I would have, in effect, reached my destination before the bus I was waiting for even started. QED!" Mah Step said triumphantly.

"Ingenious!" John said laughing.

"But seriously, the government does not subsidize public transport. People have to pay for the real cost of all public utilities here. But to be fair to the government, the people do not have to pay any income tax either," explained Mah Step.

"No income tax at all? Not even for the rich?" John was incredulous.

"No. At the time of independence from the British, the "no tax" offer was made to mollify our tribe and get us to accede to the union. We get funds from the central government to cover our expenses."

They reached the gate of the house and stepped into the compound to find Nora sitting on her haunches surrounded by two large aluminum basins and two plastic buckets.

"Good afternoon, Mah John," she called out a little self-consciously as she tugged at the *sainjyrshah* out of modesty.

"Good afternoon, Nora! What are you doing?" responded John.

"Washing clothes," she said lifting her suds-covered hands to show.

"Mah Step, I thought you said you had a washing machine?" John asked.

"We do but Nora prefers to wash clothes by hand. She says it cleans better that way."

"If I had known I would have washed my clothes myself," John said remorsefully.

"Don't worry, John. Nora is happy doing it and she will be done soon."

As she scrubbed the clothes and dipped them into the first bucket and then the other, Nora had many questions for Mah Step about their trip to the town. It was a joy to see Nora work energetically; from watching her you wouldn't think washing clothes by hand was a chore. From time to time, she would move her arm across her forehead to wipe away the perspiration. John found that especially fetching.

"Let's go in," Mah Step suggested.

Ma was in the kitchen and after the exchange of the usual *Hooblei* they moved on to the sitting room. She brought them a carafe of cold water and two glasses. All the walking and the mountain air had made John thirsty and hungry. The water was refreshingly cool, and he was delighted when Mah Step mentioned that lunch would be served as soon as Nora completed the washing, which didn't take very long. When they entered the kitchen, John could see through the windows the clothes all hung out to dry on lines that crisscrossed the compound.

Nora, looking fresh as a daisy, her face freshly scrubbed, had changed into a dry, new *sainjyrshah* with red checks, and was there ready to serve them lunch.

"I am going to try and eat with my fingers today," announced John wiping his hands with the towel offered and passing the aluminum washbowl to Mah Step.

"You couldn't have chosen a better time. We are having fish for lunch," said Mah Step. "Be forewarned: these fish have plenty of bones!"

The fish was delectable. It had been lightly fried first and then added to a reddish-yellow gravy. Luckily for John, the bones were not that difficult to pick. The initial lack of coordination in eating with the fingers slowly faded as the meal progressed. The biggest difficulty John had was in keeping the soft rice from falling off his fingers. The vegetable was okra cut into thin slices and deep fried. John was never a fan of okra, but he liked the way it was cooked here.

Lunch over, Mah Step and John debated about going back to the verandah for another long chat but ultimately decided against it. John thought he needed a nap. He must have repaid much of the sleep-debt because when he awoke it was already dark and the house was quiet.

Chapter 4: Off to the Boondocks!

In spite of the afternoon nap, John slept like a log after a hastily eaten dinner served by Nora who had stayed up for him. Mah Step and his parents had already had their dinner and turned in for the night thinking that John had decided to skip dinner. Other than greetings and 'thank you' and a few words here and there, the rest of the communications between Nora and John so far had been by gestures. Nora giggled at some of John's gesticulations but nonetheless they got through the dinner without any serious difficulties.

The rampaging pack of barking dogs woke him up briefly, but he went back to sleep again easily to wake up with the morning sun streaming through the glass ventilators. He quickly ran through the motions of the morning ablutions and went to the kitchen to find Nora alone by the fire.

"Good morning, Nora!"

"Good morning, Mah John!" she replied brightly.

John was pleased to note that she was getting to be more at ease with him with each interaction.

"I never slept so much in my life," John said.

“You must have been very tired,” Nora replied.

“You speak English!” John was incredulous.

“I studied English in college but ...” she was lost for words.

“But you never got a chance to speak it?” John helpfully completed the sentence for her.

Nora accented nodding her head vigorously.

“Now wait a minute. Did you just say you have been to college?”

“Yes, I studied for three years for BA.”

John was thunderstruck. He found it impossible to understand how a college-educated girl like Nora could be happy doing menial chores. “What a waste of ability and talent,” thought John.

“I'll give you tea,” she said oblivious to his thoughts, moving the charcoal brazier in his direction.

There was an unspoken intimacy as they sat in close proximity sharing the warmth of the same fire, excited as much by the vast differences between them as by the tenuous common ground that had developed unbeknownst to them. John yearned to be able to communicate freely with Nora, but he realized that she was bashful about speaking in English, and he did not want to embarrass her by forcing her to converse in a language that she was not comfortable in. So it was that they continued to communicate that morning more by smiles and gestures than by words. Nora's pleasure was obvious as she handed him a cup of tea with cream crackers by the side on the saucer.

“Thank you,” whispered John as he took the cup.

As he sipped the hot tea and munched the cracker, John marveled at the sea change two days had brought about in his perceptions. He could not explain the deep sense of peace that had descended over his being. He knew he was on the right track and felt as buoyant as Jason did closing in on the Golden Fleece.

When Mah Step joined them a little later, they moved to the verandah with fresh cups of tea.

"You've caught up on your sleep by now, haven't you?" asked Mah Step.

"I think I have. And the dogs didn't bother me too much last night. Sure, they woke me up but I went right back to sleep," replied John.

"We will be moving to the village today. Maybe later in the afternoon. Do you want to go to the town before that?"

"Hmm, let's see. I need to buy some toiletries and fresh batteries for my camera," said John.

"We can go about the same time as we did yesterday, then."

The talk soon turned to religion. Mah Step explained how missionaries had come to this remote region from England, Scotland, Wales, America and Australia nearly two hundred years ago.

"In spite of the differences in theology and though each denomination may have believed that the others were destined for perdition, they amicably divided up the tribes between them so they wouldn't have to compete against each other. It never ceases to amuse me each time I think about how they compromised their theology in preference to negotiated monopolistic territorial rights. Because of this the Baptists, the Southern Baptists, the Australian Baptists, the Welsh Presbyterians, The Scottish Presbyterians, the Methodists, the Lutherans, the Seventh Day Adventists, they all set up their own distinctive domains. At one time, each tribe had its own denomination. Talk about predestination!" said Mah Step.

"Is that how the Welsh Presbyterians got your tribe?" asked John.

"Not exactly. A Welsh missionary by the name of Roberts was the first foreign missionary to reach this remote area. By the time the American Baptists arrived he had already set up a small church in our land. So, they let the Welsh Mission keep our tribe. In recent times, new denominations and cults have sprouted in all tribes and the tribes are not denominationally homogenous as they once were."

"Were the missionaries good people?" asked John. "Or did they alter your culture and customs?"

"I know, in this day and age there is considerable repugnance towards proselytization, but you must remember that all this happened over a hundred and fifty years ago. Even if it were today, our faith would still be a precious gift. There is no question about that. The only difference would be that in the present age missionaries would probably be a little bit more sensitive to changing local customs and traditions."

"How so?" asked John.

"Well, all hill tribes had a tradition of communal singing and dancing. By dancing, I mean customary dancing, not modern-day dirty dancing. The missionaries put a stop to all dancing. In the case of the Tsomi tribe, the missionaries banned the *thuang*, a very large drum, from worship services.

The *thuang* has made a comeback in recent times. The Tsomi Baptist church decided that the use of that musical instrument did not contravene Christianity. They have also restored traditional festivals, including the most famous of them all, the harvest festival, and revived folk dancing on these occasions. Their bamboo dance is a real treat to watch with colorfully dressed girls agilely avoiding their ankles getting caught between two rhythmically clashing bamboo poles held parallel at ground level."

"Is that true for the Sakhis too? I mean the revival of tradition," asked John.

"No, sadly not. You see, the Sakhi religion was well established unlike that of other hill tribes. The other hill tribes were all pantheists with differing religious customs. The Sakhi religion, on the other hand, was highly developed and organized. There is still a small core of devout indigenous Sakhis. The traditional Sakhi festivals and dances are associated with the Sakhi religion. In the case of the other tribes they had converted en masse to Christianity. In our case, it was more at an individual or family level. Their celebrations are more social than religious. We also lost the art of weaving, but that wasn't due to the missionaries. It was due to the import of textiles from the mills of Manchester and other English industrial cities. The Sakhis fell in love with the plaid and the tartan pattern."

"It seems such a pity that you lost part of your tradition."

"No, we didn't lose much actually. Anything that had religious connotations had to be changed. There was no way out. I don't blame the missionaries for that. At least they didn't make us wear funny clothes ill-suited to the weather as they did in parts of Africa!"

"What about your traditional dance forms?" asked John.

"There has been a revival in recent days of our spring and harvest dances. There is still an element of traditional religion to it. The female dancers hardly move! They look gorgeous in silk and gold ornaments, but they stand like statues and wiggle their toes inching forward demurely with their hands unmoving by their sides. The men, though, are warrior-like with feathered headgear and they prance around like peacocks waving long swords."

"Other than bringing in Christianity, what good did the missionaries do?" John asked.

"Well their two biggest secular achievements were education and health. Roberts—that first missionary—gave us the Roman alphabet that we use today. Our forefathers had a fable about the tribe crossing a large expanse of water on rafts and a hungry dog eating up the parchment on which was the original Sakhi alphabet. An interesting aside here. Anthropologists believe that my tribe has similarities with the tribes of Melanesia and have no anthropological connections to the other Tibeto-Burman tribes that surround us. Racially and linguistically, we are an Austroasiatic island in a sea of Tibeto-Burman tribes."

"Interesting! And do you think the story of crossing the water was probably your forebears crossing the sea on rafts á la the *Kon-Tiki* or *Ra*?"

"Probably. We don't know for sure. We are now landlocked, surrounded by these other tribes.

Anyway, the Welsh missionaries brought us education and translated the whole Bible into the Sakhi language. They also taught us hygiene and took care of our health. If it weren't for them our children wouldn't be so healthy today. Later, we came under British rule and the government then built roads, hospitals, and schools. British rule was very beneficial for our land."

"That is a whole new perspective on colonization and proselytization," mused John.

"In a way, it is. Even if the colonial power had done us harm and looted our resources, we would still be grateful to their missionaries for bringing Christianity to us. That is the dearest gift. The Christian faith has made us what we are today. By and large, with a few exceptions, the British administrators were benevolent rulers in the Sakhi Hills. But the people of the plains clung to Buddhism and Hinduism and rejected the missionaries as allies of the colonial government."

"Are there missionaries from America in these parts still?" John was curious to know.

"No, not for the last thirty years. The government thought they were subverting the people politically in addition to converting the people to their religion and banished them. They barred entry to all foreign missionaries. I kept up a correspondence with a Southern Baptist missionary from Georgia. He was with the neighboring Pangama tribe and for many years had traversed the hills on his Harley Davidson."

"Good deal! A missionary on a Harley Davidson! My mind conjures up a totally different picture of motorcycle riders," John said shaking his head.

Later they walked again to the town center to buy the things that John needed.

"Things are so cheap here," exclaimed John when the shopkeeper handed him the bill.

"Didn't I tell you, you could live on five dollars a day here?" asked Mah Step.

After getting back home John checked his email again and sent one out to friends telling them he would be out of email contact for some weeks. It was a curious feeling. He could not remember a single day in the past six years that he had not accessed email. This disconnection was going to be the severance of the umbilical cord, he realized. The cell phone itself wasn't much of a big deal. He used it very seldom anyway and was not going to miss it as much as he was going to miss the Internet and email.

Nora brought his clothes to his room after lunch. Not only had she washed them by hand the previous day, she had also ironed them neatly, every single piece, even the vest.

"I haven't ironed clothes for as long as I can remember. Thank you so much!" said a surprised John.

Nora was pleased with the appreciation.

"Who ... who irons your clothes?" she asked hesitantly, gesturing with an imaginary iron in her right hand.

"No one!" laughed John. "I just use the washer and dryer."

This appeared to confuse Nora a bit.

"The machine irons your clothes?" she asked incredulously, her eyes widening in surprise.

"No, the dryer only dries the clothes. Not many people iron clothes anymore in the US."

It was only weeks later that John realized that ironing clothes was still de rigueur in this part of the world and that even in the villages people used charcoal heated irons to meticulously press their clothes.

The taxi arrived a little after three in the afternoon. To John's surprise, it turned out to be a green SUV and not a regular black and yellow taxi. Ma, whom he had seen only at meal times, was formally dressed for the journey. She had on a tartan shawl that she wore like a cape around her shoulders, but which also covered her head. She also had on shoes that made her look even taller than she was. Ma was at least six inches taller than Pa, reckoned John. The formal attire made her appear more severe than she normally looked, although she was by nature a very shy and bashful person.

Nora was, by contrast, an absolutel delight in the green *sainlem* and white blouse and high-heeled shoes. The only makeup she had on was lipstick.

Mah Step wore a black leather jacket and carried a small bag. John carried both his bags to the car. Ma and Nora wanted the men to take the front seat, but John would have none of it. John and Mah Step sat in the rear and they were off.

"We are ahead of the evening traffic," said Mah Step.

"How long will it take to get to the village?" asked John.

"We should be there in about an hour and fifteen minutes. It is about forty kilometers from here," replied Mah Step.

The car sped quickly through the town and in less than ten minutes they were on the outskirts of the town, with smaller houses set in the midst of a profusion of pine trees. As John looked out from the window, the blue of the sky alternated with the green of the trees as the car followed the winding road climbing steadily uphill. The whine of the engine increased as they reached a long straight stretch with no curves to break the ascent. After another twenty minutes of this slow climb, they were at the top of the mountain with Kyllang, the Big Town, laid out below. They stopped for a minute for John to take in the view.

"It's breathtaking!" said John watching the city traffic moving around below like a chain of tiny matchboxes.

The wind was much stronger and cooler at this altitude and John pulled his jacket together as he got back into the car.

"We are at the top of the plateau now. My village is at the very edge of this same plateau. The hill section of our road begins here. I hope you are used to mountain roads," said John.

The road quickly narrowed as it curved around the sides of denuded hills. Soon a deep gorge opened up on the left side of the road and John could see green paddy fields and shiny tin roofs way down in the valley glinting in the afternoon sunlight. John felt a twinge of anxiety as he considered the speed of the car, the width of the road, and the steep drop to his left.

"This road was built by the British. They were excellent engineers," said Mah Step making conversation.

"It hasn't been rebuilt or redesigned since then?" asked John.

"They resurface it every year but have not made any major changes like increasing the width. The best thing about the road is the gradient at curves. The car just eases into the curves, it's such a pleasure to drive. Those British engineers were perfectionists."

That certainly appeared to be true, as the car seemed to naturally lean into the curves. The s-curves and the blind turns did not seem to bother the driver as he moved the car along at a fair clip. Ma had fallen asleep and her head lolled about with every turn the car took. But Nora was awake, and she chatted with the driver and offered him *kwai*. She offered one to Mah Step also, but he declined. There were farmers working on the steep hill ahead.

"Pineapples," Mah Step explained cryptically.

Soon they came to a saddle in the road that bridged two hills. The short straight stretch had gorges on either side but on reaching the other hill the steep drop was on the right side as they climbed the new hill in the opposite direction. The fascinating view dispelled the fear that John had initially felt. They passed through small villages with a church or two by the roadside. Free range chicken flapped out of harm's way and pigs rooted by the side of the road. At one turn they nearly ran into a herd of miserable looking cows and the young cowherd had to run up and down brandishing a large stick to get the cows to stay to one side and let the car pass. Soon they came to a stone quarry that initially looked like the end of the road. Workers were smashing the rocks set on the hillside with sledgehammers and the broken chunks lay strewn about the road. Two boys ran from stone to stone moving them out and creating a path for the car to pass through.

"We are almost there. Another twenty-five minutes," announced Mah Step.

In a short while, the ravine vanished as the road left the edge of the plateau and turned inwards, transforming itself into a snaking black ribbon in the middle of a rolling green plain, with paddy fields on either side. The small church was the first building to come into view followed by a clutch of small huts, some thatched, some tin-roofed. Further on, to the center of the village, there were a few shops with a string of taxis and jeeps waiting for passengers. The road began to slope down after that and ahead lay a small group of nicer looking houses, much like the ones in the Big Town. Mah Step's house was a little farther away and as the car turned off the bitumen-topped road onto the rocky ground that led to the house, a group of children gave up their play and ran alongside the car waving. John's waving back seemed to excite them even more and they broke out into screams of delight. When the car stopped about twenty feet from the house, Mah Step, the first one out, had to gently shoo the children away so they could unload the baggage. The children watched intently from a distance as the white *sahep* got down from the car after Ma and Nora. Pa came out of the house to welcome John into the house, saying "*Hooblei!*" as he shook John's hand warmly. The house was much smaller than the one in the Big Town. The front porch had three doors opening on to it. The white washed walls of the house contrasted with the red tin roof with the flaking paint. Mah Step paid off the driver and led John into the house.

"You must remember this house is much more modest than the other one. I hope you will not be uncomfortable," said Mah Step apologetically.

"No, please don't apologize! You already told me about this in our online chat. I am easy!" John replied.

"I sincerely hope that is true and you won't find life here an inconvenience."

"I don't think I will," John said resolutely.

The house was literally a row of parallel rooms with the kitchen at one end. By the time John and Mah Step reached the kitchen on their walkabout, Ma and Nora had already had the kettle over a wood fire.

The room next to the kitchen turned out to be the bathroom. The room had no tiles and was quite unlike any bathroom that John had seen before. There was no shower or tub; just a cemented two-inch deep, three-foot square depression on the floor, which John surmised was the bathing area.

"Remember there is no running water in the house or even the village for that matter. You wash yourself by sitting on those wooden stools and pouring hot water from a bucket over your body," Mah Step explained.

The wooden stools were only about nine inches high but that wasn't going to faze John.

"I think I can cope with this!" he replied chirpily.

"The other thing is the toilet. We don't have it inside the house. The traditional way is to have an outhouse. And that is what we have. Come let me show you," Mah Step said as he led him out to the backyard.

About fifty feet away was the black, tin covered outhouse. John realized that the tins were of the same size as the tins he had seen on the huts on the way.

Noticing his look Mah Step said, "Those are from old oil and kerosene tins. The tins are cut open and beaten flat and provide sturdy protection against the heavy rains during the monsoon. Some of the houses, you may have noticed, are made of tin too."

"Yes, I saw that. Excellent recycling!"

The outhouse itself was made of wooden planks covering a hole in the ground. John hoped the planks were strong enough to hold his weight. Instead of a roll of toilet paper, there were strips of newspaper speared on a length of metal wire hanging from a nail on the wooden post.

"Poetic justice for yellow journalism and the gutter press!" thought John with a smile.

The land behind the house was very nearly flat with shallow hollows here and there. Pigs, chickens, and goats could be seen grazing on the plentiful grass. There weren't any trees to be seen except in the far distance.

They went back inside the house to John's tiny room at the opposite end of the house. John thought it was only a little bigger than his walk-in closet back home. The room being so small, John pushed his two bags under the low wooden bed to have enough space to move about. A small bare table about three feet by two with no drawers stood against the wall by the side of the bed with an armless chair in front of it. The utilitarian furniture reminded John that life here was going to be truly spartan.

The staunch admirer of simplicity that he was, John could not resist the temptation to say, "Thoreau would have been happy here."

"Yes, that's true," Mah Step nodded in agreement. "And there are no taxes, either!" he added laughing.

"You are good! Now how did you know that!" said John joining in the laughter. "But seriously that's why I am here, aren't I? To see if I can leave all the gadgets of modern technology and the non-essential compulsions of modern life behind and still survive."

"True," agreed Mah Step. "But it might be more difficult than you think as the days pass."

"I'll do my best to cope. I see you have electricity here. Do you also have a landline?" John asked.

"Don't be fooled by the wiring and the bulbs. The electric supply is intermittent. It goes off every now and then every day, sometimes for hours. If there is a strong wind or heavy rain, it is days before the fault is repaired."

"What happens to the food in the refrigerator?" John asked.

"There *is* no refrigerator!" Mah Step laughed. "We cook for each meal. But because of the cool climate, any excess food actually stays well overnight, or till the next meal. So, there is little waste. And meat and vegetables are fresh—and all organic, I might add."

"Good deal!" exclaimed John. "What about the telephone?"

"As I told you yesterday, we are out of range of cell phones here. As for the landline, they don't work anymore because some villagers stole the copper wire! The government phone company replaced the lines twice but finally gave up. It was too expensive and there was no way they could prevent future thefts."

"How do you stay in touch with the outside world?" John was curious.

"The bus drivers and taxi drivers carry personal messages to the city. If you have mail to post, they will carry that as well. You don't need to know them personally. They do it for everybody. For free. Once it reaches the city they leave it with someone at the market who gets in touch with the addressee."

"How fascinating! And since I don't see any TV in the house I presume you can't receive any channels here."

"That is correct. Sometimes though when the atmospheric conditions are just right stations from Thailand and Burma come through. I used to watch the Burmese stations for some cross-cultural education, though I don't understand a word they say. We don't have a TV here now. But if one could afford satellite TV it would be possible to watch TV here."

Squatting down to pull his bag from under the bed, John took out the radio he had brought and handed it to Mah Step.

"What a lovely radio! Is it digital?" John hadn't seen Mah Step so excited before.

"Yes, it is. It is a Sony *ICF 77,* one of the finest portable radios ever made," John said proudly. "I remember you telling me how radio was the only source of information in the village and I decided to bring this cutting-edge piece of technology. Brought some rechargeable batteries to go with it as well."

"Wow! This is simply wonderful!" gushed Mah Step.

"Turn it on and see if you can catch any station?"

John had to help Mah Step turn the radio on and extend the whip antenna but once it was on Mah Step was quick to tune the radio to the BBC.

"John!" said Mah Step dramatically throwing wide his hands. "I present the BBC, loud and clear from their relay station in Singapore, without any electrical or electromagnetic interference or even the ignition noise from vehicles."

"It's almost as if we were right there in their studios," said John marveling at the clarity of the sound.

"Yes," exulted Mah Step, "the studios of Bush House, London. How pure and clear and strong!"

"It is, isn't it?" agreed John.

"My life revolves around the BBC," continued Mah Step. "It gives me the news every hour and it also has wonderful music programs and even drama on weekends."

"I listened to the BBC a lot when I was at Cambridge," said John. "But they don't broadcast to the Americas anymore and I haven't gotten around to buying that satellite stuff."

"I keep forgetting that you studied in England. You mentioned this in one of our chats, but I had forgotten. How many years were you there?"

"Seven years. I studied English literature for my undergraduate and my master's. I try and visit England at least once every other year, especially the Lake District."

"You are a Wordsworth fan, aren't you?

"Yes, I am. The "Ode on Intimations of Immortality" has strong religious overtones for me."

"But you are working on your Ph.D. thesis on Philip Larkin, right?" asked Mah Step.

"Yes, that's right. I'm glad you remember. Larkin's wit and poetic felicity are amazing. His poems 'Money,' 'Toads,' and the sequel 'Toads Revisited' are absolutely perfect. He is quite metaphysical. 'High Windows' is another of my favorites. I do my research mostly on weekends at the Greenbelt library. My day job has nothing to do with literature. I need it to pay my bills. You will love that library. They let you borrow up to seventy books at a time."

"Seventy books! Per person? Here I can borrow only two books at a time and that too for a week!"

"For a bibliophile like you, there's nothing better than the American library system. And it's all free."

"It seems so unfair when we compare our library here with yours! Anyway, you are lucky to have facilities like that. No doubt about it. Anyway, your living in England explains your 'international' accent, if I can call it that. Your accent is not the typical American accent nor is it purely British. It is somewhere in between."

"The term 'International English' is now used derisively to mean a kind of pidgin English spoken by non-native speakers from various parts the world," said John.

"I didn't know that. And I didn't mean to offend you," Mah Step was apologetic.

"No offense taken," said John laughing lightly. "By the way, the neutral British-American English is referred to as the "mid-Atlantic" these days."

"Is that right? That's news to me!"

"Do you think listening to the BBC has shaped *your* accent?" asked John.

"I don't know. Maybe to a small extent. You tend to speak the same way others around you speak, you know. And as another American said famously once, 'Asian accents go all over the place.' I speak much like everybody else speaks here."

"That's not quite true. You are so much easier to understand than the others. You don't go up and down like the rest. And you certainly have a much better vocabulary than I do," John said.

"Thank you! Though, that's probably not true. You are too generous," Mah Step responded in his self-effacing manner.

"You know what? You remind me of Conrad!" exclaimed John.

"Most assuredly, I am unworthy of that comparison. Conrad, or Korzeniowski to use his Polish name, was a great man. I never cease to be amazed at how he mastered the English language well enough to find a permanent place in English literature. I think I mentioned this to you in one of our online chats—*Lord Jim* is one of my favorite novels. The technical perfection of the long story *Heart of Darkness* is no less remarkable."

"Yes, I remember that. You never told me how you learned English. I have always been curious of that," said John.

"It's a long story. It was my grandfather who taught me to write. I learned my alphabet in the mud. My grandfather guided my hand that held a twig as we squatted in the wet front yard after a rain. He would smooth the mud flat with his left hand and I would start all over again. Children like to play in the mud. I *learned* in the mud. My grandfather couldn't afford slates or books for me to write on at that time. I get emotional just thinking about that."

"Your grandfather knew English?" asked John.

"No, he did not. But remember, the Sakhi language uses the Roman alphabet. He could read and write in Sakhi. The missionaries had taught him to read the Bible. When I was in middle school, my parents sent me off to a government boarding school in the Big Town. We didn't own a house there then. The school had exchange teachers from England funded by the Nuffield foundation. It was Mr. Whitfield, my chemistry teacher from Scotland, who ignited my love for the English language."

"This is utterly unbelievable!" John made no attempt to hide his astonishment.

"Yes, it is rather unusual. After finishing school, I devoured books from the only library in the Big Town and listened to English programs on the radio. English is the most genteel, precise and perfect language in the world!"

"You are quite an Anglophile. You do love English, don't you?"

"Absolutely. Remember the American lady I told you about? The one that backpacked through South and Southeast Asia? She told me quite bluntly that I had an accent."

"You are kidding, right?"

"No, she actually did. She said this to me in the Big Town. She didn't come here to the village," said Mah Step.

"And how did you respond?" John was curious.

"I told her evenly that when she was in my country it was *she* who had an accent—not me!"

"Touché!"

"We also had a small argument about phonetics."

"What was that dispute all about?" John asked.

"Well, she hadn't heard of phonetics and said she didn't see any need for another language (as she called it) merely for pronouncing words! I lost that argument. I couldn't convince her. This was before the Internet reached our town."

"Mah John, would you like some tea?" interrupted Nora. John hadn't heard her come in because all the doors (including the front door) were always open.

"Yes, of course, Nora. That would be lovely! Thank you! Tea is always welcome," John said. "I am so getting used to life here," he added to Mah Step.

After tea, they went for a walk around the village. There was still about an hour left before sunset, but the farmers were already trudging back home from the fields or from the market. Almost everyone carried on their backs large round-mouthed cones made of bamboo strapped to their foreheads. Mah Step explained that the cones contained produce from the fields, farming tools and implements and purchases from the market. John discovered later that the loose sling that went around the mouth of the cone and the forehead of the bearer held the cone safely without the need for any additional securing. He also found out that these cones were sturdy and could carry a lot of weight. Most of the men puffed on pipes while the women walked in groups chatting and chewing *kwai* and tobacco. The children ran up to them and delighted themselves in calling out "*Hooblei!*" to John before trailing excitedly behind the towering white 'giant'. Everyone they met smiled warmly and talked briefly to Mah Step and bowed shyly to John. When they had crossed the last huts, the green paddy fields came into view, swaying gently in the cool evening breeze. It was so quiet that John could hear the water dribbling down the open pipes some distance away.

"The ingenious gravity-fed irrigation system was made by the villagers themselves. It wasn't designed by a highly paid college-educated engineer; or by an exorbitantly priced foreign consultant. It is all indigenous ingenuity. The open pipes are bamboos slit length-wise and propped up on bamboo legs. One hundred percent indigenous! A hundred percent bio-degradable!" exclaimed Mah Step.

"How does the water climb without a pump?" wondered John.

"That is the cleverest part of the system. The weight of the accumulating water opens sluice gates at collection points where the water has to climb in small incremental steps. Somewhat like the locks in the Panama Canal."

"Amazing! Where do they get the water from?" asked John.

"There is a natural spring and reservoir on the next hill. We get our drinking water from the same source."

Just then a taxi pulled up alongside and the driver accosted Mah Step. After Mah Step and the driver had exchanged greetings, Mah Step introduced John to Mah Aks.

After the car had moved on John asked Mah Step, "Isn't "Axe" a rather unusual name? Is he the godfather type?"

"Noooo! Mah Aks is one of the nicest and kindest human beings in our village. His name is diminutive for "Accelerator", his given name. In our language, it is actually spelt a-k-s—Aks. We have neither "c" nor "x" in our alphabet."

"Is that really his name—Accelerator?" John asked dubiously.

"Yes. His father had worked as a handyman and driver to a rich contractor in the Big Town and he could think of nothing else to name his son when he was born than something related to driving."

"What could be more logical!" murmured John dryly.

"But Mah Aks didn't follow the advice of Johnny Cash's "Boy Named Sue" and name his children normally. He stuck to the same pattern as his father in naming his children," continued Mah Step.

"I will be darned! Now how did you know that Johnny Cash song?" John was incredulous.

"Heard it on the radio!" replied Mah Step with a disarming smile.

"Ask a silly question! OK, what *did* he name his sons?"

"Mah Aks has three sons and a daughter. He named his sons First Gear, Second Gear, and Third Gear in that order!"

"You're kidding!" John said as they laughed together.

After they had gone a few more steps John stopped and turned to Mah Step.

"And what did he name his daughter?"

"I thought you would never ask. "Clutch"! He named her Clutch!" said Mah Step cracking up as they both erupted into peals of uninhibited laughter.

When their laughter had subsided Mah Step said, "Seriously, there are other strange names too. 'Morning Star' and 'Bright Star' are fairly innocuous. There are also names like 'Scholar', 'Intelligent', 'Innocent', 'Respectful', and for girls, 'Beautiful', 'Gently', 'Faithfully', 'Sincerely', etc. There's even a guy called 'Help Me'. Whenever I call out to him I feel as if I am sending out an SOS signal or making a distress call!"

They walked back to the house in the dusk, their shadows lengthening behind them. John was hoping to write his daily journal on his computer after dinner but got no opportunity for that as a steady stream of visitors poured into the house to take a look at the white *sahep* who had come from the other side of the world.

John learned an invaluable lesson about the system of social intercourse here. One didn't have to let someone know beforehand that you would be coming to visit. An invitation, even informal, was wholly unnecessary. You just dropped in. It was open house every day of the year. One subordinated one's tasks to the social needs of good-neighborliness. The village headman, the Presbyterian pastor, the middle-school headmaster, the postman, the only government officer who lived in the village, the local nurse ... they all came to see John. They all had the same questions after the *Hooblei* and the handshake. "How old are you?" "How many children do you have?" "Why are you not married?" Like Mah Ap, the inquisitive headman of the Big Town locality, they appeared perplexed, even disconcerted, by the fact that he had no spouse or progeny and, worse, showed no inclination to redress the situation. They all seemed to be quite at home sitting on whatever was available in the kitchen and sipping endless cups of unsweetened red tea. As the discussions were all in a language he could not comprehend and as prolonged squatting on the low bamboo stool was beginning to hurt his back, John excused himself and retired to his room. He got his laptop out but try as he might he could not locate the adapter for the plug. Ultimately, he gave up and decided to turn in for the night. As in the city, the sounds of animals woke him up briefly. In addition to barking dogs, he thought he heard the howling of wolves and a growling that he could not identify. He thought he also heard the sound of distant drums, but he wasn't sure if he was awake or asleep.

Chapter 5: Exploring the Neighborhood

John got to see the bottomless fissures the next day.

But first, he had to navigate the outhouse. His fears of the previous day did not seem unfounded as the wooden planks sagged under his weight. He noticed in the dawn's early light that the wooden planks were laid over a bamboo lattice. As if crouching on his haunches was not bad enough, the low roof (designed for people eight to ten inches shorter than him) caused him to bend awkwardly forward as well. At least, he consoled himself, it was better than being out in the open and being chased around the countryside with his pants around his knees by rooting pigs.

After this the bathroom is going to be a breeze, thought John; but it wasn't quite that easy. For one thing, there was no washbasin. For another, there were covered aluminum and brass vessels along the sides of the wall filled with clean water. John had to again squat so as not to splash soap or water on the pitchers. This was probably the first time he had brushed his teeth squatting. But try as he might he could not keep his feet and legs from getting wet, though his pajamas, rolled up high on his thighs, stayed dry.

After the morning brunch, Mah Step and he went out for a stroll. This time they forsook the road and climbed the hill towards the tree line in the distance. It was on the flat ground on the other side of the hillock, not too far from the village, that Mah Step pointed out the cracks in the earth. Some of them were only a few inches wide but there were three that were at least a foot across and ran along the ground far into the distance.

"These crevices appeared after an earthquake in the fifties. But our worst earthquake was in 1897. Elders speak of the earth opening up and entire villages being swallowed up in that terrible calamity," said Mah Step. "These cracks are bottomless. You drop a stone and you cannot hear it hit the floor."

John picked up a stone and dropped it into the gap. Sure enough, there was no sound.

"Didn't hear a thing. This is scary. I have never seen anything like this before," said John.

"We try our best to keep the children off this area. So far we have only lost some farm animals here."

"How many people died in the big earthquake?" asked John.

"No one really knows. There were no censuses done those days. Folklore puts the number at over twenty thousand, but we will never know. But we did lose a sizeable portion of our tribe. Much like losing an arm or a leg."

"It must have been a terrible calamity."

"It was. Many took it to be divine retribution."

"Was there a falling off?" John asked.

Mah Step was confused. "What do you mean?"

"Wrong choice of words. Sorry. I meant did people lose their faith in God?"

"No, on the contrary, there was quite a revival of faith. There was a big spurt in conversions and new churches sprang up in many villages. The five years following the earthquake recorded the highest growth in Christianity. Since this area is highly seismic we also have some natural hot springs not too far from here, about thirty kilometers away. They are very therapeutic."

"If they are anything like the hot springs of Japan I'd like to go there sometime."

They found a small grassy knoll further ahead with a perfect view of the village and the paddy fields below.

"I feel as if we are in the middle of a power outage," John remarked.

"I don't understand," Mah Step replied.

"When there is no electricity—and that happens very, very rarely in the US—there is a deathly quietness. All electrically powered appliances—TVs, stereos, washing machines, refrigerators—everything shuts down. When the constant background hum of all these machines is gone, it is a strange feeling. It is like that now. It is as if everything has come to a standstill. Even time."

"It is much quieter than the Big Town here. That's for sure!" said Mah Step.

They could hear only the twittering of birds and the sighing of the breeze in the trees behind them.

"Crickets!" John smiling.

"What?"

"I heard the chirping of crickets."

"Oh, yes, there are plenty of them around here. Cricket is also a popular sport that the British left us."

"I know that game. I played it at Cambridge on weekends. Flannel trousers and cream-colored sweaters and dark green or blue caps. Quite the gentleman's game."

"It is my favorite. Nothing more satisfying than hitting a ball clear out of the ground for a six," said Mah Step holding his hands together and swinging at an imaginary ball.

"There's also the phrase 'I can hear crickets' which means that things are pretty quiet or nothing much is happening. It can also mean the lack of any response from the other side to a query or request."

"Deathly silence, huh?" suggested Mah Step.

John lay back on the grass and watched the white puffs of cloud drift across the blue sky. "This is the real life; the total banishment of the hurly-burly and desperation of everyday urban life," thought John contentedly.

In a little while, when they started chatting again unhurriedly, their discussions turned to religion again.

"One basic difference between Christianity and the Sakhi tribal religion is forgiveness," said Mah Step.

"Why, is there no forgiveness in the Sakhi religion? I thought you said the traditional religion and Christianity were quite similar."

"Yes, they are. And forgiveness is a part of the Sakhi religion. The core of the traditional Sakhi belief lies in earning righteousness. In doing good deeds. Our elders teach us that there is nothing more precious in this world than honesty and righteousness. Christianity, on the other hand, has salvation by faith as one of its fundamental principles. Grace is the core of the Christian faith."

"My friend's wife would love your religion," remarked John.

"Why, what does she believe in?" asked Mah Step.

"This couple are close friends of mine. Their daughters have flown the coop and they are enjoying their freedom again. No more college fees to pay. No more tantrums or arguments. They are into yoga and other esoteric things. They go for lectures on a wide variety of topics. They support PBS and NPR. They also found religion recently."

"How did it happen?"

"They attended a 'Purpose Driven Life' workshop and came back converted. Well, at least Bob did. Cindy liked everything else about Christianity except the forgiveness-of-sin part. She loved the 'love your God' and 'love your neighbor as thyself' bits. But she could not understand how Jesus' death could bring forgiveness to everyone. She wondered how a person who did not know her and whom she did not know, could pay the price on her behalf. She questioned the universality of forgiveness of sins."

"That is a difficult concept for some," conceded Mah Step.

"What are your thoughts on this, Mah Step? How would you explain this to Cindy?" prodded John.

"It's not easy. Some people of my own tribe wrestle with this issue. Socially, we are taught to earn righteousness and at church, we are told salvation is free and comes by faith. I'm not sure how I would explain this to your friend Cindy. I need to think a bit."

They then talked about other things. John lay back again on the grass with his hands and legs spread-eagled, fascinated by the azure sky and the cotton-candy-like white clouds that floated by. The quietness was peace itself. Mah Step, however, was deep in thought like Rodin's *Thinker.* He kept pushing back the bridge of his glasses and pursing his lips.

"I think I have a possible answer for Cindy," Mah Step announced after some time.

"Do tell. I'm all ears," replied John.

"This is more like a parable but is a true story nevertheless. Some years ago, we had a drought and our crops failed. That year the crops failed not only in our region but also all over the country. It's a kind of famine that comes once in forty-eight years. Farmers all over suffered heavy losses. They had no means to pay back the agricultural loans they had taken from banks. The government imported food, reduced grain prices and stepped up rationing through the public distribution system. This helped everybody. But the debts of the farmers remained unpaid. The overdues mounted with interest and late payment fees. In the plains, a few farmers committed suicide rather than face the ignominy of being declared bankrupt. Some of the farmers in our area sold their valuables, mostly gold, to repay their loans. But in the majority of cases, the loans were insurmountable. Then one fine day our finance minister made a surprise announcement over radio and TV. Newspapers carried the news as banner headlines the next day."

"What was the announcement?" John asked.

"The announcement was this. The government had decided to forgive the debts of farmers up to a limit of $350 per farmer. Ninety-five percent of the farmers in the country had loans below this amount. You must remember that our farms are small, and they are labor-intensive with the farmer's family providing most, if not all, of the labor. Remember also that it was not the government that gave the loans. It was the banks that had lent the money. But the government, a third party, decided to forgive the debts of all farmers in our country. The government paid the banks the bulk of the loans. The banks wrote off their bad debts up to the equivalent of three hundred and fifty dollars per farmer. Here is the moral of the story. The farmers in this village did not know the finance minister personally. Some of them may not even have known his name till this amnesty was declared. But that did not prevent the pardon from being effective. All that a farmer who trusted in the government's announcement had to do was go to the bank and claim that pardon. It was as simple as that. The forgiveness of the debt was universal and at the same time, it was also personal. The Christian concept of forgiveness of sins is quite similar to that."

"A neat parable. I like your story;" said John enthusiastically raising himself on one elbow. "Do you believe that your own sins are forgiven?"

"Yes, I do. I try to do good deeds and to be honest and upright in the tradition of my tribe. But I also believe that nothing I do will ever earn total forgiveness for me. The Christian concept of forgiveness and pardon is a huge, huge comfort. It takes the weight—the pressure—off me. I strive to do good deeds because I am saved not because the good deeds themselves will save me. It is grace, amazing and beautiful grace, all the way," said Mah Step quietly.

John reflected on that for a while. Finally, he said, "I wish someday I have your assurance and certainty in matters of faith," John said.

"I hope so too," replied Mah Step. "You know what I find really mystifying?"

"What?" asked John.

"Isn't it ironic that people have no difficulty believing the fictional sacrifice of Sydney Carlton in *The Tale of Two Cities* but have a problem with the substitutionary concept of Christianity?"

John laughed. "This is the first time I have seen Dickens used as a theological reference point!"

The other big event of the day was the tasting of the *kwai*. But it was nothing like the wine tasting parties that John had attended in DC. When Nora brought out the plate of *kwai* after the 'evening tea', John decided to give it a try. He remembered Mah Step's explanation of how *kwai* was steeped in tradition. The Sakhis chewed it all the time. John noticed that the Sakhi women had a tiny cloth or plastic bag slung over their shoulders that contained *kwai* and, he was to learn later, tobacco for chewing. Men carried *kwai* in plastic pouches or stylish shiny metal boxes along with their cigarettes and pipes carved out of wood or bamboo. Not only were guests and visitors always offered *kwai* but also, John noticed, it was a practice to exchange *kwai* when meeting a friend on the road.

With that kind of importance, there was no way John would not have tried the *kwai*. After all, he had tasted the horrid smelling durian fruit when in Malaysia and lived to tell the tale.

Mah Step demonstrated by first taking a piece of areca nut and a folded betel leaf from the plate that Nora held out. Opening the leaf, he showed John the white lime smeared on it.

"My daily dose of calcium," he joked. "It is the lime and the juices from the leaf that combine to produce the deep crimson color."

"What does it taste like?" John asked.

"It's difficult to explain. One gets used to it, you know. Definitely an acquired taste. But it does sort of warm the body up. Makes your ears tingle," replied Mah Step.

"That ought to be interesting! Tell me, does it stain the teeth permanently? It does not seem as if pearly whites are valued here," remarked John.

"You are right. Since practically everybody eats *kwai* here, perfect white teeth are not the norm. The opposite is! But eating *kwai* once in a while won't stain your teeth."

"How diametrically opposite are our values when it comes to teeth!" John said. "To think in the US, we spend a small fortune and suffer braces and painful procedures for whitening and perfecting our teeth!"

"There is no dentist in this village and even in the Big Town, there are not many. People go to a dentist only when they are in pain with an infection or a broken tooth or something. Cosmetic dentistry is unheard of here."

"Amazing!" was all John could say.

"And *kwai* is part of our tradition. Nowadays doctors tell us that it can cause oral cancer especially if tobacco is chewed along with it. But it is a difficult custom to break. As a symbol of hospitality, every guest is offered *kwai*. As I already told you it is considered bad form to refuse. If we gave up *kwai* we would need a new substitute for hospitality."

"You know what? I'd like to try it. I want to see what *kwai* tastes like. This is as good a time as any. Let's go for it!" John said smiling.

"Are you sure?" Mah Step asked. "Absolutely sure?"

John was not to be deterred. Nora held out the plate and John helped himself to a piece of nut and a folded leaf. Tentatively he took a small nip of the areca nut. It tasted like a piece of mildly acidic wood. "This is harmless," thought John as he popped the whole quarter piece into his mouth and chewed it.

"Definitely an acquired taste," he said to Mah Step.

"Now you chew the leaf as well. But take some of the lime off the leaf," suggested Mah Step.

There wasn't much lime on the leaf, but John took half of it off and, since there were no paper napkins to be seen, put it on the edge of the ashtray on the center table. He then rolled the betel leaf with the remaining lime into his mouth.

The very next moment, he regretted his action. He felt the blood rush to his head and his ears turned crimson as if on fire. His tongue burned as if it had been scalded. The room seemed to wobble and spin as he felt the gorge rising in his throat. He sensed and vaguely saw the anxiety on the faces of Mah Step, Nora, Ma, and Pa.

"You had better lie down," Mah Step said as he cleared the wooden settee and held him by the shoulders. Lying down with his head on the arm of the sofa reduced the giddiness only a little. The ceiling still spun, and his mouth was full of the bitter-tasting mixture of bits of areca nut and betel leaf. The *kwai* stained his lips a bright scarlet giving him the ghoulish look of a vanquished vampire.

Nora ran out of the room and came back with a tin from the yard.

"Spit out the *kwai,*" Mah Step said, and John was glad to do just that, turning on his elbows on the settee. The relief was palpable. Ma offered John a glass of warm water. John rinsed his mouth and spat that out into the tin as well.

"I think I need to rest a bit," John said and lay back with his eyes closed. The feeling of nausea still lingered, and he desperately wanted to avoid vomiting.

It seemed like ages but must have been about twenty minutes when the giddiness slowly receded.

'That was some adventure!" John said sitting up with a sheepish smile, sweat pouring down his forehead and face.

"Unforgettable may be more like it? Like the famous Alec Guinness movie."

"What?" asked John puzzled.

"*The Bridge on the River Kwai.* That famous river has the same name as what you just ate. Or at least tried to."

"Of course! Now why didn't I think of that? By the way, Alec Guinness played a fabulous role in that movie."

"Yes, he did. One of my all-time favorite movies—after *Casablanca*, of course."

"Is that your favorite movie?" asked John.

"It is. That is *the* perfect movie. Humphrey Bogart and Ingrid Bergman both played the roles of their lives."

Just then Nora came in with cups of tea on a tray. John was grateful for the tea. It removed the last vestiges of the awful taste from his mouth and at the same time revived his spirits.

"What are the favorite Sakhi sports? Other than cricket and soccer, I mean," asked John.

"Traditional sports are dying out. But one that has still retained its preeminence is archery."

"I didn't know that! How is it played?"

"Actually, archery is nowadays linked to gambling. It is gambling that is driving the sport now. You may have seen two numbers displayed on many shops in the Big Town. They are the archery results of the day. If you bet on the winning number, you may win a lot of money."

"Is it government controlled? We have State-run lotteries in America. Sometimes the jackpot runs into millions of dollars. The profits are used for funding education and other worthwhile causes."

"That doesn't happen here. It is not government controlled. It is largely illegal. The poor people are the worst sufferers. They bet their day's wages and, more often than not, lose it all. It's a pity."

Chapter 6: Meeting the Neighbors

The next day was a Sunday and John accompanied Mah Step and the family to church for the eleven o'clock service. When the church bells began to peal at a quarter to eleven people streamed in decked in their Sunday best. John suggested that they sit towards the rear so he could watch the whole service unobtrusively. Ma and Nora sat towards the middle and Pa sat in the front pew. Unlike the church in Greenbelt that he sometimes attended, where on some pews there was just one worshipper or none at all, the church here was packed to capacity. John was wedged tightly between Mah Step to his right and the village headmaster to his left.

The choir was enthralling. John realized that the Sakhis had a deep love for music. When he mentioned this later Mah Step had said, "The tonic sol-fa was another of the legacies the missionaries left behind. The Sakhis became so adept at choral singing that the Sakhi Presbyterian Choir has sung not only in Wales and England but also in America."

"If I had known I'd have traveled cross-country to hear them sing. What about traditional Sakhi music?" John wanted to know.

"It is still in existence and it has a devoted following. But sacred music is sung only in the western tradition."

The service dragged on for over two hours. The children in the congregation were a little restive but they sat through the entire service. The sermon itself was close to an hour. John did not understand a word of what was said but he recognized familiar hymns like 'Nearer my God to Thee', 'Amazing Grace', and 'Just as I Am' from the many hymns that were sung. During the offertory, John realized that Pa was one of the elders of the church as he went from pew to pew with the other elders collecting the offerings of the congregation in purple velvet bags.

When the service ended, John was surprised at how quickly the church emptied. There was no after-church fellowship or refreshments. No coffee hour. The congregation simply dispersed as quickly as they had come. The pastor came over to speak a few words to John. Pastor Highborn was a dapper and soft-spoken man who could easily have passed for a neatly dressed middle-class Englishman with a high tan in a dark tweed suit. He spoke with a slow deliberateness that became his calling.

"I'm so glad you could come for our service today. Mah Step told me about you. While you are here please join us for worship every Sunday. If you would like to preach during one of our services we would be happy to accommodate you," said Pastor Highborn.

"I'm happy to be here. But preaching is not my forte. I don't preach. I am just a seeker. But I will try and attend the service when I can," replied John.

On the way back, Mah Step then told him of the Sakhis' reverence for the white man. As he was wont to do he pressed the bridge of his glasses against his forehead with his left index finger and looked thoughtful as he spoke.

"Ever since the missionaries came to our land, studied our language, gave us our alphabet, translated the Bible, compiled the first dictionary, set up schools for education, provided medical care and, most importantly, introduced us to Christianity, every white person is an angel, a messenger of God. To them, a *sahep* can do no wrong. Totally unthinkable. The British rule did not seem like colonialism to us. If we had our way, the British would still be here. They may have been vindictive and cruel in the plains. But up here in the hills, the affection was mutual."

"That's a whole new perspective on the Raj!" said John.

"Yes, it is an inconvenient fact. But times have changed. In the Big Town now the Americans are the clear favorites. The movies, the music, the soaps on TV are all American. The US is considered the defender and protector against all the evil forces of the world."

"This is quite the opposite of how Americans are perceived elsewhere in the world," John said.

"That's right," Mah Step continued, "To us, there is no such thing as an 'Ugly American'!"

"Awesome!" John said but, grimacing, quickly reverted to a more British response. "I mean, that's splendid!"

Mah Step smiled and said, "But the villagers do not differentiate between American, British, French or German. For them, they are all white men—*saheps*. We have a joke here about our nurses in the

Big Town during the Second World War. They were so enamored of the white allied soldiers and wanted to have white—I mean, fair-skinned—children. The Tommies had it so good they didn't want to go back home to England! To the Sakhi every white person is a devout Christian and in the present day also a kind and generous American."

"If only they knew the truth!" muttered John sotto voce.

"The TV reality show *Cops* was an eye-opener to many here. They didn't believe that there was any such thing as 'white trash'. Many of them still think that that show is staged or rigged and not genuine. The same people think that all the wrestling they see on TV is real! To most Sakhis, all Americans are born-again Christians. I sometimes think this is the safest place for Americans, America included."

"Then this must surely be the best-kept secret!" John replied.

Then Mah Step told him of the visit of the German scholar a year earlier. Helmut Wege had come to study the Sakhi language and its grammar. He had a theory (subsequently discredited) that it was an offshoot of the Indo-Germanic family of languages and a derivative of Sanskrit and was not a part of the Mon-Khmer group.

"One day the pastor and the elders of the church requested Helmut to preach at church the following Sunday. This happened during the third week of his stay here. Helmut vigorously refused. They attributed Helmut's rebuff to modesty and redoubled their entreaties in the following weeks. Their persistence finally upset the German. The upshot of the whole thing was that Helmut abruptly left the village in a huff, his research unfinished. The villagers never really understood why Helmut was so upset and why he refused to preach the gospel. Later the professors from the university in the Big Town narrated the reason. Helmut, the linguist, was in actual fact an atheist who actively detested Christianity. But that was beyond the comprehension of the villagers. 'How can any human being not believe in God?' they had said when they found out later. 'And how can a *sahep* not be a Christian?' These two issues confounded the villagers for weeks afterwards."

"Is the belief in God universal?" John asked.

"Yes. Absolutely. I don't think there is even one person in the whole village who doubts the existence of God. We live in such close communion with nature and we are so vulnerable to natural phenomena that we have an unshakeable faith in God."

"How different is the traditional concept of God from the Christian version?" John asked.

"That's a good question. We are surrounded by people who believe in a multiplicity of gods. Their pantheon of gods extends into the thousands like the innumerable gods of the Hindu tradition. There are millions in the plains who worship idols. To us that is anathema. The Sakhis worship the one true God—not objects of stone or wood made by hands. Neither do we worship animals or creatures or natural phenomena. Nor do we deify our intellect as some fancy atheistic so-called churches do these days in your country. We are unique. The traditional Sakhi religion holds that there is only one God—the one true God."

"Was this notion something the Christian missionaries brought with them?" John asked.

"No! This was already there. That's the beauty of it. It is our own belief. The followers of the traditional faith hold the same belief even today."

"Interesting!" remarked John.

"Yes, so much so that the Unitarians in America and England have vied with each other for the allegiance of the traditional believers here. The difference is that most western Unitarians these days are either atheists or universalists accepting all religions. They are not theists like the Unitarians of Transylvania or the Sakhis here. Both sides tend to downplay the differences for their own reasons."

"Did the belief in one God make it easier for the Sakhis to accept Christianity?"

"In a way, yes. But it really goes deeper than that. The Sakhi moral code is very, very close to the Christian principles of loving God and loving our fellowmen. The Sakhi code of ethics is centered around the phrase: "Know God; Know Man". Every Sakhi child is taught that at an early age. The other important moral code is difficult to translate into English in a few words. It teaches us to respect not only our own clan, which is our mother's clan because we are matrilineal, but also to respect equally the clan of our father. That takes care of all relatives on either side of the family tree. I already told you of the strong emphasis we place on earning righteousness. The strong moral code is so akin to the Christian principle of loving God with all our heart and mind, and loving our neighbors as ourselves, that it makes even non-Christian Sakhis appear to be Christians from their actions."

"You mentioned the Unitarians. What about the relationship with the Presbyterian Church in Wales?" John asked.

"Our relationship is still very strong. We are independent now with our own Synod. But we have a very active relationship with our parent church in Wales. Their representatives come for our annual conferences and our choir goes there almost every other year. The church also sends some theological students to Wales once in a while. But ironically our roles have been reversed now."

"How's that?" asked John.

"At the last Synod—something like an annual conference—we had a speaker from Wales. He broke down in the midst of his sermon and explained how our relationship had come full circle. It was the great revival in Wales that prompted them to send missionaries abroad, including to our land. The church here has grown in stature and is continuing to grow. The church in Wales, on the other hand, has steadily declined. Membership is dwindling. They are a mere shadow of what they once were. The speaker from Wales tearfully said the time had come for us to send missionaries to Wales. And we are doing that now."

"That is ironic!" agreed John. "Christianity is declining in the west. In Europe now there are many empty or defunct churches. But in the US the church is still vibrant and growing."

"So, when are you going to preach?" teased Mah Step.

"Quite frankly I have no intention to preach. You know that. What can I preach about? My doubts? My existential dilemma? That will make no sense to the pious village folk here," said John.

"Don't worry, you don't have to preach. I was only teasing you. I will talk to the pastor about it.

But at least I am sure you will not commit the mistakes of most foreign speakers," said Mah Step.

"And what's that?" John was curious.

"Most of them begin their sermons by describing their journey here. They talk about jetlag and connecting flights and layovers at London, Amsterdam or Frankfurt. They forget that most of the villagers have never even seen a plane let alone been in one. Matter of fact, only very few of them have been to any town other than the Big Town."

"Have no fear. I will never speak of those things. You can be sure of that. If I absolutely must speak, you will have to be my interpreter! Maybe you should do all the preaching on your own and I'll just mumble," John added smiling.

Sunday afternoon was the laziest day that John could remember in his life. Mah Step had gone on some errand. The whole village had come to a standstill. There was nothing to do, nowhere to go. He was tempted to turn on the radio to find out what was happening in the world. But he had come to a difficult decision the previous night: he would keep away from the radio and would shut out the outside world as completely as he could. He marveled at the important role the radio still played in the lives of these village folk. The government station broadcast news in their language only twice a day; once in the morning and again in the evening at seven thirty. Since they left for their fields by daybreak the only newscast most of them could listen to was the evening broadcast. Almost the entire village would be tuned in at that time, avidly listening to the news. John did not understand a word but that did not bother him. It was a sight to see them listening intently. He also learned that this was not the time for small talk.

Without keeping up with the news, he might return a two-month Rip Van Winkle, but he didn't care. He wondered at how much he had changed in just a week. "What if I don't ever go back to the high-pressure life?" he asked himself that afternoon. "What if I elect to stay here and savor life and renounce the sheer headlong rush of desperation?"

As usual, it was Nora who broke his reverie. She, attentive as always, brought him tea and cookies. Mah Step had not yet returned. Nora surprised him by bringing a *lora* (he had learned that that was the Sakhi name for the round cane stool) and sitting down by his side on the verandah. John was pleased and at the same time a trifle apprehensive not knowing how to manage the communication.

"Is the tea sweet?" Nora asked hesitantly.

"Yes, it is. Perfect," John replied sipping the tea.

"Have some more biscuits," offered Nora holding out the plate of cookies.

"Thanks!" said John taking one.

Their conversation ended there as each sipped their tea. Nora would look at John from time to time and smile shyly and John would smile back. But neither said a word. This was the first time that John really looked at Nora. The dark brown hair, the beautiful eyebrows, the high cheekbones, the flawless skin, the bee-stung lips and the dark expressive eyes set deep in the oval face. "She's beautiful!" John thought.

It was John who finally ventured to break the silence.

"You never told me what you studied in college."

"I studied botany, zoology and chemistry, and also English," replied Nora.

"You studied science! And did you ever work after finishing college?" asked John speaking slowly.

"No, I came back home to look after Ma and Pa. I am the only daughter."

"That's right. Was it your decision to come back home?"

"Yes. My parents wanted me to go for further studies, but Ma was unwell at that time and I decided to stay home for a year," Nora spoke haltingly. "I might go back to college next year or look for a job in the Big Town."

"Which do you like better, the village or the 'Big Town?'" asked John.

"The 'Big Town is good for shopping. There are restaurants. But the village is much safer. It is very quiet and relaxed here. Also, less pollution."

"Good deal! Can I ask you a personal question?"

"Yes," Nora replied looking a trifle anxious.

"Forgive my asking this. At what age do people get married here?"

The moment he uttered the words he knew he had made a mistake.

Nora blushed a deep red and looked into her cup. "I don't know how to answer your question. But some of my friends are already married."

"Are marriages arranged by the parents here?"

"No, not usually," replied Nora.

John decided it was safer to change the subject.

"Your English is not bad. Not bad at all!" John complimented her.

"Thank you, Mah John. My English is very bad. It is difficult for me. I am very uneasy speaking in English, I have to translate every word in my head before I speak. Sometimes I cannot find the correct word," Nora said tapping her head with her right forefinger.

"Let's make a deal. You teach me Sakhi and I will speak English with you every day."

"I hope you won't laugh at my mistakes!" said Nora.

"Believe you me, the mistakes I'm going to make speaking Sakhi will be much bigger!"

Nora laughed, her eyes crinkling, her face relaxing.

"She's incredibly beautiful!" thought John again but only smiled.

"Some more tea?" Nora asked solicitously.

"No thanks. I'm good."

"OK. Let me go then!"

And with that, she was gone, carrying the cups and saucers and the leftover cookies.

Mah Step arrived just before dusk, looking very pensive. John joined him in the kitchen, where Ma and Nora were cooking dinner. Pa sat on a *lora* puffing away at a pipe. At a signal from Mah Step he tapped the pipe against the brazier rim knocking out the tobacco and ashes on to the tin base-plate.

"I remember you told me you didn't like second-hand smoke," said Mah Step.

"Thanks. Looks like you had a tough day," remarked John.

"Yes, it was more difficult than I thought. I'm glad I didn't take you with me," said Mah Step.

"Why, what happened?"

"I was requested to mediate in a dispute between two farmers. They are actually related to each other. One of them had borrowed money from the other and hadn't paid it all back," explained Mah Step.

"That's not uncommon," commented John.

"True. The fact that they are related complicated matters. The borrower had already paid a good sum as interest and most of the principal. The lender wanted to sell the gold that he was holding as security and keep all the proceeds for himself because of the default. The borrower wanted more time, quoting crop failure. I tried to persuade the lender to lower the interest rate a little and give some more time for repayment. Or otherwise to return the excess amount from the sale of the gold."

"That sounds reasonable."

"Unfortunately, they called each other names and did not agree to a settlement. They will now take the case to the village council."

"Is that like a court?" John asked.

"In some ways, yes. But there are no written laws. It is all based on oral tradition and common sense. But the decisions of the village council are absolutely binding. They even have powers to seize immovable property and banish someone from the village."

"Wow! They are powerful!" conceded John.

"Yes, they are. But they cannot play favorites. All the village council members are elected, and they can be removed at any time. Dispute hearings are conducted in the open and all can attend. Nothing is held in camera."

"That sounds like true, grassroots democracy."

On Ma's instructions, Nora cleared the low center-table and started to lay the table, a clear signal that dinner was about to be served. Dinner was, usual, a silent affair. But the food was, as always, superb.

After dinner, Mah Step dropped a bombshell. He thoughtfully tapped the bridge of his glasses with his forefinger.

"I need to go to college tomorrow. May have to stay there the whole week and come back only on Friday," said Mah Step.

"That's OK. I will be fine. I will be well taken care of here, I'm sure."

"If possible, I will try to come someday in between. But I will need to go back by the first market-bus the next morning,"

"You don't have to. You already told me about your work. I'll be fine. Besides, I don't want to be overly dependent on you or anyone else," said John.

"How about some red tea?" asked Nora, holding out a tray.

Mah Step took a cup and passed it on to Pa. As they sipped the tea they talked of other things.

"Do you miss emails?" asked Mah Step with a smile.

“Actually, no. As long as the out-of-office message works. That way nobody would be left wondering about my silence.”

“Let me know if you need anything from the Big Town,” offered Mah Step.

“No, I think I’ll be fine. Even if I do run out of anything I will still manage. Remember, I’m trying to lead as simple a life as possible. To relive, so to speak, the life of my hero Thoreau. Except, I will still have to pay my taxes to Uncle Sam, which I don’t mind at all.”

“I admire your ideals. It’s not easy I know to give up the creature comforts that one is accustomed to,” said Mah Step.

“That’s true. But the incentive is the freedom and the inner peace that you get as you let go of the non-essentials. By the way, I found that adapter I was looking for. Want to see my laptop?” asked John.

The two of them walked to John’s room. John fished out the laptop from his bag under the bed and handed it to Mah Step.

“Go on. Turn it on. It’s going to be yours soon,” said John.

Mah Step placed it gingerly on the table and sat down. He watched intently as the computer screen lit up. After John had keyed in the password, Mah Step began checking the computer systematically, starting with the system information and then moving to the control panel.

“How much did you pay for this?” Mah Step asked John.

“Just $500. It is refurbished.”

"For that price, this is a good machine," he said finally.

After Mah Step had left the room John sat down at the desk typing out all his experiences after Bangkok. There was more to write than he thought. With no brazier to warm him, he felt so cold in a little while that he had to sit wrapped up in the quilt, drawing his cold hands inside from time to time to warm them before resuming the typing again. It was late and the house was quiet as he turned in for the night. He slept as soundly as he did the previous nights except for being woken up by the howling of wolves from the forest and the faint sound of distant drums in the middle of the night.

Chapter 7: A Moveable Feast

Mah Step left the next morning by the first market-bus to town. John was up early, and they had tea together with Nora. Mah Step was visibly agitated.

"It is nothing. Each time I have to go on a journey, I'm like this. Plus, this time I am also worried about leaving you on your own," he explained when John asked him what was bothering him.

John said he would walk him to the bus. Mah Step tried to dissuade him but finally agreed on the condition that Nora would accompany them also and walk him back home.

The bus was filled to capacity with all kinds of produce. There were sacks of potatoes commingled with gunny bags of rice and jute sacks filled with charcoal. Live trussed-up pigs and chicken in bamboo restrainers that looked like large mesh bags were on top of the sacks or in the aisle. Women covered in thick dark shawls occupied the front seats. Men lounged around on top of the bags inside puffing their country pipes or climbed to the roof of the bus, already precariously piled with sacks of vegetables and broom. John wondered if the center of gravity of the bus was low enough to negotiate the curves. He wouldn't want to ride on this bus with a deep ravine on one side of the road! Mah Step found a seat near the front of the bus. Formally attired as he was, he looked quite out of place with the rest of the unkempt and shoddily dressed male crowd on the bus. The bus was slated to leave at 6:15 but it dawdled with the engine idling until a woman arrived running and out of breath. Mah Step waved as the bus pulled out, the engine whining with the strain of the heavy load.

John was happy walking back with Nora. Her happiness was infectious. She smiled at him and at all the passers-by and did a little skip now and then like a little girl. It was a beautiful morning. The warmth of the sun's rays had driven the chill away. The whole place glowed under the orange-red glare of the morning sun.

"Are you hungry?" Nora asked as they were nearing the house.

"No. I'm good," replied John.

"What would you like for breakfast?" asked Nora.

"You know what, I think I will switch to the Sakhi custom of a meal of rice in the morning," replied John.

"Are you sure?"

"Yes, I am. If I have to stay eight weeks here I might as well get used to the local customs."

For the next five days, Nora was his companion and confidante. Her diffidence in speaking English disappeared gradually with each passing day as she was involuntarily thrust into the role of interlocutor in her brother's absence. While his own attempts at learning the Sakhi language was floundering miserably, John took delight in watching Nora's learning-curve rise steeply, with the long pauses of translation-in-the-head yielding place to the reflexive choice of words that rolled off less self-consciously off her tongue. John recognized that the rapid rise of Nora's skill in speaking English was because she already knew how to read and write the language but had lacked the occasion to speak it conversationally.

John also had to admit that he was being, slowly but surely, drawn to Nora. Her unspoilt, virginal innocence reminded him of the stanza from Gray's 'Elegy Written in a Country Churchyard'.

Full many a gem of purest ray serene,
The dark unfathom'd caves of ocean bear:
Full many a flower is born to blush unseen,
And waste its sweetness on the desert air.

He thought of all the time she spent doing chores around the house every day. It seemed to him so terribly unfair that that was her entire life; sitting on her haunches doing the dishes or washing clothes; crawling on her hands and knees swabbing the floor spick and span; or squatting uncomfortably on a tiny six-inch high wooden stool in a smoke-filled kitchen. "What a waste of talent! Nora deserves a much better life than this," he said to himself. "She fits the 'Lucy' image of Wordsworth to a T."

A violet by a mossy stone,
Half hidden from the eye!

Whenever she was outside the house, and sometimes even when she was inside working, children from neighboring houses would drop by to talk to Nora. She had a soft corner for children and they liked being with her. The children had such cherubic faces in spite of runny noses or grime on their cheeks. The torn clothes they wore, if anything, further accentuated their beauty. They were free spirits and radiated the happy innocence that Blake wrote about and etched. That was another thing that John noted. Children were free to be children here. Although public displays of affection amongst adults were totally absent, children were bestowed with it all the time. They were constantly hugged, kissed and carried about. Mothers had their small babies on their backs in a sling made of a shawl tied securely across their back and knotted in front at the chest. The babies slept or looked around as their mothers worked in the house or even out in the fields. It was initially a strange sight for John to see girls in their teens carrying siblings on their backs. The children roamed around in complete abandon. Ten and twelve-year-olds even went outside the village alone to play on the edge of the forest or to fish and swim in the nearby stream. They showed no signs of fear or mistrust. The adults too didn't seem to have the faintest anxiety about the safety of their children. Obviously, child predators were unheard of here. Nora was confused when he asked her about this and John quickly decided not to pursue the subject further. When Mah Step got back he would ask him about crime levels in the village and town. But in the meantime, he was happy to watch the untrammeled innocence of the children as they laughed and flitted about enjoying unfettered freedom.

The five days passed quickly. By the end of the week, John had met many of the villagers, explored the surroundings on his own, been invited to lunch on four out of five days and had generally insinuated himself, without really trying, into the village consciousness. He would have a lot to share with Mah Step when he got back.

It was dusk on Friday evening when Mah Step returned from the city. "I'm back," he called out matter-of-factly as he entered the kitchen where John sat by the fire with Pa, Ma, and Nora. There were no hugs or kisses. John had already noted that the Sakhis were not physically expressive though innately affectionate. "Definitely not touchy-feely," he told himself. Nonetheless, even if unspoken, fondness and trust were always very palpable.

"How are you?" Mah Step asked, formally shaking hands.

"I'm good," John responded. "How did your lectures go?"

"They went well. They were well received. I had to also correct some test papers. Did you have a good time?

"Yes, I did. I was invited out to lunch four times. I also got to go for a short hike in the hills with the school teacher Mah Listrin yesterday."

"Good! I'm glad you are settling in. I need to have a wash first. The road was too dusty. I'll be back with you and we can talk at length."

But first, it had to be a hot cup of tea and crackers. After tea, Mah Step was off with a bucket of hot water from the fire.

The Sakhis adored John—or so Mah Step had told him before he left on Monday. John had not believed him then but the last five days had proved that it was indeed within the realm of possibility. This was wholly unexpected. Never in his wildest imagination did he dream that he would one day be the recipient of public adulation, the like of which he thought was reserved for movie actors or pop stars. So far in his life, he had tried to live a simple life and had shunned the spotlight. But here he was—like it or not—the cynosure of all eyes.

But funnily enough, he did not feel intruded upon. Instead of feeling his privacy and personal space being violated, he felt the opposite emotion—that he was being accepted and graciously welcomed into their lives. In his encounters with the Sakhis he had felt genuine affection being offered without the slightest hesitation or reservation and he felt impelled to reciprocate with kindness and gentleness the best way he could. For one thing, he smiled a lot more. Everybody smiled here. Back home it was the regulation "How're you doing?" or a plain "Hi!" when you met someone. But here the *"Hooblei!"* and the smiles were more than mere social courtesy. They seemed to come from the heart and opened the doors to genuine human interaction.

He had, for the first time in his life, felt connected to a whole society—and not just a single individual—by a band of affection that was almost familial. He was treated like family by men, women and children—all total strangers—proffering their hands shyly and saying, "*Hooblei!*" when they met on the road. And when they came to Mah Step's house to see John, they did not come empty-handed. They would bring eggs that their free-range chicken had laid; or freshly plucked vegetables from their garden—a head of cabbage, small tomatoes, a bunch of supple okra or tender French beans—all organic and not genetically modified. In the beginning, he was tempted to decline the gifts, but

Mah Step had gently pulled him aside and told him it was rude to refuse presents. John could only hope that he conveyed his heartfelt gratitude adequately as he accepted their gifts. He became quite good at it, holding both hands together and saying "*Hooblei*" with a faint bow. But he always felt guilty that he had nothing tangible to offer in return.

People dropped in at Mah Step's house at all times of the day and night to spend some time in the vicinity of the white man, the s*ahep.* It was open house all the time, every day, almost twenty-four seven. Ma or Nora offered them *kwai* and tea or even a small bowl of rice.

He realized later on, that it was more than mere curiosity on their part. Mah Step explained that the reason they came was to share and participate in his presence in their midst, in their village. They would sit near the kitchen fire on low wooden or cane *lora*s and talk unhurriedly with Ma. But every so often they would turn to look at him unabashedly and he was disquieted when he saw admiration and even awe in their eyes.

"I really don't deserve this," John told himself. "I'm just an ordinary guy. Nobody gives me a second look back home but here I am being fawned upon like a celebrity!"

The previous weekend when Mah Step was around he had willingly assumed the role of interpreter. But the triangular conversations must have begun to tire Mah Step after a while because he had begun to provide many answers on his own, without any input from John, who had been left smiling vacantly or nodding sagely, depending on the tenor of the conversation, without a clue as to what was being discussed. John had retired early the first time when Mah Step was present. But he thought later that that was not the right thing to do and since then had sat through these visits, even if the low *lora* was uncomfortable for prolonged use. Since Mah Step was away in the Big Town they chatted mostly with Ma in the kitchen, sharing *kwai* and small talk with Ma and Nora. Before leaving they would invariably come around to shake his hand and say, "*Hooblei*" and wish him a good night's sleep with *"Phiah sook"*.

"A far cry from the American experience, isn't it?" Mah Step had asked after the visitors had left.

"Absolutely! If people back home dropped in on each other unannounced as is done here, there would be a steep rise in the homicide rate," John replied dryly.

"In the village, it is still open house as far as neighbors are concerned. Till as recently as five years ago, locks were unheard of. People would go to the fields just shutting their doors and leaning a stout piece of wood against them to prevent animals from getting in. A spate of thefts by out-of-state thieves changed all that. But even now no part of one's house is out of bounds to the neighbors. They are free to roam around all the rooms, including the bedroom. In the Big Town things are different. Everything's so formal now. The old traditions have all but disappeared."

His shower done, Mah Step joined him looking fresh and relaxed. They had just begun to converse about the week when Nora came in and said something in Sakhi to Mah Step, nodding respectfully to John as well. John understood what she said. It was time for dinner. This time Pa joined them also. Ma and Nora, as usual, would eat later.

Nora did all the serving at her mother's bidding. John never failed to be moved when grace was said. But especially so when it was the father as he doffed his cap and prayed in such gentle and earnest tones. John was deeply touched to learn later from Mah Step that he always prayed for John's health and happiness.

That the dinner was a silent occasion was not a surprise anymore. There was roast beef; and pork in a thick black sauce of ground sesame seeds. John was happy to be served a third helping by Nora. After dinner Mah Step and John retired to the sitting room with mugs of hot green tea, leaving the kitchen for the women to have their dinner.

"The food was excellent," said John. "I'm getting to be quite fond of the pork-and-sesame dish. Ma and Nora cooked it for me twice this week at my request."

"My mother is a good cook. Her entire life is centered around the kitchen. Nora is learning from her."

"I see that. By the way, you don't waste much food here, do you?"

"No, we don't. Food is never taken for granted. It is considered a sin here to waste food."

"In the US, a lot of food is wasted every day. I can remember only one instance where I saw a similar attitude like yours to food. It was at a Sunday afternoon lunch with the family of a friend. An elderly aunt couldn't bear to see the food left on my friend's plate and finished it off for him. She had been through the Great Depression, she explained, and couldn't let food go waste."

"We have devastating famines every forty-eight years," Mah Step said.

"Every forty-eight years?" John could not hide the skepticism in his voice.

"Yes, every forty-eight years. I told you of this before while explaining the universality of Christian forgiveness but did not explain how the famine occurred. It comes like clockwork, they say, with the flowering of the bamboo. For some reason, it is referred to as "gregarious" flowering. Not sure why. We call it *kowtam*. Anyway, it comes every forty-eight years. And when that happens, rats and bandicoots multiply—literally multiply, proving the Malthusian principle. Nothing can stop them. Not poison, not traps. Suddenly, there are so many of them. And they are everywhere. The rats raid grain and seeds stored in thatched huts and we run out of food. And there are no seeds left for planting the following year. The famine used to be terrible in earlier years but now the government brings in food and seeds from elsewhere."

"I never heard of this before! Never knew flowers could start a famine," John said.

"Enough about famines. Tell me about your adventures while I was away."

"I stumbled on an intriguing mystery and solved it. I also learned a new skill," John said with obvious happiness.

"What was the mystery? And what's the new skill that you picked up?" Mah Step perked up.

"Well ... the mystery first. On Tuesday I was invited by Mah Listrin—the school teacher—to his house for lunch. His wife served the two of us in the sitting room. She did not join us. We sat on regular chairs—not *loras* or small wooden stools—at a round table of normal height. The table had a plastic tablecloth with red and white checks. They had also thoughtfully provided silverware for me—a spoon, a fork, and a knife. The lunch was delicious. There was curried chicken, thick lentil soup with butter, fried potato slices, steamed carrots and peas, and yellow turmeric-flavored rice."

"That must have been a very good lunch. Mah Listrin's wife is a good cook. But what was the mystery that you solved?"

"Patience! I'll get to that in a minute. But you are right about the lady's cooking skills. She is definitely outstanding. Now about that mystery. The next day's lunch was at the pharmacist's house. The house was full of kids. He told me he had seven children. There seemed to be a lot more than that! They were running around and chasing each other and raising quite a ruckus. The elderly parents and a spinster sister also live with them. A real extended family, if ever there was one! Anyway, my lunch was served again in the front room. I sat there alone at a round table similar to the previous day's. Even the chair looked familiar. The stainless-steel spoon, fork, and knife were of the exact same design as the school teacher's. I had to eat alone again but the food was great! The chicken was scrumptious. I half expected the pharmacist to come up and join me, but he didn't. He stayed in the kitchen with his wife and the rest of the family except to come and see if I needed anything."

"That's not uncommon for honored *saheps* and *mems*. By the way, a *mem* is a white person of the feminine gender. The Sakhis are a little shy to eat at the same table with their foreign guests," Mah Step explained.

"I could've done with some company. Eating alone is no fun. Yesterday's lunch was at the village headman's house. Mah Jo spoke only a few words of English and he seemed terribly self-conscious sitting with me. When lunch was served, I had to eat alone again. He escaped to the kitchen to eat with his wife and kids. In the middle of my lunch, I suddenly realized that the table and chair and the cutlery and the tablecloth were all of the same design as at the other two houses. Then it struck me. These things—the china, the cutlery, the table and chair, the tablecloth—were indeed the same at all the three houses. They were being moved from house to house for my sake. Quite literally, a moveable feast!"

"You're quite observant, aren't you?" Mah Step laughed. "As a matter of fact, everything belongs to the Mah Listrin, the school teacher, the one you had lunch with the first day. The others do not have high tables or chairs. We prefer the low table with the cane stools. And everybody eats with their hands. Nobody uses silverware here. They wanted to make you feel at home. To have the same comforts they think you are accustomed to. Mah Listrin generously lent these free to others when they invite you for lunch. I remember the same thing happened when the missionary from Wales was here."

"I was touched by their concern for my comfort. To think they would go to all that trouble," mused John.

"What was the skill you learned?" Mah Step could not restrain his curiosity.

"Half-way through the meal at the headman's yesterday, I decided I had had enough of eating alone. I took my plate and went to join them in the kitchen. When I reached the kitchen, there they were, the whole family, sitting around on *loras*, eating from plates balanced on the flat palms of their left hand. On seeing me Mah Jo nearly dropped his plate. He was very concerned. He asked me if anything was wrong and I said I wanted to eat with them. Actually, it was less words than gestures and a lot of vigorous shaking of the head! The family was all excited. I think only Mah Jo understood what I was getting at. He offered me a *lora* and made space for me right next to him. In the beginning, they all seemed a little self-conscious, but they got over that pretty quickly. Since they were all eating with their fingers, I decided to do likewise. Soon we were enjoying the food and each other's company."

"But you already knew how to eat with your fingers," interrupted Mah Step.

"True. I had already learned that. That wasn't new. The new skill I learned was surviving in a room full of smoke. Their kitchen did not have a chimney like yours and the smoke from the wood fire stayed in the kitchen. They kept the top half the door open but there was still too much smoke inside for comfort. The smoke got in my eyes and tears ran down my face as I ate. Still, it was good fun!"

"I'm glad you are so flexible. That's why they like you so much. Beware, most kitchens do not have a chimney."

"I'm beginning to enjoy eating food with my fingers now. The food acquires one more sensory quality—that of tactility. You miss that with the fork and spoon!"

"You are talking like a Sakhi now," laughed Mah Step. At whose house did you have lunch today?"

"At the pastor's. He is a really nice person. He told me of his theology studies in the Philippines. It's been a very good week. I have never been so relaxed and yet so connected in my life."

"I wonder if you realized one other thing. I'm not saying this to make you feel guilty or anything. Just letting you know."

"What's that?" John asked.

"You know, the people are not rich here. Some of them are dirt poor. They live a hand-to-mouth existence. Yet, given a chance, they all want to invite you to their home for a meal. What it costs them sometimes is a good percentage of their assets," explained Mah Step.

"I don't understand," John protested.

"Suppose a family has two pigs and twenty chicken. That—plus the hut—are all the assets they own. And in your honor, they kill a chicken for dinner. Since their total assets add up to very little, the cost of the dinner works out to a good chunk of their total assets. Maybe ten percent in some cases."

John was shocked. "Oh, my gosh! That's the equivalent of a middle-class American spending ten or twenty thousand dollars on a guest, which no one in his right mind would do. How can I compensate them?"

"Well ... I don't know. It's not good form to refuse either. It's a difficult choice. Maybe you can present them with some gift if there is a birthday in that family. Or maybe give them some money as a gift. I don't know. It's difficult."

"The more I think about it the more upset I become. Very few Americans would spend one dollar on a hale and healthy stranger—especially if the stranger was a hundred times richer."

"It all has to do with our values of hospitality. Strangers and travelers are always treated with kindness and generosity. Even the Good Book exhorts us to entertain strangers because we may be entertaining angels unknowingly!"

"I am no angel, Mah Step. That's for sure."

"A little bit of trivia here," said Mah Step with a smile. "Did you know that chicken is the most expensive meat here?"

"You're kidding! And which is the cheapest?"

"Beef is the cheapest. Pork and chicken are about even, with pork slightly cheaper."

"That's the exact opposite of how it is in the US. Beef is horrendously expensive. And chicken is the cheapest."

"Here chicken is the most expensive."

"That explains why the bones were picked clean like a piranha!" said John.

"It's not every day that we have chicken," said Mah Step. "And I told you before we don't waste food."

"One thing I didn't like was the smoking," said John.

"Yeah, public opinion here hasn't moved against smoking like it has in the West. Most men smoke and a large percentage of women chew tobacco. Smokers here don't even ask others in the room for permission for smoking. It is considered acceptable to smoke anywhere."

"What about the incidence of cancer?" asked John.

"It's on the increase; especially cancer of the esophagus. The government needs to start an awareness campaign."

Nora brought in tea at that time. She smiled warmly at John as she handed him his cup.

"I am beginning to like black tea," John said.

"We call it red tea here. The decoction is actually red, not black."

"That's probably true. It's just a turn of phrase."

"I'm glad you had a very good week. I'm even more happy that you have assimilated yourself nicely into our society," commented Mah Step.

"I'm glad to be here. This is Shangri-La for me. When you used that term in our chat I dismissed it as hyperbole. Now I know it's true."

"We will talk more tomorrow. It's getting late. The bus ride has worn me out," Mah Step said suppressing, as if on cue, a yawn.

"See you in the morning, then. *"Phiah sook!"* John said rising and putting away the *lora* in the corner.

"Good night, Mah John! *Phiah sook!"*

John went to his room and turned on the naked overhead bulb. He didn't feel like reading but sleep wouldn't come easy either.

He lay on his bed staring at the spots on the white cloth ceiling. He wished he had a long enough brush to paint the ceiling as Chesterton had wished. But painting was never his forte.

He could not help marvel at the past two weeks. "I could stay here forever," he thought, "No Beltway traffic, no deadlines, no pompous but mediocre bosses, no insufferable colleagues, no junk mail, no telemarketers, no mindless TV, no compulsive shopping in sprawling malls, no crawling traffic on a backed-up highway cocooned from nature and fellow man in one's car, and—best of all—no choices to make!" He had every reason to smile in contentment.

He turned off the light and prepared to sleep. Just then Wordsworth's immortal lines came to his mind:

> *The world is too much with us; late and soon,*
> *Getting and spending, we lay waste our powers...*

Chapter 8: When Laptops Grow on Trees

John felt as if he had transformed himself into a child of nature as he woke with the breaking dawn to the crowing of roosters and the chirping of birds. "Who needs artificially created natural sounds here?" he thought. It was colder than previous mornings and he was the first to get to the outhouse. By now the strangeness of the outhouse and the washroom had worn off and neither seemed precarious or wearisome. On previous days, he had found a kettle of hot water that Nora had thoughtfully placed before he got back from the outhouse. Today she was not up and there was no hot water. He brushed his teeth as quickly as he could and washed his face with the cold water, squatting on the floor so as not to splash water on his pajamas or the vessels lined up against the wall.

Back in the kitchen, he debated what to do. Should he try to light the wood fire and make tea? Or should he wait till Nora or Ma got up? He decided to wait. He went back to his room, plugged in the laptop and began to write his journal.

A short while later he heard a timid knock on the door. It was a contrite Nora.

"I'm very sorry I got up late," she apologetically.

"Not to worry! It is I should who should apologize for waking up so early. Good morning!"

"Good morning, Mah John! I'm really sorry," Nora said again.

"Please don't apologize. I am good," John tried to comfort her.

"There is a fire in the kitchen. I am going to make tea. If you're feeling cold ...," she trailed off.

"Just the thing I want on a cold morning. I'll be there in a minute."

Quickly shutting down the laptop John hastened to the kitchen. The charcoal in the brazier glowed invitingly as Nora tried to get the wood fire going.

"Here, let me help," offered John.

"No, it is OK. I'll do it," Nora said.

But John would have none of it. Reluctantly she handed him the black cast-iron blowpipe and John, kneeling down to get close enough to the fire, started blowing furiously. He had not lit a fire since his Boy Scout days. The first essay was a disaster as he blew the ash all around. But soon he got the hang of it and had a moderate fire going. The exertions, though, had winded him. He sat on the *lora,* holding his hands over the brazier and watched Nora put a kettle on the fire. Once the water boiled Nora lifted the kettle lid and dropped in tea-leaves from an old tin. She then reached up for the cookie tin so that the table was set for the morning tea by the time the kettle whistled.

It was a pleasure to sit around the fire with Nora. "This is the best incentive for getting up early," thought John and smiled to himself. Her unspoken trust amazed him no end. He reveled in the quiet assurance that she displayed with neither the assertiveness nor the defensiveness that his female colleagues at work exhibited. "There is no trace of guile in her," he concluded.

Mah Step woke up later than usual. He suggested that they go to the market immediately after tea.

"Today is our market day. It comes every eighth day," said Mah Step.

"I'd love to see what the village market looks like. Are there markets on Sundays too?" asked John.

"No, when it falls on a Sunday it gets moved automatically to the following Monday."

The market turned out to be a much bigger affair than the daily village market. The whole street was jammed with buses, jeeps, and cars. The cacophony was deafening. Buyers haggled with farmers over vegetables, pigs, and chicken.

"All the people are not from this village. On market days, buyers from the Big Town and neighboring villages come down here. The biggest buyers are middlemen from the plains. They are all frauds and they gang up to cheat the farmers."

Mah Step purchased two kilograms each of potatoes, tomatoes, French beans, onions, and okra. The large cloth bag sagged under the weight of the purchases.

"You may notice we don't use plastic bags here. They were banned two years ago. Not bio-degradable," said Mah Step.

"In the Big Town, too?" asked John.

"Yes, remember the toiletries you bought? The shopkeeper handed them to you in a bag made from old newspapers."

"Yes, that's right!"

"We are a little ahead of the curve in terms of environmental awareness. Plastic bags became a nuisance clogging up the drains in the Big Town and dirtying the streams in the countryside."

When they got back Nora was ready with a lavish brunch.

"I have something special for you today," said Nora happily.

"What is it?" John was curious.

"Taste it and tell me if you like it."

"It is fish and it is good!" John said taking a bite.

"It is deboned fish ground with herbs and mild spices," explained Mah Step.

"I'm happy you like it," Nora said delightedly.

After brunch, Mah Step and John walked to a small hillock on the other side of the village. John lay on his back on the grass watching the blue sky and the floating clouds while Mah Step leaned back on his hands and studied the horizon.

"It will rain this afternoon," said Mah Step abruptly.

"It has been raining almost every day in the afternoon. So, what's new?" John asked lazily.

"Those were mere showers. The usual convection rains. This one is going to be big. Look at the horizon," said Mah Step.

Sure enough, ominous dark clouds were slowly rising up in the far distance in the direction of the sea, turning the distant horizon nearly black.

"It'll be another four or five hours before the rain hits us. We don't need to hurry back," said Mah Step.

"Good deal! So we can talk for some time?"

"Of course. What do you want to talk about?"

"Something has been puzzling me. The howling of wolves wakes me up in the middle of the night. I also hear distant drumbeats at the same time. Who beats drums at 2:00 in the morning?" asked John.

Mah Step looked at John thoughtfully. He kept pushing his glasses against the bridge of his nose. It was some time before he spoke.

"You are very observant. The drumbeats are barely audible. I am impressed. You have asked a very difficult question," he paused for a minute. "OK. I will tell you all I know. But you may find it too fanciful and fantastic. There is a myth in our tribe that people can become filthy rich by appeasing or worshipping a serpent with supernatural powers. The catch is, the serpent needs to be fed human blood."

"Are you saying there is human sacrifice going on here?" John sat up aghast.

"Look, I told you it's a myth. I don't believe it myself and I haven't seen any proof of it. But people are mortally scared of *pdin* and *pdin* worshippers. *Pdin* is the name of the snake devil. They are afraid that *pdin* worshippers will snip off a lock of their hair or the fringe of their clothes and offer it to *pdin*. People believe that that will cause them to fall sick and die. Unfortunately, this superstition causes the nouveau riche to be viewed with extreme suspicion, regardless of their hard work or business acumen."

"What are the drumbeats then?"

"It is believed that at the time of the blood offering *pdin* worshippers beat drums to appease the *pdin*."

"You can hear the drumbeats and yet you don't believe this practice exists?" John was skeptical.

"I have not met anyone who admits to hearing these drums in their own village. It is always from afar. At least one village away. I never heard these drums close at hand."

"Have you had people disappear in your village?" John asked.

"No, not one. But we have had healthy people suddenly take ill and die. They thought it was because of *pdin*. But I think that was due to other natural causes," said Mah Step.

"Hmm. This is a mystery. If you know of anyone who knows more about this, let me know. I'd like to dig a little deeper."

"Not many will be willing to talk about this. In the next village, a couple was lynched on suspicion of being *pdin* worshippers. It was later discovered that they had nothing to do with the disappearance of a young girl. As a matter of fact, there was no child missing. It was all hearsay."

"Sad. Very sad. It is so peaceful and so serene here it's difficult to imagine anything macabre like that happening."

"I know. Guess every society has its dark side."

"Anyway, there is something else that I wanted to ask you today," said John.

"Shoot."

"This is a profound question. It goes back to what we discussed the other day regarding your tribe's strong faith in the existence of God."

"OK. What's the question?"

"This is a personal question and you don't have to answer it if you don't want to. Mah Step, you are an educated person. Do you personally believe there is a God?"

The question had a stunning effect on Mah Step. For a while, he appeared to be nonplussed as he kept tapping the bridge of his glasses with his forefinger. He sat up straight from a supine position and plucked at the grass. He then looked up at the skies. John wondered if he had pushed him too far.

Finally, Mah Step turned to John and said with a tone of finality, "I do believe that there is a God. Believing in the existence of God has nothing to do with one's education. I do not for a moment think that only the uneducated believe in God. If anything, what I learned at the university made my faith stronger. Just look around us. What we see is proof enough that God exists."

"I'm sorry if my question upset you," John said.

"No, the question did not. But the fact that you thought education would weaken my faith in God is what baffled me."

"Maybe I should have phrased my question better. But you know there is an ongoing dispute between evolutionists and creationists in the US."

"Yes, I have heard of the "Scopes monkey trial"," replied Mah Step.

"Whoa! How did you know that! You are amazing!"

"It's nothing. That trial was world famous. I'm aware of the continuing dispute between evolutionists and creationists, between fundamentalists and liberals. Man has tried from time immemorial to prove or disprove the existence of God. More than the metaphysical writings, what I found most fascinating was Descartes' attempt to produce a mathematical or geometrical proof of the existence of God. But to me all attempts at finding physical proof of God's existence will be unsatisfactory. The reason being, we are using temporal tools to measure something that is eternal and infinite. It's like using a test-tube to measure Mount Everest. Or like using a stopwatch to measure the volume of the Pacific Ocean. For one, it is the wrong dimension. For another, the tools are puny compared to the enormous size of object that is being measured. Using finite tools, however sophisticated, to measure an infinite God is slightly ridiculous. So are human arguments, however erudite or learned."

"How then can one be sure that there is indeed a God?" asked John.

"For me, the basic proof of God's existence is nature itself. Entropy is a proven scientific fact. Things tend to decay, to fall apart, to degrade. There is no automatic upward movement towards improvement. I believe it is the divine force that makes that happen. Man himself is such a complex creation. I find it incredibly asinine to believe that man was created by some fortuitous set of circumstance. Just look at the trees and the animals and the sky and that fast-approaching storm. Could it all have just happened?"

"There are many—some well-educated—who think nature is the result of evolution and God does not exist."

"Are you referring to the "God is dead" claim of Nietzsche?" asked Mah Step.

"Yes."

"You see, I have very little sympathy for the nihilistic Nietzschean theory. Man is not superman. There is no such species. We are extremely vulnerable and fragile. Man attains self-actualization only through the Divine."

"What about the argument about nature being the result of evolution without God? Is that an educated hypothesis?"

"I can only say that wisdom and education are two different things. A highly educated person can have the stupidest personal beliefs. It's almost like there is a veil that is hiding things that are in plain view of others more spiritual. An argument regarding the existence of God is never satisfactory because our limited rationality is insufficient to explain the limitless being that is God. It has got to be intuitive. I have often wondered how Descartes attempted to prove the existence of God with a mere triangle. I am more sympathetic to the 'leap of faith' of Kierkegaard and the 'wager' of Pascal."

"Ultimately it boils down to personal belief, doesn't it? More faith than proof?" suggested John.

"Not really. To me, God's existence is so self-evident that it doesn't need to be proved. The whole universe is proof that God exists. The other day I visited a friend of mine who is an apiarist. He did not study beekeeping at school or college. Everything he knows he learned through personal observation. And he knows a lot! He showed me a honeycomb and explained how the hexagonal shape produced the optimum space, how accurately the bees constructed it at an angle on opposite sides for high tensile strength, how sterile the atmosphere inside the hive was, and how intricately the temperature was controlled. He said a beehive was more hygienic than a hospital and better climate-controlled than a scientific laboratory. I have been asking myself since then: 'How did the bees figure all this out?' It is nothing short of amazing! If one can look at the ceiling of the Sistine Chapel and marvel at the work of Michelangelo, how can one fail to see the Master's hand in all the wonders of nature?"

"I'm not sure if you've heard of this theory. Knowing you, I'm fairly positive you have. There is a school of thought that wonders why we can't think of ourselves as little gods evolved in the same manner as the complex universe?"

"John, I don't think we are gods. The smallest microorganism that we can't see with our naked eyes is enough to kill us. That's how puny, how powerless, we really are. If we can conquer all diseases and our own aging bodies, we would be close to being gods."

"What about all the progress we have made? Air and space travel? Atomic energy?"

"None of that has made us immortal. We could die at any moment. A small cancer is enough to kill us. If we were gods, we would be in control of everything. A truly divine being is eternal and omnipresent. A truly divine being, by definition, is also the incarnation of the highest form of goodness. How can we be gods? Our desires can sometimes be so base even by our very low standards."

"I don't know. I am a skeptic," said John.

"We are even captives of our emotions!"

"That I completely agree with!"

"Let me give you an example. The laptop you brought with you from America is a very complex and intricate piece of equipment which took the geniuses and skills of many persons and many years of research and scientific progress to create. Do you think that is a fair statement?"

"Yes, it is. That can hardly be disputed."

"If that is incontrovertible, if you can believe that your laptop computer was not an accident of nature that kind of magically popped up when the right climatic conditions came together, why is it difficult for you to believe that man and all creation—all of which are far more complex than a laptop—are the products of a Creator? I read the other day about what a wonderful piece of engineering our knee is. How much more complex is the brain, the eye, the heart, the whole human body?"

"I guess I'm a doubting Thomas," smiled John.

"You know when I will believe there is no God?"

"When?" asked John, curious.

"When laptops grow on trees and PDAs sprout from grass, then I will believe God does not exist."

"Whoa! That's profound!" exclaimed John.

"You know what the height of irony is?" asked Mah Step.

"No. What?" asked John.

"The height of irony is an evolutionist expounding his theory and shaking a fist at creationism while wearing on his wrist an expensive, intricately designed Swiss chronometer with many perfectly balanced jewels and precision movements."

"Man! You are in terrific form today!"

"Thanks, John. Do you want to stay a little longer here? Or should we go back now?" asked Mah Step.

"That cloud looks ominous. Let's go back," suggested John.

Walking downhill was more tiring than climbing up because of the steepness of the path. When they reached the footpath at the bottom of the hill a strong breeze, the harbinger of the impending rain was, already blowing. At the house, Nora was busy taking in all the washing off the clotheslines. She placed the still wet clothes carefully in the large aluminum basin that she had used for washing earlier. Ma and Pa were still at the market meeting friends from other villages. They sat in John's room and talked. The computer and the radio rested on the table.

"Have you been listening to the radio?" asked Mah Step.

"No. The funny thing is I don't have any inclination to find out what's happening in the outside world anymore. At least while I'm still here. I have sort of tuned out," said John.

"Any particular reason?" queried Mah Step.

"No, not really. It's just that I am content with living the simple life like the farmers here. I am at peace."

"When you go back to America you will need to make huge adjustments," cautioned Mah Step.

"I know. But I don't want to think about it right now. If you like you can borrow the radio," offered John.

"Are you sure?" asked Mah Step.

"Absolutely. Here you go," said John handing over the radio.

"Many thanks! I will listen to it while grading the papers I brought from college. See you in a short while."

"See you in a bit," said John. More than anything he felt like a nap. The bracing mountain air and the brisk walk had made him drowsy.

It was the thunderclap that woke him up. He felt as if a tractor-trailer had crashed full-speed into the house. The after-rumbles set the furniture chattering. The skies had darkened and lightning streaks cleft the sky. And then the rains came. What started as a patter on the tin roof had, in a matter of minutes, built up into a deafening crescendo. John walked to the window and watched the puddles turn quickly into pools of water. Very soon there was muddy water speeding along the ground following the line of least resistance. The rain came down in buckets. John felt as if he were at an aquarium looking at an artificial waterfall. All that was missing were the fishes.

Nora came in with Mah Step to find out how John was doing.

"Are you OK?"

"I'm good. The thunder woke me up. I haven't seen rain like this."

"It is pretty heavy. But there are times when it rains harder than this," said Mah Step.

"How could that be possible?" wondered John.

"Would you like some tea, Mah John?" Nora chipped in.

"Tea is always welcome, Nora. Thanks!" John replied.

Just then another crashing thunderbolt shook the house and lit up the outside in an eerie electric-blue light.

Mah Step went to fetch the brazier and he went back again to bring two *lora*s. The temperature had plummeted. It was comforting to sit by the fire and chat while nature raged outside.

"What do people do when it rains like this?" John asked.

"We are compelled to stay indoors. The rain sometimes goes on for days. When that happens, it is like being in prison. If there is a brief respite, you get to run out and feed the chicken and pigs, and also get some provisions for yourself."

"Will the shops be open?" asked John.

"The owners live behind the shops. In fact, a shop is usually the converted front room of a house. So, it is only a matter of getting to the shop. The owners will serve you any time except on Sundays. No transactions on the Lord's Day."

"Must be difficult to pass time cooped up indoors with no TV or entertainment."

"It is difficult. Many men go on drinking binges. Not that there has to be rain for that," said Mah Step.

"Is drinking a problem here?"

"Actually, it is *the* major problem we have. A high percentage of men become enslaved to alcohol and die young."

"That's a pity," remarked John.

Nora came in with the low table which she placed between John and Mah Step and went back for the tea.

"Instead of biscuits I have rice and minced beef!" announced Nora brightly.

John waited for Mah Step to say a brief grace for the food. The lightly spiced mince with diced potatoes was delightful.

"Getting back to the problem of drinking. What is the favorite drink here?" asked John.

"The cheapest is the traditional rice-brew. But most people now drink rum or whiskey which they consider more fashionable."

"I didn't see any wine shops here."

"They brew the local stuff in their houses and sell it out of the back door. Rum and whiskey are sold in the Big Town, but some shops here sell it on the sly. It is illegal but everyone turns a blind eye to it."

"What does the church do?" John asked.

"The church offers counseling and suspends members who are habitual drunkards or cause a public nuisance,"

"But that doesn't solve the problem."

"No, it doesn't. Drinking fermented rice-brew was an old tradition. It was an integral part of celebrations and all formal occasions. Everybody drank a little, but nobody got blind drunk. The missionaries put a stop to that. People began drinking secretly and they soon switched to whiskey and rum. For some genetic reason, my tribe has a lower tolerance for the imported stuff than the local brew. Just last week a brilliant teacher died of cirrhosis. He was only thirty-five. It was a tragedy. He was the best math teacher we had."

"That is sad," responded John.

Mah Step went back to the kitchen with their bowls for more rice and mince. He came back with a big smile and big second helpings.

"Tell me something about the missionaries who lived here," said John.

"The early missionaries were highly committed. They came with an intention to live their lives out here. A few actually lived here until their death. The others went back to Wales when they fell seriously ill or when they turned old. But curiously, at least in two instances, there was reverse conversion."

"What do you mean?" asked John.

"Those two missionaries came here to convert us to Christianity, but they found our tribal way of life and our beliefs so much more attractive that they renounced their faith, accepted our traditional beliefs, and lived with us until their deaths. The man married and raised a family. The woman missionary never married. But she taught school and brought up young girls. She is a legend in our area. She set up many schools. When she cooked dinner, she would count the number of people coming to eat and cook the exact number of potatoes. People found this preciseness very funny. They talk about it to this day."

But John could not contain his curiosity. "There were no black sheep?"

"How do you mean?" Mah Step asked.

"No foreigners with sexual peccadilloes or proclivities? No scandals?"

"You mean taking advantage of innocent village damsels?"

"Something along those lines. I guess homosexuality would not be very prevalent here!" John countered with a laugh.

"You are right. Homosexuality is totally unheard of here. If it's there, it's very well hidden. But nothing can really be hidden in this village. In all my life, I haven't heard of a single incident of homosexuality in the village. I wouldn't be so sure about the Big Town. But nothing overtly offensive like the gay pride or anything. We had some gay foreigners visit us, though," Mah Step added with a wicked laugh.

"Really? How did you know they were gay?"

"One of them was originally from Oklahoma; a minister, if you can appreciate the irony of the whole thing. One evening over an after-dinner coffee at a restaurant in the Big Town he gave me a manila envelope with five of his sermons. The first of which was a strong defense of alternative sexual preferences and was titled 'Coming Out of The

Closet'. Two others made passing references to gay themes. The next day I asked him about the stance of his church on gays and the priesthood and to my surprise he confessed to being gay. I was quite surprised. I had not in the least suspected that he was himself a homosexual."

"Did he tell the others about it?" John asked.

"You see, that's the thing. He told me he had had a hard time coming out of the closet in his church in Oklahoma. He made it public after his wife of twenty-seven years unexpectedly died. It seems some of the congregation were offended (as much at his infidelity while his wife was still alive as his gay confession after) and cut him off. In the end, he had to move to another church in more liberal California."

"So, he kept it a secret here?" John asked.

"He implored me not to breathe a word to anyone. His main concern was that the Sakhis would ostracize him if they knew. He had enjoyed their affection and trust all these years and didn't want to lose that. I think he was slightly disappointed that I wasn't gay. He was curious to know if there were any gays I knew," Mah Step laughed.

"How many years ago was this?"

"Oh, it's been five years now. He used to be a frequent visitor, coming every year. Last I heard he had found himself a partner from Germany."

"No straight liaisons between missionaries and Sakhi women?"

"Just two that I can think of—excluding the Catholic priest from Spain, of course."

"What about the Catholic priest?"

"He got off scot-free. Nine families in his parish each had a white child. The mothers were all young girls but nobody said anything. In our society, there is no stigma attached to children born out of wedlock, partly because we are matrilineal. And a priest is to be respected. No complaints were ever made but the Catholic Church suffered. People preferred the Presbyterian Church. The concept of asceticism and life-long abstinence is alien to our culture. Sexuality is an accepted part of the human condition even if it's not openly discussed or flaunted."

"Is he still here?"

"No, he went back to Spain two years ago and never came back. It was the American who caused me the most trouble."

"Which American is this?" John asked.

"A fellow by the name of Dan. He was a single man in his early 50s. He accompanied the gay minister on his last trip. Dan wasn't gay, though. That was clear from the beginning. In his very first week here he started an affair with a twenty-three-year old girl just out of college. All this happened in the Big Town. But she was from this village. And the following week he proposed."

"At least he was a gentleman. What was the problem? His age? Did the girl's family object?"

"No, they were pretty thrilled about their daughter marrying a white man and going off to America. She was happy too. She wanted to go to America. It was I who objected."

John was taken aback. "What? Were you in love with her?"

"No! Absolutely not! The chap insisted that she sign a prenup."

"What?" John was incredulous, "A *prenup*? Was he nuts or what?"

"Yeah, it was crazy. I hadn't even heard of prenuptial agreements. Found out from the Internet what it was. Dan went back to the States and sent the girl the agreement for her to sign. She brought it to me for my advice. After reading it carefully I thought the whole thing was unfair to the girl. I informed the girl's rich aunt who lived in the Big Town. She called Dan and asked some tough questions. And the next thing I know I get a letter from Dan's attorney threatening a million-dollar lawsuit for meddling in his affairs."

"Did he really do that? Take you to court?"

"No, that was just a threat. I told her I didn't want to get involved. She signed and mailed it back. About three months later she left for the States on a fiancée visa."

"Interesting! I'm surprised more Americans haven't hot-footed here for the same purpose."

Mah Step didn't say anything but only looked at him quizzically.

Realizing that it had not come out the way he meant, John corrected himself.

"I didn't mean it that way. I mean, I wasn't suggesting sex tourism or mail order brides or anything like that. I am truly surprised that Americans have not taken advantage of the goodwill they have here. We are generally very quick to exploit the slightest opportunity. We don't lose any time at all!"

Chapter 9: When it Rains, it Pours

The rain continued unabated. Nora had hung the wet clothes on lines that crisscrossed all rooms except John's. In the center room where the heavier garments were draped, she had also placed a brazier to get the clothes to dry faster. So, getting from one room to the other became as intricate as navigating a maze and you never knew who you would bump into on the other side as you parted the hanging clothes to cross over. To complicate matters the lines were not tied very high and John had to stoop low as he moved from one point to the other. The worst part of the rain was getting to the outhouse. John had to roll up his trousers to knee level as the whole ground was covered with calf-high water. The big, sturdy umbrella was no protection for rains of this intensity that blew laterally. He came back soaking wet and (he found the pun irresistible) completely pissed off.

The thunder and lightning did not last long but the rain did not let up. It seemed to vary in intensity, but it never did actually stop. The family had an early supper, which was fortunate because the power failed just when they had finished. Candles were fished out and placed on tins taken from the pantry. John hit the sack early but the incessant drumming of the rain on the tin roof kept him awake very long.

When he awoke the next morning, it was still raining with the same vigor as of the previous day. "This is unbelievable!" he told himself. "Now I know what a monsoon really is." As he trudged through the muddy water to the outhouse he recalled the book *Chasing the Monsoon* and admitted to himself, "I'm no Alexander Frater."

In spite of the rain, Pa, Ma, Nora and Mah Step went to church. No amount of cajoling would get John to accompany them. Power was still off. This made his decision easier. He got in under the quilt and slept all morning.

When they returned from church, John got up to sit by the fire for tea and rice. The rain had come down to a drizzle which made talking a little easier. Unfortunately, the high humidity in the air prevented the clothes from drying, the heating notwithstanding. What was worse, even dry clothes absorbed the moisture in the air and gave off a damp and musty smell.

The tea done, and nothing else to do, they resumed their conversation. Predictably the discussion quickly veered around again to religion.

"I was quite impressed by the Sakhi concept of earning righteousness," John said.

"Yes, it is appealing, in a way. People who value self-reliance and independence would, given the choice, prefer to work out their own salvation," stated Mah Step.

"But that is not what you believe as a Christian?" asked John.

"You are right. As a Christian I believe that salvation is the gift of God. I don't think one can earn it through good deeds."

"Because of original sin?" asked John.

"Yes. I think we are innately so prone to falling short that all our good deeds would not tip the scale."

"What use are good deeds then?" John persisted.

"We do good deeds because of our inner compulsion to love and help our neighbor as ourselves. Not because by doing that we will save ourselves. Good deeds are the fruit of salvation not the root or the cause of it. The true Christian's motive is purely altruistic."

"It's certainly idealistic," said John.

"I agree it is. Look at it this way. It is somewhat like credit card debt. If one is too deep in it, it is almost impossible to get out of it on one's own steam. You need external help."

"Does God keep scores? Does he have the time for that?" John asked.

"It is human nature to think of God as an implacable accountant posting to the debit all the wrong things each person does. The analogy may not be perfect, but do you think the President of Bank of America personally keeps track of all your credit card expenses?"

"No. What's your point?"

"One of these days you may use your credit card in the Big Town. You may charge expenses to it in Bangkok or New York or Frankfurt or Johannesburg or Sydney or any other place on earth. It doesn't matter where. If you are able to complete a transaction you can be certain that it will be accurately recorded in your account. The President of the bank has nothing to do with the posting. In all probability, no human being does anything manually to record the transaction. It is all automatic. If mere mortals can have such an intricate system to keep track of something as mundane and prodigious as millions of credit card transactions every day—or night—at *any* place in the world, don't you think heaven can have something far better?"

"You would make an excellent apologist!" laughed John approvingly.

"Oh, no! I am not a patch on C.S. Lewis, the one I admire most. Have you read him?"

"No, I haven't."

"His *Mere Christianity* is an absolute gem. Actually, I found the story of his life equally compelling. It is a very strange love story. You might want to watch a video of his life after you return to the States," said Mah Step.

"I'll check if the Greenbelt library has a copy after I get back."

"Back to our discussion. With your permission, I'd like to push the credit card analogy to its limit. What is unique about Christians is that their account will never be overdue or maxed out. It is paid in full, from an inexhaustible fund. In an instant, they are out of credit card debt—debt that an entire lifetime would not have been able to repay."

"Wow! You are amazing!" John said with genuine admiration. "You know what? You could take this up another level."

"I don't get you," said Mah Step confused.

"You could throw in the credit score as well."

From the blank look on Mah Step's face, John realized that he hadn't heard about credit rating agencies. John discovered that they did not have such a system in Mah Step's country; so he explained how it works in the US.

"That's good, John. You're catching on too!" laughed Mah Step when John had finished describing how credit rating worked.

"You know there are people who don't believe in the concept of sin. They think it is wrong to make people feel guilty and ashamed of themselves."

"Who can deny there's sin in this world? Every day we read of murders, rapes, robberies, to say nothing of pedophilia, incest, and subjugation."

"That's all evil," said John.

"Evil and sin are intricately intertwined. We all have the element of evil within us. Golding's *Lord of the Flies* exemplifies that better than anything else. It is this proclivity to evil, that causes sin. When the conscience gets hardened, we deceive ourselves into believing that there is no such thing as sin. How can we look at the child-soldiers of Africa, the child prostitutes of Asia and South America and say there is no sin? Greed and promiscuity are sins. Sin exists individually and collectively. Violence is a sin. If the terrorist bombings by Islamic terror groups is not sin, what is? Forgive my saying this. Slavery was sin, pure and simple. So was the subjugation of the Native Americans. The napalm bombing of the

Mekong Delta and all the collateral damage inflicted on the innocent civilians of Vietnam and Cambodia was sin. Don't get me wrong. I'm not against your country. No one is perfect. In spite of all its faults, America is still the best nation there is. But to me any falsehood is sinful. Telling a lie is a sin."

"Whoa! That's pretty intense!"

"Pardon me. The idea that there can be no sin rebels against the very core of my Christian belief and Sakhi ethic. What horrifies me most these days is child pornography. Just the thought of it makes me sick. How wretched is the human condition! Let's stop. Enough talk about these repulsive matters. Tell me about your town Greenbelt."

"OK. Here goes. Greenbelt is about ten miles outside of Washington, DC, on the very edge of the Beltway that circles the capital. It takes me only twenty minutes to drive in to DC to work every morning," John paused.

"So, what's unique about Greenbelt? I remember you telling me there was something unusual about your town."

"I'm glad you remember. The old Greenbelt was in fact built by the federal government! Can you imagine the government getting directly involved in housing? The town was constructed as a planned community in the 1930s under the New Deal of Roosevelt. In 1952 when the federal government decided to pull out of real estate, the residents formed a cooperative and bought the federal holdings. It still remains a cooperative. Very unique for the United States."

"Is it like the Russian cooperatives?"

"Heavens, no! I'm not certain exactly how the system works but owning a house in old Greenbelt is different from owning a house elsewhere. I do not live in the cooperative myself, obviously. I live in a condo—short for condominium—built in the late '70s."

"What's a condo? How's it different from an apartment?" asked Mah Step.

"It's just a fancy name for an owned apartment. It is a multi-dwelling building in which you own your dwelling and share the common costs of air-conditioning, maintenance, garbage collection, etc. with other fellow owners."

"What else is special about Greenbelt?" asked Mah Step.

"Well, let's see, Greenbelt is a city in the Prince George's county of the State of Maryland. Prince George's county goes back a long ways to the year 1695. It was named after Prince George of Denmark. Probably the most famous establishment located in Greenbelt is the NASA Goddard Flight Center. It is not widely known that the world's oldest continuously operated airport is only three miles from Greenbelt. It is at College Park. Wilbur Wright was a flight instructor there and this airport also operated the world's first airmail service."

"When you first mentioned Greenbelt in our online chat, my mind went to Wangari Muta Maathai."

"Who is that?" asked John.

"I'm surprised you haven't heard of her. She won the Nobel Peace prize for protecting the environment. She is a Kenyan and is the founder of the Green Belt Movement."

"Talking about the environment and Greenbelt, it was the greenness of the place that attracted me initially. There are many trees and wooded areas. A beautiful sight in spring is the blooming of the ornamental Bradford pear trees planted by the roadside. Overnight the green trees turn pale pink with the blossoms enveloping the whole tree. And it happens all at once. It is breathtakingly beautiful again in the fall when the leaves change color."

It did not look as if the power was going to come back anytime soon. Mah Step hunted for an old raincoat to go buy some candles. Then he realized that it was Sunday and the shop wouldn't sell even though the owners had access to the shop. To stretch their stock, he extinguished some of the candles.

"Rain or no rain I need to go to college tomorrow," said Mah Step.

"Will the buses run in this kind of weather?" John asked dubiously.

"Unless there is a landslide blocking the road the market bus will go."

"Are there frequent landslides here?"

"The soil in our province is firmer than that of the neighboring province. They have landslides that sometimes take weeks to clear up. We have one spot on the road to the Big Town that is susceptible to landslides."

"I know where that is," interjected John.

"Where is it?" asked Mah Step.

"It's where the stone quarry is, isn't it?" John said triumphantly, noting from the surprise on Mah Step's face that he had guessed right.

"You are a keen observer!" complimented Mah Step.

"Tell me one thing. Back home just three inches of rain is enough to cause floods and devastation. What happens to all the water here?"

"We are fortunate because of the altitude. All the water runs off into the plains and they have roof-high floods for days."

"How many inches of rain do you get on average?"

"The average annual rainfall—believe it or not—is 360 inches," Mah Step said quietly.

"360 inches?!" John was incredulous. "You're kidding!"

"Yes, that's right. I'm not exaggerating. Look it up in the encyclopedia."

Dinner was quieter than usual. Instead of the usual meat or fish, Ma and Nora had made egg curry instead. And after supper, there was no sitting around drinking red tea. As soon as Nora had finished washing the dishes by candlelight, they all turned in for the night. In the middle of the night, John got up with an urge to urinate. He could not bear the thought of traversing the route in the rain and mud to the outhouse in the dark. He didn't know what to do. Finally, he opened the creaking window as gently as he could and peed into the rain. When he told this to Mah Step the next morning, Mah Step laughed till tears came to his eyes.

Mah Step then told John of the story of his friend who had been drinking late into the night at a neighbor's house after a day of fishing together.

"It was too late at night for the friend to go back to his own house. They were both punch-drunk by the time the rice-brew was finished. My friend kept insisting on going to his own house but was finally persuaded to sleep over. The two of them tiptoed through the parents' bedroom to get to the bedroom at the far end of the house. The bed was too small to accommodate both of them and so they slept on the floor. All the drinking soon caused my friend's bladder to distend. He decided the outhouse was too far to go in the middle of the night and decided instead to open the outside door and pee into the night. Groggily he pulled himself up, opened the door and started to pee. The next moment there was a loud bellow of rage and my friend was soon running for his life chased by the enraged, machete-wielding father of the house. In his drunken stupor, he had opened the wrong door—what he thought was the outer door turned out instead to be the connecting door to the parent's bedroom!"

Nora had got up early as usual and had cooked lunch for Mah Step to carry, just in case there was a landslide and he was stuck in the middle of nowhere for hours. Mah Step left in the steady drizzle to catch the bus. It stayed cloudy and foggy and continued to rain the whole day. Without electricity, it was too dark to read. It was too wet and slushy to go out. John's only pleasure was sitting with Nora and watching her work.

The sky did not clear up even the next day as John had hoped. The rain had subsided a bit but had not really stopped. John was afraid to step out into the water outside as it carried all the debris from the pigsties and the chicken runs. The dismal fog and the lugubrious gray clouds together conspired to block the sun out completely. John was sure that the rain would stop today. But to his disappointment, it did not. When he woke the next morning, instead of letting up, the rain had redoubled in intensity. It was raining cats and dogs again and he slept most of the day. "So, this is what torrential rain is all about, huh?" he asked rhetorically. The only silver lining was the time he got to spend sitting with Nora in the kitchen.

But he warned himself against falling in love with Nora. Love was what spoiled relationships. To like each other, to be even fond of each other was fine; but when the feeling turned to love, it changed everything. And in this case, the situation was impossible. She belonged here, and he would soon have to go back to the other side of the world.

The laptop battery had long since run out. The radio still worked but the rain-dance on the roof drowned out the audio. He turned the radio off, saving the batteries for any emergency.

When Thursday came around the rain was still there, but the skies had lightened a bit. Nora went to the shop under a large native umbrella made of bamboo and leaves called a *tnup* that covered her back like a large leaf from her head to her knees. John marveled at the *tnup* as he tried hanging it from his forehead. The light frame reached just below his waist. By bending forward, it was possible to protect most of the torso from the rain, which did not seem to deter the villagers. They hurried about barefoot under *tnup*s looking like large leaves scurrying about on their tails with the stems stuck in the air. "The Sakhi version of Birnam Wood," mused John.

Friday was a lot better. The sun's rays pierced through the clouds by mid-morning. John's cabin fever was at breaking point now. He just *had* to get outside. He envied the children who played soccer in the mud and rain. But he was afraid of catching some infection from the muddy water that covered the ground and stayed indoors.

Mah Step arrived about an hour later than expected. After holding up for six days a massive landslide had finally blocked the only road to the village. Passengers had to climb the precarious hill on foot and catch the bus waiting on the other side of the landslide. Mah Step was extremely tired and irritable. Electricity had still not been restored and there was no way he could grade the papers at night as he had hoped to. He had to wash and change his muddied clothes by candlelight. Nobody was in any mood to talk. A very disappointed John turned in right after a simple supper.

And then the rains stopped.

John woke up the instant the hitherto incessant pattering on the tin roof abruptly ended.

The silence was so profound that it awakened John. It took a while for him to figure this out in the dark. He could not hear any dogs barking, or wolves howling. There wasn't any spooky drumbeat even. It was all silence except for Mah Step's breathing in the next room. It was then that he understood. It was the sudden silence, the lack of noise, that woke him up. And he lay awake rejoicing that the weeklong rain had finally ended.

"The rain has stopped! I can get out of the house in the morning!" he felt like yelling out. It was difficult to go back to sleep again. The anticipation was stronger than caffeine. He wanted to be rid of the cabin fever that had plagued him for seven days now. "I won't just go out for a walk, I will jog!" he told himself. He always carried a pair of jogging shoes wherever he went because he believed that running was the best and simplest exercise there was. A morning run would bring back his energy and raise his spirits. He hugged his pillow and screwed his eyes shut in a vain effort to sleep. But sleep eluded him till early morn. It was close to daybreak when he finally dozed off.

He woke again before the rooster crowed. Last night's thoughts came flooding back. "I am going jogging!" he told himself. He jumped out of bed like a man possessed. The rest of the house was asleep as he rushed through the morning ablutions. He slipped on his Reebok jogging shoes and slowly crept out of the house through the back door. It was dark when he had stumbled to the outhouse but now there was a faint rosy glow above the eastern hills. The chickens were already out of the coop. The pigs were rooting in the sties behind the houses. As he walked down the narrow path towards the road he felt a strange happiness. The despair of cabin fever had lifted.

The market bus to the Big Town hadn't arrived at the village center yet. The mist lay heavy and the ground was still soft and squishy from the rains. He would have to run on the road, he told himself. As he took the road to the right he could see there were already a few people about swathed in those ubiquitous blanket-like shawls. In the fog, he could not recognize any of them. They must not have seen him either because there was no customary greeting. His T-shirt was no protection against the goose-pimpling coolness of the morning. He broke into a trot to warm himself and was petrified by the immediate volley of barking that erupted. The dogs came out of the woodwork, six or seven of them;

mongrels of varying sizes and shapes. They came running after him full tilt. The last thing he wanted was to get bitten by one of these dogs that had never got rabies shots. John stopped and turned around. The dogs stopped too but kept on yelping. Without breaking eye contact John bent down, picked up a few stones and slowly backed away. The barking gradually died down as the dogs, one by one, turned and wandered away growling.

Soon he was out of the village. There was more light now and the fog was lifting. The pureness of the air and the serenity of the scene overwhelmed him. He had a lot to be grateful for, he told himself. There, ahead of the bend in the road lay the fields; rising up the hill to the left of the road and sloping down to the valley below on the right. The road gradually snaked its way up the side of the hill towards the Big Town forty kilometers away.

He slowly began to run. He hadn't run in months. The first steps were almost painful. The ankles seemed strangely soft and the muscles in his hips hurt. But twenty steps later the knees and ankles moved better, and the jog began to be exhilarating. The wind in his face ruffled his wavy hair as he spurred himself on.

He saw them as he came around the next bend in the road. They were headed out in the same direction, about five hundred yards ahead of him. He saw them first on the other side of a small ravine, around the inside of which the road curved in a U-turn. "These women must have woken up early," he thought. There must have been about ten of them, with bamboo cones on their backs and *tnup*s dangling from their heads. Laughing and chatting the women were striding along briskly, strung out in two uneven rows across the road, when one of them looked to her right and saw him. Abruptly they all stopped to turn and look in his direction across the ravine. They were too far off to be heard distinctly. He wondered if it was his imagination that they had become more animated on spotting him. He waved airily in their direction and continued jogging nonchalantly. None of them waved back but they turned and continued on, picking their speed up a little bit, he thought, while stealing looks in his direction. By the time he completed the curve and was on the other side of the gorge, they were out of sight, gone past the next bend.

He saw them soon enough again after the next turn. They were walking again but the moment they saw him appear behind them, they broke into a trot, giggling loudly as they did so. John involuntarily slowed down. "Are they playing tag?" he wondered as he kicked the ground pointlessly and switched from running to walking. Curiously, the women slowed down to a walk too, warily looking over their shoulders. After a while, John decided to ignore them and resumed his jogging. The moment he did so, one of the women excitedly shouted to the others and they all started running too. "This is crazy!" he thought as he slowed down to a fast walk. The women slowed down too but their excitement seemed to have gone up a notch. "They are having a lot of fun with this," John thought. He recalled George Orwell's (a.k.a. Eric Blair) account of being chased down a Rangoon road early one morning by a Burmese woman with her sarong raised around her waist. This was that in reverse. He wondered if they thought he was so sex-starved as to have (forgive the pun) gone around the bend? "Or maybe this was their idea of some harmless fun?" he hazarded a guess.

He would have to tell Mah Step about this when he got back. Even if he caught up with them he could not have held an intelligent conversation with the women. Just then the women disappeared around the curve ahead and John thought it safe to resume his jogging again. He tried to focus his mind on the vista around him rather than the distracting gaggle of women up the road. The rain-softened gravel road felt a little like the rubberized track at the local high school in Greenbelt where he ran a lap or two at five o'clock every morning before driving to work. The warm rays of the morning sun had by now completely lifted the fog. The plants by the roadside were still wet from the rain. There were no trees in the vicinity. Slash-and-burn agriculture had taken care of that. It was a good thing they believed in preserving community forests. Sloping up the hill on the left were pineapple fields in some semblance of order though the rows were a little wavy here and there. On the edges stood clumps of plantain trees. Falling off to the right were vegetable fields. There was a small lot of mustard and another larger field of maize, but all the rest were potatoes. He was nearing the bend now. "Better slow down," he told himself, "You don't want to cause a scandal here."

To his surprise, the women had disappeared! "Where could they have gone? They can't have speeded up that much." The next bend was much further off. He looked up the slopes to the left and then to the valley on the right. There was no sign of them. He felt a vague sense of disappointment. The whole incident had ended with a whimper with no resolution. He smiled at how the women had drawn him into their mysterious game. "I had better run another mile and then get back to the house," he told himself as he picked up the pace again.

He had hardly run twenty steps when he was startled out of his wits by loud shrieks that would have done Macbeth's witches proud. As he stopped and half-turned in startled alarm he was flung to the ground in a fierce tackle worthy of the Green Bay Packers.

Winded and stunned and his face muddied, he chided himself: "You have done it now. You just had to go out alone and get mugged. Maybe this was the kidnapping of another naïve American?" The weights of the bodies were off him the instant he relaxed submissively. Resignedly he turned himself around and sat up, wiping the mud off his brow, to face his attackers. To his utter surprise, he saw that it was the group of women he had seen earlier that had brought him down, sans their bamboo cones, *tnups*, and thick shawls. They must have been lying in wait for him in a hollow beside the road. The women giggled embarrassedly amongst themselves but watched him keenly. John could only look back at them uncomprehending.

They clearly did not intend him any harm. In fact, they seemed terribly self-conscious about the whole thing, covering their faces shyly. One of them, possibly the oldest of the lot, spoke to him in the Sakhi language. The only word he could decipher was the word for "sorry". He realized that they were trying to apologize to him. "Why would they jump on me like a bunch of screaming banshees, throw me to the ground and then say 'sorry'?" As he tried to stand up the women rushed to help. They led him to the boulders lining the culvert and bade him sit down. The one who had spoken to him earlier spoke to two younger women who excused themselves and went down the side of the hill. They quickly clambered back up to the road carrying the *tnups*, the thick blanket-like shawls, and the bamboo cones.

"I should be going," he said in English and made as if to rise. The women would have none of it. They gently gestured to him to sit and pointed in the direction of the village. "Mah Step", one of them said but John could not be sure in what context his friend's name was mentioned. "All right, if that's the way you want it. I will just sit here and wait till you go off to your fields," he murmured softly. But they did not seem to be in any hurry as they made themselves comfortable on dry stones and opened their betel leaves and areca nuts. "I hope this is not going to be a long morning." he sighed. The women chattered on, throwing glances in his direction every now and then. He decided the only thing he could do was sit back and enjoy the beautiful daybreak.

At the direction of the leader, one woman dug from within her cone her 'brown bag' (green banana leaves, actually) lunch. The elder woman opened her lunch wrap and brought it to him. There was white rice mixed with pieces of curried meat. As politely as he could he gestured by rubbing a hand across his tummy, waving his hand, and shaking his head that he wasn't hungry. The last thing he wanted to do was rob them of their lunch. He had already realized he was in no danger, but why were they not letting him go? Why were they holding him against his will in some kind of citizen's arrest? "What law have I broken?" he wanted to ask them but could not figure out how he could make himself understood through mere gestures. It was all too complicated.

John had turned away from the women to watch the morning sunlight spread over the distant blue mountains when he heard the excited mention of Mah Step's name. Turning around he saw in the far distance Mah Step walking up the hill along with a woman. He guessed she was a member of this group who had been sent back to the village to summon Mah Step while the ambush was taking place.

It took a while for them to get there as they climbed uphill. Mah Step had concern written all over his face.

"Are you all right?" he asked anxiously. "This woman here came back to the village to ask me to come and get you."

"Come and get me? Why? What's up with the women here?" John demanded a little testily.

"Tell me what happened?" Mah Step asked softly trying to calm John down.

"They snuck up on me from behind and threw me to the ground. Can you believe that? I have no clue why they did that. Absolutely none! And why are they holding me against my will and not letting me go? What did I do?" John could not hide a trace of exasperation.

There was some talk amongst the women and Mah Step. Finally, Mah Step asked gently, "What were you doing out here at this time of the morning?"

"I was jogging, for Pete's sake! Can't you tell?"

Mah Step looked nonplussed for a moment. Then he broke out laughing. He laughed uncontrollably till his whole body shook, and tears streamed down his face. John had never seen Mah Step in this state before.

"Why, what's so funny?" John asked.

"The women here thought you had lost your marbles ... ha, ha, ha ... gone off the rocker ... ha, ha, ha ... soft in the head ... ha, ha, ha ... they thought you were running away ... ha, ha, ha ... from the village without ... ha, ha, ha ... without ... my knowledge ... ha, ha, ha ..."

He could not go on. When his laughter had subsided, he explained to the women what happened. But they did not seem to be very amused.

"John, nobody jogs here. We don't need to. We get enough exercise with all the walking and work we need to do every day. When I explained to the women about jogging, one of them asked me 'Why would anyone run for no reason?' They really think you lost it."

It was John's turn to chuckle. "I'll be darned!" he said over and over again as he and Mah Step turned to trudge back to the village and the women picked up their cones and headed in the opposite direction to their fields.

Chapter 10: Of Snakes and Leprechauns

The rest of the day compensated for the misadventure of the morning. Pa and Ma, and most especially Nora, were very relieved to learn that John hadn't gone loco.

"John, you have the dubious distinction of being the first man in this village ever to run for no reason! 'Fleeing when no man pursueth', as it is written!" teased Mah Step. "I thought you had either gone cuckoo or had a very severe attack of seasonal affective disorder."

"Noooo! I only wanted a little exercise after being cooped up inside for so long."

"You know what, there's something else you need—a haircut."

John ran his fingers through his hair.

"Yes, I do need a haircut. This is the longest I've kept my hair since the '70s. Is there a barber here?"

"No, people are not so style-conscious here. They just cut each other's hair. Or they get it done at a barbershop when they go to the Big Town on one of their trips."

"Maybe I should do the same. But it seems so pointless going there all the way for a haircut!"

"Instead of going to a barbershop in the Big Town, I could do it for you," offered Mah Step

"OK, I'll take you up on that. I'm not going anywhere for the next two weeks. So even if you botch it up, it's no big deal. As long as you don't snip my ears!"

So it was that John soon found himself seated bare-chested on a *lora* at the center of newspapers spread out in the front yard and Mah Step hovered around him with a pair of scissors and a long comb.

"You can cut it real short at the top but don't take too much off on the sides. I don't want to be looking like a horse, as Saroyan once said."

"All right, I'll do as you say," said Mah Step as his scissors began to nimbly skim over John's head. Soon there were clumps of blonde and gray hair strewn all around the *lora* on the newspapers. Ma and Nora came out to look and so did the children of the neighborhood when they saw what was happening. As they circled around laughing and giggling they found the golden locks irresistible. The children darted in to pick up the longer strands as souvenirs. John found this very amusing and smiled and waved his hands at the children.

"You must sit still. These scissors are very sharp," Mah Step cautioned.

When it was all over Mah Step lightly swatted John's neck and shoulders with a folded-up newspaper before letting John back inside the house for a bath.

"Not bad, Mah Step! Not bad at all!" John said when he emerged from the bath and had looked in the mirror. "The long hair was kind of an irritant. We must do this once more before I go back. Thanks much!"

After brunch Mah Step suggested they go explore the forest. Nora packed towels and soap for them in a cloth bag and Mah Step recommended that they carry a change of clothes. It was a long walk to the woods. They walked on narrow slippery footpaths bordering vegetable fields, were stung by the sharp edges of pineapple leaves as they took a shortcut up a steep hill and got mired in the water of paddy fields before they got to the edge of the forest.

"Forests are sacred to us," said Mah Step. "Scientists complain about our slash-and-burn method of agriculture. We are accused of indiscriminately burning up the green cover. But this is completely untrue. Forests are sacred to us. Our population is minuscule and how much forest can we destroy with our bare hands? The mechanized razing of the Amazon is fueled by human greed. We cultivate the way we do for our survival, for food. We even rotate our crops by letting the land lie fallow after seven years and allowing the forest cover to grow back."

"Who owns the forest?" asked John.

"That is the best part. All forests and all land are owned by the community. The village council allots lands to families for homesteads or for farming. Individuals do not have absolute title to any land. It is all owned by the community. They can keep it for their use but if they don't use it, the land reverts back to the community."

"What about the poor and the homeless?" John asked.

"There are no landless or homeless people in our tribe. They may be poor, but they are never landless. They have their own piece of land."

"That's unique," said John.

"Some of the other tribes do not have this system. In their areas, land is individually owned. They cut down all their trees for profit and have no forests anymore. Their denuded hills are covered only with grass and shrubs. They have some landless people as well. Our sacred groves are treated with respect. No one can hunt or fish or cut wood in the sacred forests. In the other forests, there are no restrictions. You can hunt and fish all you want."

Climbing further downhill they heard the babbling of a brook.

"Reminds me of Tennyson," said John.

"Yes, "The Brook's Song" is indeed a beautiful poem."

For men may come and men may go,
But I go on for ever.

"That's what I like about you. I don't have to explain anything. You get what I'm talking about instinctively."

"Thanks for the compliment. But that's not really true. The brook was fairly obvious," said Mah Step modestly.

The stream was a beauty. The water was so clear one could see the sand and the smooth round pebbles below. It looked green from the reflection of the trees that arched over both banks to form a canopy.

"How safe is this?" asked John cautiously.

"Very safe. You can actually drink the water. You can also swim. The flow is not strong. No danger of being swept away or anything."

"Are you sure?" John needed reassurance.

"Absolutely. You can take my word for it. Watch me."

With that, Mah Step stripped down to his shorts and jumped in. After the slightest hesitation, John followed suit. The water was not as cold as John had anticipated. It felt good to be in the water. The sun's rays piercing the leaf cover dappled the waters as Mah Step and John swam around. When he turned on his back and did the backstroke he could see pieces of the blue sky between the leaves. After some time, they trod water gulping in lungfuls of air.

"You know that saying about a tree falling in the forest and no one hearing it? This is where it could happen," said John.

"This is not as isolated as you might think," replied Mah Step.

"But it's absolutely idyllic."

"That I agree."

"Hey, I didn't know you had curly hair!" said John.

"Yeah, when it gets wet it goes all curly," said Mah Step.

"You are brachycephalic," opined John looking at Mah Step's round head with his hair plastered to his scalp.

"And you are ... let's see ... dolichocephalic, aren't you?" countered Mah Step.

“Touché!” cried John. “I’m tired of saying how amazing you are.”

“I appreciate your compliment but there are no geographical or cultural boundaries when it comes to knowledge.”

“Don’t get me wrong. Didn’t mean to offend you. I’d have been impressed even if you were an American.”

“No offense taken. But I’ve received some very patronizing compliments from Americans before.”

“I wasn’t being patronizing, Mah Step” John said evenly.

“I didn’t think you were. And allow me to compliment you as well. You are very cerebral. You are a thinking human being.”

“Thank you. You are a scholar and a prince.”

“Thank *you*! That’s the finest compliment I ever received.”

After a long while, they got out of the water. Mah Step took out two leaf-bound packages from the shoulder bag.

“I don’t know about you, but I am hungry.”

“I’m hungry too. Hey, is that food?”

“It most certainly is! Nora packed lunch for us.”

“Brown bags, huh? Bless her soul!”

The green banana-leaf wrapping opened to reveal rice, chicken and fried vegetables packed tightly together. Mah Step said grace before they tucked into the food. The red gravy-soaked rice was manna for the hungry men.

"I don't know how I will go back to eating American food again!" exclaimed John.

"I'm glad you like our food so much. I've said this before. You are so adaptable, it's amazing," Mah Step said.

"Now *you* are being patronizing!" laughed John.

"No," said Mah Step embarrassedly.

After they had eaten Mah Step showed John how to dispose of the bones and the banana leaf wraps at the base of the nearest tree.

"Everything is biodegradable," said Mah Step

"I like this. Very eco-friendly," agreed John. "What do we do for water?"

"The stream water is potable. But I wasn't sure about your immune system. I had Nora put in a bottle of boiled water for you."

As they lazed on the grass John remarked, "I am beginning to think that religion is probably a function of one's environment."

"What do you mean?" asked Mah Step.

"Back home in America, I'm so insulated from natural phenomena. There is climate control at home, the office, and the car. The only greenery I see are carefully cultivated and well-maintained gardens. Almost all my food comes pre-packaged. If I fall sick I am surrounded by machines that monitor my body by the minute. I am totally screened from the natural world."

"I haven't been abroad, and my experience is limited to what I read and see on TV or in films. Probably there is a lot of truth to what you say."

"I am beginning to think that the spiritual part of man is suppressed in the modern world and that's the reason there is a falling away of faith," said John.

"John, you are beginning to sound a bit like Matthew Arnold!" laughed Mah Step.

"As in "Dover Beach"?" asked John.

"See! Now it's my turn to be impressed."

"What was that verse again?" asked John.

"This may be the one you are looking for? *The Sea of Faith / Was once, too, at the full ...*"

"Yeah, that's the one. Who was with him at the beach? Who was he speaking to in the poem? Was it his sister?"

"No, I don't think it was his sister Jane. Must have been Marguerite or Mary Claude or his wife Fanny Lucy. I'm going to have a bath in the stream before we go back."

Mah Step and John got back into the water again and bathed. John had to dive below the surface to retrieve the soap that slipped from his hands into the water. After changing into fresh clothes, they were ready to trek back home. But they were in no hurry; the leisurely walk took them a lot longer, but John was happy to be outdoors again after the forced incarceration during the monsoon rain.

Dusk was falling as they neared the village. The men and women from the fields had all gone home. From their vantage point on top of the hill, they could see the stragglers winding their way home. From this height, the village below looked so pastoral, so peaceful, with smoke rising from the roofs of chimney-less houses that John stopped to drink it all in.

"Look, Mah Step! Electricity is back!" said John pointing at the lights in some of the houses.

"That's good! Life is back to normal then, isn't it?"

Instead of taking the winding road Mah Step suggested that they cut across the fields. The short-cut would get them home before it got completely dark. They traversed fields of potato before reaching the uncultivated stretch, with clumps of earth and untended plants growing wild.

Suddenly Mah Step stopped and gestured to John with a finger to his lips. Though he did not understand why, John obeyed Mah Step's directions and froze. For a minute or so they both stood like statues, frozen in time. But to John, who had no clue as to what was happening, it seemed like an eternity. He instinctively knew that something was seriously amiss. He watched as Mah Step furtively removed his shirt. Just as abruptly as they had stopped, Mah Step threw the shirt about five feet to his right and hissed, "Run!" The next instant they were both running pell-mell downhill towards the village, jumping over small thickets of grass and shrubs. By the time they got to the edge of the village John was winded. They both stopped. With his hands, akimbo John bent down and gulped in large chunks of air.

Still bending down, he asked, "What happened? What was that all about?"

Mah Step, shirtless though he was, did not appear as tired as John was. He smiled, "What do you think it was?"

John straightened up panting. "I don't have a clue. I didn't see any animals around so I'm guessing it was a snake."

"You are right it was a snake. It was actually a cobra."

John was surprised. "How do you figure *that* out? Did you see it?"

"No, I didn't."

"Then how can you be so sure there was a snake there, let alone a cobra?"

"I smelt it. There was a smell of freshly cut tapioca and there are no tapioca plants in the vicinity. The tapioca is the same as the cassava plant. A friend from a neighboring tribe told me that the breath of the cobra smells like tapioca. And after we had killed one in the forest I realized what he said was true."

"You must have an acute sense of smell. Amazing! But why did you throw down your shirt?"

"The cobra has a far more powerful olfactory sense than humans. The odor of my shirt and its warmth trick the cobra into believing that I'm still there. It repeatedly strikes the clothes thinking it's a human being."

"Olfactory? There you go again with your vocabulary! But thanks for saving me from a snake bite."

"We are lucky we escaped getting bitten. There is no anti-venom in the village. By the time we get a victim to the government dispensary in the Big Town it's usually too late. A tourniquet is the only thing we can do and that cannot be used for all parts of the body. If you are bit on the torso you are as good as dead."

"Whew! This is scary."

"Yeah, there are no poison treatment centers and no emergency number like 911."

"What about medical facilities?" John asked.

"That is one of the big tragedies of rural life. On paper, we have a doctor, a dentist, a vet, an agricultural officer, a public works engineer, and an electrical engineer. The trouble is they don't stay in our village. They all live in the Big Town. Some of them come once a week. The more brazen ones come only once a month to collect their salaries."

"That's terrible!" exclaimed John.

"Yes, it is. Some of them even have their own private practice in the town. They get their government salaries for no work and, on top of it, they also get their private income. It is criminal," Mah Step said with unconcealed disgust.

"Can't something be done about it?" John ventured.

"Corruption is difficult to root out. The wealthy and the powerful gang up together." Mah Step added despondently, "There's very little the poor can do."

Nora was waiting when they reached home. The shirtless Mah Step briefly narrated the encounter with the cobra. Nora raised a hand to her mouth in alarm and gave a little gasp of horror. She looked at John with such apprehension that Mah Step assured her that they were both safe. "Except for the loss of a perfectly good shirt," he added in English. John found her concern touching. Nora said something to Mah Step and hurried away to the kitchen.

"Nora says she has cooked a special meal for us. Good thing we didn't get bitten!" Mah Step laughed.

When they entered the kitchen, there was Ma sitting on the *lora* stirring something on the fire. She said "*Hooblei!*" with a smile in John's direction and then launched into a rapid-fire, staccato monolog aimed at Mah Step, once even waving the ladle above her head. A visibly chastened Mah Step bore the berating stoically and said to John, "She is upset with me for risking your life." But as abruptly as it started, the tirade ended, and they sat down at the table for the evening meal. "Pa has gone to town and will come tomorrow morning," said Mah Step. In Pa's absence, it was Mah Step who said grace.

John started with the steel spoon but laid it aside to eat with his fingers.

"This is good!" John said to Nora right after he took the first bite of the meat.

"Thank you. It is nothing special. Just ordinary food," replied Nora in the usual self-deprecating manner but she was obviously pleased with the compliment.

The meat was a tad more spicy than usual and John made no secret of how much he relished it.

"Wonder what the spices are?" John said. "There is definitely a bit of cardamom in addition to the staple turmeric and cumin."

"You will have to ask Nora for the recipe after dinner," said Mah Step light-heartedly.

But John could not contain his fascination with the main dish. His curiosity got the better of him.

"It's not just the spices. Even the meat is different. It is definitely not pork or lamb. And it doesn't taste like beef. If you don't mind my asking, what meat is this?" John asked Mah Step.

Before Mah Step could answer, Nora jumped in, "It's horsemeat!"

Mah Step looked at her and they both laughed. The usually reserved Ma joined in too. John smiled too but he wondered what the joke was. Ultimately, he decided to let it pass and did not press the issue.

Nora was her usual attentive self and she heaped more meat and gravy and rice on his plate. John could hardly protest.

"This food was absolutely divine," John said again at the end of the meal. Nora blushed with pleasure.

When they had finished eating, Nora brought around the aluminum basin again and John and Mah Step washed their fingers in the warm water. As John lifted the towel from Nora's forearm his fingers brushed her hand and she turned crimson. "I'm sorry," mumbled John embarrassedly. After the table was cleared, Ma offered *kwai.*

"I think I'll pass," John said with a wry smile.

While Ma and Nora sat together and had their dinner in silence holding their plates in their hands, Mah Step told John the story of Mah Zan.

"About our encounter with the cobra. I am reminded of my friend Mah Zan," Mah Step said.

"Do I know him?" John asked him.

"You may not remember him. He was among those who came to see you the second day. He will be coming again. He is a good friend of mine. His full name actually is Tarzan." Mah Step said with a smile and added, "But as with all Sakhi names it has been shortened to "Zan" colloquially."

"Did he encounter a snake too?" John asked.

"That is not an uncommon experience. Snakes are aplenty here. But Mah Zan did something unique. He spoke to the snake."

"What?" John asked incredulously.

"Sounds unbelievable, doesn't it?" Mah Step said. "But as I already told you our tribe has a very close bond with nature. It has been handed down to us by our forefathers that we are inseparable from the environment we live in. Which is why we have community forests where it is considered taboo to cut wood or kill animals. Out kinship with Nature is almost Wordsworthian. You already told me how much you love his "Ode on Intimations of Immortality". That poem captures the Sakhi philosophy of nature like no other."

"Good deal! The line I like best goes like this: *But trailing clouds of glory do we come ...*"

"From God, who is our home: recited Mah Step completing the next line.

"Very good! Let's see if you can do this one: *Whither is fled the visionary gleam?*"

"*Where is it now, the glory and the dream?* Isn't that how it goes?"

"Mah Step, I am really impressed!" said John with admiration.

"Thanks, John. You are pretty good yourself. Anyway, to get back to what I was saying. This affiliation with Nature transcends religion. Whether Christian or traditionalist, nature is accorded the same respect. To come back to Mah Zan's story. He was walking on foot to the next village on a secluded footpath when he came across this cobra. It was a big one. About eight or ten feet long, it had its hood flared and its head raised about two feet above the ground. And it stood right there in the middle of the footpath. It must have been about eleven in the morning. Mah Zan stopped in his tracks about twelve feet from the snake. The cobra and Mah Zan looked at each other. Neither moved. They continued this way for what seemed a long time. Mah Zan told me the story later. He said, instead of feelings of fear or hate for the reptile, he began to see nature's beauty in the venomous snake. Finally, he spoke softly but firmly to the snake. *'What have I done to thee? Why dost thou block my path and bare thy fangs at me? I have no quarrel with thee. Go thou thine way, and I'll go mine.'* He said this and waited."

"And what happened?" John asked.

"The cobra appeared to consider what Mah Zan had said. After a few minutes, it slowly and majestically lowered its head to the ground and slithered away into the underbrush."

"Do you think the snake understood what Mah Zan said?"

"If you mean whether it understood the verbal language, I don't know. But I do believe that the harmony of nature would have allowed them both to communicate nonverbally."

"You really think so? Most Americans would find that hard to believe, you know."

"In spite of them speaking to their pets?" Mah Step asked with a glint in his eye.

"Well said!" laughed John. "Talking about communications between animals and humans, there's the story of Balaam's ass—I mean, donkey."

"How true! I hadn't thought of that. Thanks!" said Mah Step. "If you stay here with us long enough, you will believe this and more. A lot more."

"Like what?"

"Do you think gnomes or leprechauns or fairies—whatever you call them—exist?"

"Only in fairy tales," John replied laughing.

Mah Step had a faint smile on his face as he said, "I have not seen any myself, but both my father and mother saw these tiny creatures—humanoids, really—many times when they were young. And Nora once saw a leprechaun under the rose bush when she was ten."

"You are joking, right?"

"No, I'm not. I'm a little skeptical myself because I haven't seen any yet. But I believe Nora. And I also believe Ma and Pa."

"How come you don't see them anymore?" John asked.

"Development," said Mah Step. "Pa says human dwellings have pushed back the forest line. All forests were interlinked before and wild animals moved from one forest to the other through these links. Now that many of these connections have been severed, the dwellers of forests are mostly confined to isolated pockets. Gnomes and leprechauns won't wander out too far from the forest. They come out briefly to inhabited areas but hurry back to their haunts quickly. Once in a while, you hear of people bumping into them in the community forests. But like I said, I have never seen them with my own eyes."

"Reminds me of Blake," John said quietly.

"You are in good form today, Mah John!" said Mah Step appreciatively. "Yes, Blake spotted angels on tree tops and met God on the staircase. I love his *Songs of Innocence.*"

Nora brought out the red tea.

"Today was an eventful day," said John.

"Yes. In the morning, you were captured trying to run away. And in the evening, you ran from a snake," said Nora with a smile.

"Yes, that's true. I'll never forget the morning encounter. Mah Step and I had a good time swimming in the stream. And to top it all the dinner was terrific! I loved the horsemeat."

At this Nora laughed uninhibitedly and Ma and Mah Step joined in. John could not figure out what the joke was.

"Why, what did I say?" John asked.

Mah Step looked as if he was about to say something but then appeared to think the better of it.

Nora came around with the kettle to pour a second cup of tea.

"It has been such a nice day after the rain. Before we turn in I will tell you a funny story."

"Go ahead. I love stories," said John.

"Remember I told you how attached we are to our church? We take great pride in the fact that we are Presbyterians. This story has to do with an illiterate politician who was on his first flight. He was flying business class, as politicians do, in real style. Soon after they were airborne the stewardess came around to enquire about his meal preference. 'Vegetarian or non-vegetarian?' she asked. Drawing himself up he replied indignantly, 'I'm a Presbyterian!' much to the amusement of everyone around."

"Ha, ha, ha. That's funny! You have very dedicated Presbyterians here!" John laughed.

"On that note let's turn in for the night," said Mah Step rising.

After wishing everybody good night John retired to his room and wrote his journal before turning in. And one of the things he remembered to put down was the fact that he had horsemeat that day.

Chapter 11: TLC, Sakhi Style

Pa arrived early next morning from the Big Town looking as well-groomed as he always did and showing no signs of the journey of an hour and a half by the uncomfortable public transport. When it was time for the Sunday service John hesitated only for a moment before tagging along with the family even though his heart was not really in it. He could not understand a word of what was said making the long service even more tedious. But he put aside his personal likes and dislikes because he had come to realize that in the Sakhi Hills you did what others expected of you, not just what you wanted to do. Unbeknownst to himself, he was gradually moving away from the Western egocentric mindset that had so far directed his decisions. He intuitively understood that here in the Sakhi tribe, freedom of choice and action was balanced by the responsibility to others and respect for their expectations.

The service was longer than the previous week. After church, John got to meet Mah Zan. On seeing him John immediately realized that they had met before.

"Mah Zan has just invited you for dinner on Wednesday," translated Mah Step.

John said, "*Hooblei*," thanking Mah Zan.

"This time I must find a way to reciprocate," he reminded himself.

Ma and Nora had cooked a special Sunday dinner. It was large chunks pork boiled with mustard leaves, with no seasoning except salt. John found it surprisingly tasty. The pork was more fat than lean meat. John wondered the effect it would have on his midriff but decided to throw caution to the winds. He decided to continue eating like the natives; after all, he was yet to meet one obese person in this village. And if it did not hurt them, it could hardly hurt him, he reasoned. Getting the grease off his hands afterward was an entirely different matter, requiring repeated washing with hot water and soap.

Mah Step then told him a story from World War II. "A small band of Japanese soldiers lost their way in the jungles of Burma and stumbled into a village of the neighboring Pangama tribe. Having nothing to match the deadly weapons of the intruders, the village quickly capitulated. All the males of the village were rounded up on the football field and the Japanese watched over them with their guns at the ready. The wary Japanese never let their guard down. Since neither side could communicate verbally with the other, the ensuing stalemate continued till the next day when the pangs of hunger got the better of the Japanese. Through sign language they demanded food. The village headman was a crafty old man. He called out to the women to cook pork and told them to cut the pieces really big; much bigger than usual. When food was served, the ravenously hungry Japanese fell upon the rice and pork with gusto but did not forget to hold on to their guns with one hand. But the big pieces of pork kept slipping from their fingers. They needed to use both hands to hold the large slippery hunks of dripping fat. In the beginning, they resisted the temptation and made vain attempts at holding the greasy pieces of pork with one hand. Frustration and hunger finally got the better of them. One by one they began picking up the pieces of pork with both hands and after taking a couple of bites went back to eating the rice with one hand while holding their guns with the other. The villagers watched patiently. Each time the soldiers used both hands for holding the large chunks of pork and then held the gun with one hand they were unwittingly transferring grease to the gun. Soon both their hands were covered in lard. The women, on instructions from the village headman, piled on more rice and meat, which action the soldiers interpreted to be ingratiating servility. When the Japanese had just about eaten their fill, and were sated and distended, the headman gave a shout and the men with a loud war cry jumped on the Japanese soldiers. The skirmish was brief. The Japanese, their hands still caked with grease and rice, could not hold on to their slippery weapons for dear life. The women came running out with machetes and spears and the denouement was swift. All but one of the Japanese soldiers were killed. The lone survivor ran away into the jungles and was never heard of again. Though there were reports of villagers spotting a wild man in the jungle for many years afterward. Pork won the battle that day!" concluded Mah Step.

"Very shrewd! Cunning old man!" said John. "Did the Japanese army reach their village later?"

"No, luckily the war ended before that. The Japanese had captured the plains and then they pressed on to Burma. There were some bloody battles there. Some of the American planes flying sorties to China crashed in the mountains of the neighboring Pangama tribe. I think those airmen are listed as MIA to this day."

"How did you come to know of this?" asked John.

"In one of their interior villages, I found them using shiny utensils that I had not seen anywhere else before. When I asked them about it, they said they had made it out of metal from a crashed American plane."

"I think you should report this to the American Embassy."

"If I can find out who to report this to, I will. There must be at least four or five planes that crashed on that mountain."

"We could look it up on the Internet," suggested John.

"Of course, there's that. The Pangama tribe is mostly Christian now but they were head-hunters before. On my first visit to them, I was horrified by the sight of human scalps hanging under the eaves of their huts. The more the number of scalps, the higher the status."

"Who did they kill? The people of the plains?" John asked.

"They killed anyone who crossed their paths. The largest number of scalps were of neighboring hill tribes. There were frequent and bloody inter-tribal wars."

"And Christianity changed all that?" John asked.

"I wish I could say that. But it is not a "happily ever after" story. When they are provoked the old nature breaks out and then their Christianity is forgotten. I remember they had a recent quarrel with the Duhongi tribe. It so happened that the highest government official in their area was a Duhongi. He had nothing to do with the dispute, but a large mob attacked his government residence and dragged him out and tied him to a tree and thrashed him within an inch of his life. It was horrible."

"Didn't the police protect him?" asked John.

"The mob was so big, the police did nothing. Moreover, the police belonged to the same Pangama tribe as the mob. On another visit to their area, I was awoken one morning at the government circuit house by shouts from the next room. When I stepped out warily I discovered that a group of around ten men had broken down the door of the next room and were giving the inmates of that room a severe beating. Thinking that they were robbers I got quickly back into my own room and bolted the door. After some time when I heard them all walking out to the road I came out to the balcony. There was a man naked except for his briefs and behind him a woman completely naked. The woman was completely bald. The duo was paraded around the center of town. I found out later that the man was a government official and the woman was another man's wife. And she didn't have a shaven head. As a retribution for adultery, the assailants had plucked out her hair completely."

"Absolutely barbaric!" pronounced John.

"I agree. I could not eat that day. My mind kept going back to the woman whose hair had been pulled out as a mark of shame. It must have been very painful. And on top if she was marched naked around the town. A fate much worse than that of Hester Prynne in *The Scarlet Letter.* The man at least had his boxers on."

"Does such cruelty run in the Sakhi tribe too?" asked John.

"Once upon a time—this was before the advent of Christian missionaries—the Sakhis were considered the fiercest of all tribal warriors. But we were never head-hunters like the Pangamas. For some reason, their veneer of Christianity is easily broken. We have our faults too but in comparison to the Pangama tribe we have put our violent past behind us forever."

"Did you feel safe traveling around in the Pangama province?"

"Yes, I did not face any problems. They are basically very nice people with the same tribal sense of joie de vivre. The Pangama women are especially beautiful. It is just that the men have a strong sense of revenge and a compulsion to get even that breaks through their "American Baptist" (as they call themselves) piety. The most heart-wrenching and brutal incident I ever witnessed happened in the same town too."

"What happened?"

"It was twilight and dusk was falling, and an army truck was headed back to camp. Army drivers are not known for defensive driving. This particular driver wasn't probably the worst of them. Anyway, he grazed a young girl who was walking with her mother on the road. Instead of speeding away unconcerned as they usually do, this army driver stopped the truck and lifted the fallen girl in his arms. The girl was miraculously unhurt. But the Pangamas didn't care. They pounced on him and beat him black and blue. And then, in front of my very eyes, the biggest of them lifted a large stone from the side of the road and crushed the skull of the fallen soldier. It was primitive savagery at its worst."

"Did the army retaliate?"

"The dead soldier was from the plains and the entire army was made up of plains people. By the time their rescue team arrived the body lay on the deserted road beside the vandalized truck. The people had fled to their homes and barricaded themselves in. The army's revenge was brutal. They broke into the homes and assaulted the men and raped many women and girls. In one instance a young woman was gang-raped publicly in the courtyard of her home in front of her parents and family. Five young men were dragged away. Their tortured bodies were found two days later in a grove of banana trees on the edge of town."

"I'm a pacifist. I'm against all forms of violence but most especially this kind of violence perpetrated by a government army against defenseless civilians," said John.

"I am reminded of Thoreau's objections in *Civil Disobedience* to the standing army being an arm of the standing government."

"That's a very powerful essay. I know parts of it by heart. *That government is best which governs least.*"

"To that, I must add: *A man's a man for a' that."*

"Isn't that Burns?" asked John.

"Yes, it is! I was so happy they sang it for the opening of the Scottish Parliament, though there is little likelihood that it will make it as the national anthem. That poem states more clearly than anything else the *égalité* of man."

***

Mah Step left the next day for the Big Town and John was left to his own devices again. He strolled around the village and then walked to the knoll just outside the village where he and Mah Step had sat on their first day out. The weather was perfect; bright and sunny but not warm. He reckoned it to be around seventy degrees on the Fahrenheit scale that he was familiar with. Doing some mental arithmetic, he figured it would be approximately twenty-one on the Celsius range that they used here. Lying in the grass with his jacket rolled up under his head he thought of his friends in Washington, DC, Greenbelt and Baltimore. "It must be early evening there," he thought. "They would all be caught up in the rush hour traffic right now." He did not envy them the least bit as he languidly rose and sedately sauntered back to the house.

"For all practical purposes, I'm an MIA too. Without email and cell phone one might as well be on another planet or pushing up the daisies," he thought wryly. "Except I feel like I have died and gone to heaven!"

Nora was waiting for him when he got home. She had finished washing all the clothes and was limning her soap-puckered hands with oil.

"May I make you some tea?" she asked.

"I can never say no to tea! But there's no hurry."

But Nora wouldn't wait. She quickly capped the bottle of oil and hurried off into the house. After a little while, she was back with *lora*s and a low table and bowls of rice with curried minced beef. They were the very picture of domestic harmony as they shared high tea in the mellow afternoon sun.

***

It happened on Wednesday morning. John woke up happy and eager, anticipating another day of quiet contentedness. He was looking forward to having dinner at Mah Zan's place later that day. Nora had also promised to take him to see knives and farm implements being made by hand at a traditional blacksmith's workshop. As he lay wallowing in the warmth of the quilt on that cold morning, the sense of overwhelming gratitude returned. This trip was like no other; a whole new secret world had opened up for him. The pastoral life here had validated some of the cherished personal values that seemed so out of place in the fast lane of the modern world. Loath to be a sluggard in such inimitable circumstances, John wanted to leap out of bed and greet the day with arms flung out. Throwing the quilt aside he made as if to sit upright in bed but immediately fell back clutching his back. The pain was as excruciating as it was sudden. He felt as if a muscle in the small of his back had knotted up and wouldn't unwind. After waiting a few minutes, he tried again to rise. He could not move. The muscle stayed tight and searing pain shot up towards the back of his neck when he tried to move. That was when a trace of panic set it in. "This can't be happening to me," he told himself. Only minutes ago, he had felt on top of the world with nary an inkling of discomfort and here he was now immobilized in bed with a back that seemed locked in a painful vice. "Where can I find a doctor?" "Will my insurance cover this?" "Will I have to be airlifted home for surgery?" These questions swirled in his mind. On a more practical note, "How will I manage the outside toilet?" he wondered.

He could hear Nora moving about in the kitchen. He tried again to turn onto his side. The shooting pain in his back stopped him. He worried about his treatment in the village with no medical facilities. Time seemed to hang still as he pondered over this sudden and wholly unexpected turn of events.

Ultimately, he decided to call out for Nora. She came quickly with a big smile calling out gaily, "*Hooblei*, Mah John! Good morning! You called me?"

"'Morning, Nora. I'm in a spot of bother here. I seem to have hurt my back somehow. I cannot move."

"What? What happened?" asked Nora still not fully comprehending what John had just said.

"I think I have sprained my back. I cannot get up."

This time she understood and her face blanched. She was nonplussed. This was completely unexpected; a bolt from the blue.

"Wait. I'll go and call Pa and Ma."

She rushed out of the room to return with Pa and Ma who looked as if they had just woken up. Nora acted as the interpreter as Pa asked questions about where the pain was and how he felt. On Ma's orders, Nora went to the kitchen and came back with a bottle of mustard oil and a small container of lime. Pa asked him to open his mouth and stick out his tongue. From the way Pa recoiled, John knew that his breath stank. Translating for Pa, Nora said, "You seem to have some stomach problem." This seemed rather strange to John. He thought the problem was muscular. Pa took the oil from Nora and lifting John's T-shirt applied the mustard oil gently on his stomach, rubbing it in a slow, circular motion. The mustard oil warmed his body. Pa then helped John turn over to lie face down. This was not easy, but the heat of the mustard was soothing to the muscles. Pa then rubbed oil on his back in firm downward sweeps with the ball of his palm. The knotted muscle in the small of his back twitched as Pa expertly kneaded his back. Pa then turned John again over on his back and, using the paste of lime from the container Nora handed over, drew a large cross centered on his navel. The white lime dried almost instantly into a taut flaky mass across his belly.

"That's the cross for protection against the devil," Nora explained. "Pa wants to pray for you, OK?"

Pa came over, laid his hand over John's midriff and, as Ma and Nora stood alongside, said a long prayer. When he ended John, as usual, murmured an "Amen".

The news of John's illness spread like wildfire across the village. Anxious neighbors started dropping in to see him almost immediately. John wondered idly how they achieved this level of swift communication without telephones. Nora had to prepare *kwai* for everyone who dropped in. But she didn't want to leave John's bedside either. She brought a *lora* to his bedside and commenced peeling the husk off a whole bunch of areca nuts and quartering them. The neighbors appeared genuinely concerned for his welfare. They spoke in low tones with Pa and Ma and lingered, seemingly unwilling to leave him till he was better. While Pa was speaking to a young man, Nora whispered to John, “He’s sending for the local doctor.”

The ‘local doctor’ arrived in a matter of minutes but turned out to be not the kind of doctor that John had conjectured. He had a dirty plaid shawl tied around his neck and looked more like a rustic farmer than a medic. After gently massaging his stomach and back, much the same way as Pa had done before, he announced his diagnosis, which Nora translated haltingly.

“You have a problem with your intestine ... your stomach is stretched ... this has caused your back muscle ... to tighten. He wants you to drink some medicine,” she said.

“Is he really a doctor?” John asked.

“He is a traditional doctor. The doctor for the English medicine comes only once a week. He stays in the Big Town. He has lots of patients there.”

The medicine that the ‘local doctor’ poured out of a stained bottle, stoppered with a wad of newspaper for a bung, turned out to be a bitter and pungent concoction. John hesitated briefly. But he did not forget his policy on food and drink while traveling (“If the locals can eat it and live, so can I!”) and took a swig from the proffered teacup. It tasted terrible and was difficult to swallow and keep down. He thought he would throw up but held it in check with an almost superhuman effort.

“He wants you to lie down and sleep for some time,” Nora said.

"I'm hungry. Can I have some breakfast?" asked John.

The medicine man agreed that John could have something to eat. Nora had Ma sit down by his bedside to watch over him as she rushed to the kitchen. She was soon back with a tray on which was a plate of scrambled eggs and a bowl of soft steaming rice and a cup of black tea.

"The doctor said you shouldn't be drinking milk. He wants you to drink strong red tea instead," said Nora.

Scrambled eggs had never tasted better. While he wolfed down the food, the visitors courteously stepped out of the room. When he had finished, they came back in. There were new people to see him as well. It was as if the whole village had dropped in to express their empathy. As each one left the room after eating *kwai* and talking to Ma, Pa, and Nora, they would cheerily call out, "Get well soon!" in Sakhi and John would acknowledge this by raising his right hand and saying, "*Hooblei.*"

John remembered his dinner appointment with Mah Zan and his family.

"Nora, is there any way you could send word to Mah Zan about my plight? I have a dinner invitation from him."

"Oh, I will take care of that. I think the news has already reached him by now."

Soon he fell asleep. It must have been afternoon when he woke up. He was surprised to see Mah Step sitting by his bedside.

"When did you get here?" asked a John.

"A little while ago. How are you feeling now? I have brought a real doctor to see you," replied Mah Step.

"Oh, the sleep did me a lot of good. I'm feeling a lot better now. The back still hurts, though."

The doctor turned out to be a smart young man who spoke English fluently. He took out his stethoscope and blood pressure monitor and examined John. When he was done, he said to John, "You will be fine. You have sprained your lower back. I will give you a muscle relaxant. Have you had this problem before?"

"No, this is the first time. Completely unexpected. A total shock."

"I'm going to give you some pills for relaxing your muscles and a muscle relaxant ointment to rub on your back. If it doesn't get better, you will need to come to the Big Town for an X-ray and tests."

When the doctor had finished writing down the prescription, John called Mah Step over to whisper to him.

"Do you have enough cash on you to pay the doctor? I can give you more dollars to change."

"No, we will be fine. I have enough here."

"Where will you get the medicines from?" asked John.

"I have to go to the Big Town to get it. Will have to go back to drop off the doctor anyway. There won't be any buses or share taxis going to town at this time of the day. I will have to hire a full taxi for the trip. It will be quicker too."

"Put it on my account," John said.

"Don't worry about that now. Just get well."

Before they left for the Big Town, John had Mah Step help him get to the outhouse to urinate. It was a difficult walk, but the pain had considerably lessened. Relieving himself made him feel even better. When he lay down again the pain had subsided and showed up only when he tried to turn to the left or to the right.

Nora brought him rice and minced beef to eat. John was careful not to drink too much tea till he was able to go to the outhouse on his own. The food made him drowsy again and he was glad to sleep.

Mah Step did not take long to get back as he had stopped at the Big Town only to buy the medicines, after he dropped the doctor off. John was happy to see him.

"How are you feeling now?" asked Mah Step.

"A lot better, thanks. Hurts only when I laugh."

"What?"

"Just a turn of phrase. The pain seems to be tapering off. Was the money enough for paying the doctor and buying the medicines?"

"Oh, yes, of course!" smiled Mah Step. "The whole thing including the taxi fare came to only sixteen dollars," explained Mah Step.

"What? That's impossible! Surely there's some mistake?" John was incredulous.

"No, the taxi was the most expensive at $8 both ways. The two medicines cost only $3 and the doctor's fee was $5," said Mah Step.

"This is unbelievable! The doctor travels forty kilometers out to make a house call, spends four hours of his time and still charges only five dollars? How does that work?"

"These are the costs we actually pay. The doctor did not give you a discount or anything. His usual charge is seventy-five cents for a consultation. He charged you five dollars because of the time and the travel."

"I simply cannot believe this. Is he a real doctor?"

"Oh, yes he is. He studied at a big medical school in the nation's capital and he also has a post-graduate degree from overseas. He is a qualified MD."

"I'm simply amazed. The last time I was sick and in a hospital, the doctor in ER billed the insurance company $550 for less than an hour."

"Who can afford to pay that much?" it was Mah Step's turn to be surprised. "How much was the total bill?"

"Oh, it came to about $27,000. Medical care in the US is frightfully expensive," said John. "It's all paid by the insurance company except for a small portion called deductible which the patient pays."

"And how much is the medical insurance per month?" Mah Step asked.

"That varies depending on the coverage. Mine was about two hundred dollars. But an average basic policy should cost someone about a hundred and fifty dollars a month."

"A hundred and fifty dollars a month? Even if you are not sick? That doesn't make sense," protested Mah Step.

"It is an insurance. So, you pay it every month regardless. What percentage of the people here have medical insurance? OK, I don't mean the village itself but in the Big Town?"

"Nobody in the village has medical insurance or even life insurance. Even in the Big Town, I think it would be zero for medical insurance. I don't know of anyone who has medical insurance. Maybe some of the super-rich contractors and politicians but I doubt it. Certainly, nobody else."

"How do you cover your risk then? Who pays if you are hospitalized?" asked John.

"Medical expenses are considered a necessary personal expense like any other expense. The patient has to pay for his or her own expense."

"But can they afford it? What about the poor?"

"Hospital and medicine costs are really low here as you have just seen. Maybe it is because we don't have insurance. The government-owned Civil Hospital in the Big Town charges nothing for poor patients. But most people who can afford it go to private hospitals that are more efficient. There is a cost to it but, as I told you, medical expenses are not high. When it comes to large expenses like hospitalization and surgery, family and friends pitch in to help. I don't know whether you realized it, the whole village chipped in for you."

"What do you mean?" John was surprised.

"It is our custom to visit the sick. Not doing that is considered bad manners. And when you go to see the sick you don't go empty handed. We do not have the custom of giving flowers here, but everyone takes something useful along. And for expensive treatment, many will give cash. The people who came to see you have been bringing vegetables and rice for you. Some even tried to give me money."

"I will be darned! This is so different from how we do it back home. I remember one time I fell sick waking up. I had an attack of vertigo. A loss of balance. I was completely disoriented and anxious. I couldn't walk about inside my condo let alone drive to a doctor. Nobody—just nobody—came to see me. My girlfriend called a couple of times and there was one call from the office about rescheduling a meeting. But that was it. Nobody came. Nobody helped. I was so alone. In the end, it was a kind lady neighbor who drove me to the doctor."

"You are never alone here. The society as a whole takes care of you when you are sick. It is like a hidden insurance where everyone contributes in cash and kind when there is a need. Much better than insurance!"

"I wish we had your system. It would never work, of course. People are such individualists in America. They have no time for anyone else. By the way, talking about costs, do you have many malpractice suits here?" asked John.

"I know what you are referring to. The answer will surprise you. There has not been a single—not even one—malpractice suit in our whole province."

"That's amazing! Millions of dollars are paid out in malpractice suits in the US every year. Millions! It drives up the cost of medical care and insurance."

"One reason there has not been any malpractice suits is that we believe that life and death are in the hands of God. If we truly believe that, we cannot take the doctor or the hospital to court. It wouldn't have happened if God had not intended it to happen.

In any case if the patient is dead no amount of money can bring him or her back. Why make money over a tragedy? That's our philosophy on this issue."

"This is unbelievable! It might be cheaper to fly into your country for treatment than to do it in the US. There's another thing I wanted to ask you. What about the cost of medicines?"

"You already saw I paid only three dollars for both the medicines together. Medicines are a tenth, or maybe even a hundredth in some cases, of the cost of medicines in the developed world. A classic case is the anti-retroviral drugs for HIV positives."

"Are there patent violations with the drugs? John asked.

"I'm not sure about that. But since our country signed the intellectual property rights agreement, I would think not. But I could be wrong."

"What about life insurance? Why don't people buy that?" asked John.

"Just think about it, Mah John. When you purchase insurance, you are actually betting against your own life. You win only if you die. And you are not there to receive it. If you survive, the insurance company pockets the money."

"I have never thought about insurance that way. What about unexpected deaths? Life is so uncertain, you know."

"In olden days, and to some extent even now in rural areas, our tribal society takes care of the less fortunate. The clan has first responsibility but the whole rural society pitches in to help, even for long term needs. We have our own hidden social security system that is even better than the Swedish model. But urbanization is changing all that. We look to the government more and more for welfare support instead of contributing ourselves. In the Big Town, the old social fabric is vanishing fast."

"Tell me about the "local doctor" that came in the morning."

Mah Step laughed, "He's not a real doctor. In olden days, he was the equivalent of the shaman, treating the body and the soul, driving out evil spirits. Our conversion to Christianity took the shine off the spiritual role but as the custodian of skills handed down from previous generations, he is still respected. Some people prefer his herbal medicine to the strong western medicine which has side effects. I am personally a bit skeptical of this form of treatment for complex diseases like cancer, but I have witnessed a *Doktor Makri* setting right a broken arm that was given up as a lost cause by a team of qualified orthopedics after several re-settings of the broken bone."

"What does *Doctor Makri* mean?" asked John.

"*Doctor Makri* literally translates to 'Doctor Frog', the equivalent of a quack in English. But it is not considered a derisive term. They are good at treating muscular problems also. Their expert massages can unknot muscles and reduce chronic back pain."

"Do they use western medicines also?"

"No, they don't. The best part about this alternative medicine is that it is all natural. There is nothing synthetic at all. Basil, ginger, turmeric, and mustard oil are common everyday medicines. They hunt for rare herbs in the forest."

"Are these 'frog doctors' more expensive than regular doctors?"

"No! They charge a very nominal fee, usually about half of what a doctor would. Twenty-five to thirty cents is normal."

John was left shaking his head in disbelief.

They had dinner together in John's room that evening. Nora bustled about getting food from the kitchen. Mah Step sat at a low table next to John's bed and John ate in bed. Nora's worries had been reduced by the improvement in John's condition and she expressed her happiness through broad smiles many times during the dinner as she served John.

After dinner Pa and Ma came in to see John. Mah Step translated the exchanges between Pa and John. Before leaving Pa prayed solemnly for John's relief. After the prayer, Mah Step explained that the whole prayer was about God healing him.

"As I said before, we believe that God is the ultimate healer. No amount of drugs will result in a cure unless God does the healing. We consider prayer to be an integral component of healing."

***

John slept soundly that night. When he awoke the next morning, he discovered to his utter surprise and joy that the pain had completely vanished. He could scarce believe his good fortune immediately; but after sitting up in bed and turning to either side effortlessly, he realized that he was healed indeed. He rushed to the outhouse in the dark. By the time Nora woke up he had already finished the morning ablutions and was working on his electronic journal.

She did not hide her tremendous joy when John walked into the kitchen unaided.

"Mah John! You are OK!" she shouted in joy as she jumped up from the *lora* and rushed to him holding out her hand. Even as he shook her hand formally what he really wanted to do was give her a hug: a hug of gratitude for her caring help; a hug of pure joy for being healed; and a hug of genuine affection. But, mindful of cultural mores, he restrained himself to giving her hand a gentle squeeze as they shook hands.

The others woke up early too, anxious to find out John's condition. They were as ecstatic as Nora was to discover that John was hale and hearty again. Soon the whole family was in the kitchen drinking their morning cup of tea together.

"How about a short walk this morning? Nothing too strenuous. Think you are up to it?" asked Mah Step.

"I would love that! I think I'm OK. The sprain is gone."

The ground outside was slightly damp from the showers of the previous night but the sky was clear as they walked in the warm morning sunlight by the now familiar center of the village. People they met stopped to ask after John and nodded their heads in happiness to find out he was all right.

"Today is the weekly market day," remarked Mah Step when he saw all the activity in the market area.

It felt good to be back on the grassy knoll. John luxuriated in his newfound physical well-being by stretching out on the grass.

"Will you be going to the Big Town today?" asked John.

"I'm sorry, I must. There's an important class to teach today that I cannot miss."

"I must go to Mah Zan's house for dinner tonight. He sent word yesterday that I could come today if I was all right. He seemed to think I would be healed by today."

"I will pass on the message before I catch the nine o'clock bus to town," said Mah Step.

As they walked back home John asked Mah Step, "Do you believe in heaven and hell?"

"Yes, I do," replied Mah Step.

"But don't you think it is old-fashioned and out-of-date? Can there be fire and brimstone really?"

"Our thinking doesn't change reality. And yet we often refuse to see what is right before our very eyes. It is fashionable to think that hell does not exist. But what about all that has happened and is still continuing to happen in the world right now? Who can deny hell when it already exists on earth? If the genocide of the hapless Armenians in 1915 by Turkey, the Holocaust of the Jews at the hands of the Nazis, the two World Wars, Rwanda, Bosnia, Serbia, Iraq, Afghanistan, Sudan, Ethiopia ... I could go on ... are not hell I don't know what they are. Can you imagine the plight of an ordinary, powerless human being or a family in the middle of such conflict? Isn't every waking moment pure unadulterated hell for them? When I look at pictures of Armenians starving to death in the desert or being brutally killed by the heartless Turks, both pity and anger well up in me. Injustice and intolerance of fellow human beings is hell too. Apartheid, slavery, the caste system in India ... isn't it all a living hell for the people on the wrong end of the stick? Then there are the human traffickers and the child molesters. Aren't they agents of evil? And then there's drug addiction and disease; terrorism and violence, tyranny and debasement. I do think all these are symbols or illustrations of hell right here on earth. To know of these horrors and still wish away hell is, I think, puerile. As long as there is sin, there is hell too."

"You think there's a heaven also?"

"Absolutely. By the very same token, yes; there has to be a heaven because there is heaven on earth—though we don't see it all the time. We get rare glimpses of it ... love, altruism, selflessness, sacrifice, and kindness ... these are all examples of what heaven will be like. And true justice, too. Equality and liberty as well. There has to be justice in the long run. It is the reward for honesty, truth, love and justice and the compensation for the pain, suffering, subjugation and cruelty that one may have endured in this life."

"There are many humanists who believe that heaven and hell are both figments of our imagination."

"I think that is both a denial of reality and in a way acquiescence to injustice and evil. If both heavenly and hellish situations can be experienced on earth right now, they can exist as distinct entities as well. Think about it this way. Imagine a ravaged person from lawless, war-torn Biafra or a starving destitute from Calcutta being transported to America. Wouldn't it be heaven? Likewise, if a well-fed and coddled American were moved in the opposite direction to a jungle-law state of pernicious poverty, wouldn't it be hell? Think of heaven and hell as the physical separation of all that is good and bad on earth. If heaven and hell were not there, evil would reign unfettered. Forever."

"There are some who think that hell is a state of mind," suggested John.

"That famous limerick about sitting on a pin is the answer to that!"

"Isn't that the one about the absence of pain?" laughed John softly.

"That's the one! Here's what I think. If there can be foreclosure due to non-payment of financial debt, if people can be turned out of homes and their assets repossessed for financial misdemeanors, why is it so hard for us to accept that there can similarly be punishment for depravity, brutality, cruelty, greed and every kind of moral bankruptcy?"

"You are very eloquent. And your vocabulary is showing again!"

"Sorry. I am very passionate about justice and fairness," said Mah Step apologetically. "We need to be getting back. I have a bus to catch."

"Before you leave be sure to give me the equivalent of five dollars."

"That won't be any problem. There's still money left. You don't need to change any dollars for some time."

Nora was ready with the morning repast when they got home. It was a family brunch and Pa prayed the prayer of thanksgiving for John's healing.

Mah Step left for the Big Town immediately afterward.

John was feeling so good he insisted on helping Nora with the washing. It was only when he actually got down to it, that he realized it was more strenuous than it appeared. He was afraid he would hurt his back again bending down to rinse the clothes in the aluminum basins. So, he restricted himself to wringing the clothes and hanging them on the iron clothesline to dry. He was of most help with the heavy bed sheets. As he twisted the soggy water-soaked clothes he wondered how Nora managed this work alone.

In the evening, he walked to Mah Zan's house. Squatting in the smoke-filled kitchen with squinting eyes, he enjoyed the graciousness of the host and his wife and the sumptuous food. Before returning home, John beckoned the children over and gave the eldest child a sealed envelope. Mah Zan suspected what it contained and began to protest, but John said, "This is my gift for the children. Buy them whatever they like or need."

When he told Mah Step about this on Saturday, Mah Step was pleased.

"When you asked me for the money I had wondered why. Five dollars is a lot money for us. I think you did the right thing."

Chapter 12: The Good Old Days of Radio

Mah Step asked John if he would like to go up with him to the Big Town on Monday morning. John was sorely tempted but he declined. He wanted to obliterate from his mind, for as long as he could, all those safety nets of the modern life that he had left behind and, instead, to swing free on the new trapeze of liberation that would appear extremely foolhardy to the average American.

"Let me pretend that I was born and raised here—right here in this village—without any links to the outside world," he told Mah Step.

"I belong here but that doesn't stop me from going to the Big Town for email and stuff," argued Mah Step.

"That's true. But for as long as I can hold out, I want to try and keep myself away from every semblance of contemporary advancement. Just the basic life. Not a whit more. I have fallen in love with the Sakhi way of life, can't you see?"

"That's fairly obvious. And I am happy that you love our customs and traditions. Have it your way. But is there anything you would like me to bring for you?" asked Mah Step.

"How about some chocolate-chip cookies?" smiled John mischievously.

"Wish I could. But you know we don't get them here."

"I was just kidding. But seriously, can you bring me a book?" asked John.

"With pleasure. Which book do you want?"

"Would you lend me Thoreau's *Walden*? I saw it on your bookshelf the first day."

"Yes, I do have the book. And I'll be happy to bring it for you. It would be the most appropriate book for what you are doing. For your experiment."

"It's more an experience than an experiment. I am myself the subject; the guinea pig, if you will," said John.

"Yes, that's true," conceded Mah Step. "In the meantime, you may want to read this one."

After Mah Step had left by the morning bus, John went for his usual morning walk. He took the book that Mah Step had given him, Edna O'Brien's *The Lonely Girl*. It made compelling reading. He found it hard to believe that a developed nation—that too the land of Shaw, Joyce, Yeats, Synge, and Beckett—would take offense and ban a book in this day and age.

'We are not talking about Salman Rushdie and Iran here, for heaven's sake!' he said to himself.

When he compared the condition of women in Ireland to their counterparts in this village, Irish women came up woefully short. The Sakhi women enjoyed a status that would have been the envy of any nation of the Western world.

He lost all track of time as he read O'Brien. He had come more than half way when he decided he had been away from Nora for too long. As he walked back he thought about Mah Step as living proof of how wrong the jingoistic imperialist slogan was. "Not only had East and West met in him but how gloriously!" he wondered. His reverie was broken by the greeting directed at him. As he reciprocated the *Hooblei* he was relieved to recognize the middle-school headmaster without any difficulty.

"You are the headmaster, aren't you?" asked John smiling tentatively.

"Yes, I am the headmaster," he replied clearly pleased that John had remembered him.

"How are you? Are you happy with us?" continued the headmaster.

"I am doing well, thank you. I am blessed to be here. This is a lovely place!" John replied.

"Please come to my house and have a cup of tea," requested the headmaster.

John wished the headmaster would identify himself by name but then recalled that that was seldom done as conversations were so deferential and self-effacing, avoiding personal names.

"I come home during the lunch break," he explained as he led John into the house. The headmaster called out to his wife and she came running into room wiping her wet hands on her stained *sainjyrshah* and pushing her hair back into place. John surmised that she must have been washing clothes in the backyard. Following closely behind her was a wailing child wearing a mud-spattered dress. The wife was beside herself with the excitement of having a *sahep* in their house. The headmaster spoke to her gently and she disappeared into the kitchen lifting the crying child into her arms. As the headmaster and he settled into rattan settees, John looked around the room. The posters on the walls seemed so incongruously out of place, he was startled.

"Where did you get that from?" asked John in amazement pointing at a grimy poster of Roy Rogers and Dale Evans.

"I got it many years ago, from a gospel radio station called FEBC—Far East Broadcasting Company. They used to broadcast from Manila, in the Philippines."

"And the Grand Ole Opry poster?" asked John.

"Yes, that one also."

There were pictures of Billy Graham, Tennessee Ernie Ford, and Glen Campbell. There were three smaller pictures that he did not recognize.

"Who are they?" John could not hide his fascination.

"The first one is Carl Richardson, the radio preacher on *Forward in Faith.* The other two are Phil Irwin and Pat Gates of the Voice of America. They had a program called the *Breakfast Show* many years ago. It was very good."

"Those programs were in English?"

"Yes, they were in English. They played good music. Many of us learned English by listening to the radio. The Voice of America also had a program called *News in Special English.* They would read the news very slow for us to understand. We listened to the Voice of America every day; to the news and also to the wide variety of music programs, especially Willis Conover's jazz and standards."

"Amazing!" said John in near disbelief. He made a mental note to ask Mah Step about this later.

After tea and a bowl of rice John strode back to the house eager to see Nora again. She was waiting just as eagerly for him.

"What happened? I was worried about you. Where did you go?" she blurted out.

"I lost track of time reading and then I met the headmaster on my way back. He invited me over to his house," explained John. Then seeing how worried she had been for him, he added, "I'm sorry."

"Shall I make some tea for you?" she asked.

"I had tea already at the head master's," said John and immediately regretted it, seeing disappointment cloud her face. "But I can always have another cup with you," he added and was relieved to see happiness return to Nora's face.

"I've made something special for you," said Nora bringing out the tray. "I won't tell you what it is. You taste and tell me what it is made of."

As soon as Nora had said grace in the Sakhi language John picked up a round white ball from the plate. It tasted bland as he nipped the edges and, with Nora watching him, he took a bigger bite to find there was meat inside. There could be no doubt it was pork.

"Let me guess. These are pork dumplings. Pork in steamed rice batter," John said.

"That's correct!" Nora said happily. "We use a bamboo tube for the steaming."

John relished the tea and pork dumplings, but he was happier to be with Nora again.

"I wish a little of her innocence and delight in the simple pleasures of life would rub off on me," he thought as he watched her gather the empty cups, saucers, and plates.

She came back with the wooden *kwai* bowl and made herself a *kwai*. "I'll wash the cups and plates later," she said. They looked at each other and smiled, not saying anything.

Finally, Nora asked, "Do you have a big house, Mah John?"

"My house is not very big by American standards and I will be the owner only after another twenty-eight years," explained John. He realized, to his embarrassment, that the cost of his condo would perhaps be more than the cost of all the houses in this village put together.

"Who washes your clothes? Do you give it to the laundry? Are you a good cook? Who does the sweeping?" the questions came tumbling out from Nora.

John explained how the washer was fully automatic unlike their manual version in the Big Town, which Nora did not use anyway. He then described the dryer, the dishwasher, and the vacuum cleaner but what fascinated Nora the most were the TV dinners.

"You don't have to wash or cook? The food is ready in two minutes?" Nora said unbelievingly.

"Yes, it's all pre-cooked. Just needs heating up."

John wondered how much Nora's life would be changed if she had modern gadgets to reduce the drudgery. With her talent and skills, she might even achieve something worthwhile with the time she saved. John could not imagine what Nora's reaction would be to life in America—the sheer pace of everyday life, the speeding highways, the underground metro, the blatant consumerism of the shopping malls, and the fragmented seclusion of an individualistic life.

"What a criminal waste to spend all her time and energy on just household chores the whole day, every day!" John thought. "Yet she's cheerful and uncomplaining."

"You know, Nora, I'm about half way through my stay here," John said aloud.

"I don't understand. Will you please repeat?" asked Nora.

"I was saying that in a few more weeks I would have to go back to America."

Nora looked utterly dumbfounded, her balloon of happiness deflated. She looked at John wordlessly with pleading eyes. John watched helplessly as silver teardrops snaked down her flushed face. Leaving behind the *kwai* bowl on the ground, Nora fled indoors.

"Nora, wait!" called John and rushed after Nora but she had gone into the bedroom, where John dared not enter. When he walked alone into the kitchen looking dejected, Ma realized something was wrong and she rose to go see Nora. John felt foolish; he had no clue at all what caused Nora's unexpected outburst. He wondered if Nora had been struggling with similar emotions that he had been suppressing within him.

"This changes everything," thought John as he walked back outside to ponder about this wholly unanticipated turn of events.

Later in the afternoon, Nora served him tea, as she was wont to. She had washed her face, but her eyes were still red from crying. She did not utter a word about what had happened earlier.

"I'm sorry," offered John.

Nora acknowledged it with the slightest of nods but did not say a thing. At one point when their eyes met, he saw reproach in her eyes. But that night at dinner she seemed her usual attentive self, serving him rice and curry, but when her guard was down her eyes silently spoke of an anguish she did not articulate.

***

The next morning it was as if nothing had happened as Nora and John walked together to a thatched wooden shed on the far side of the village. The shed was actually behind the owner's house and they had to walk through a narrow gap between the hedge and the house to get there. The blacksmith was already at work pumping a large, leather bellows while sharpening a knife. Sparks flew as he manually worked the knife and the water hissed as he plunged the red-hot piece of iron into it. Over in the corner, another man beat a glowing-red piece of iron into the required shape. John purchased a handmade knife as a souvenir. The folding Sakhi knife that John had seen Nora and Ma use in the kitchen was a clever contraption. The hinged blade folded into a cleft in the wooden handle so that the sharp edge of the blade was not exposed when not needed. When the blade was opened out on its hinge, a small protruding tail on the blade pressed against the wooden handle to give the knife the firmness of a fixed blade knife. John marveled at the ingenuity of the design and the completely environment-friendly way it was created. He remembered the gravity-fed irrigation system that he had seen earlier.

As they walked back to the house John noticed that the women they met on the way seemed to be teasing Nora. He presumed because of the circumstances that this in some way related to her proximity to a *sahep* but because of the previous day's incident John did not think it prudent to inquire.

But walking with Nora was very pleasant. She did not once say that he was walking too fast, a complaint that he had heard often enough from his female friends back home. The semi-formal flower-print dress that Nora wore accentuated her freshness and innocent charm. John felt happy and protective as they walked together.

The rains came again the next day but, mercifully, lasted only two days. He spent the time reading Kipling's *Kim* and lazing completely unstructured without goals, plans or schedules. "For the modern man, even relaxation has to be consciously learned," philosophized John. "So much so that even a vacation or a pastime turns into another source of stress." But here in the Sakhi Hills, it was as close as he ever got to completely emptying his being of all the burdens and obligations of a time-controlled life.

Mah Step came early on Friday. He had remembered to bring *Walden* with him.

"I have a small present for you," said Mah Step handing over a small newspaper wrapped packet.

"May I open it now?" asked John remembering the Eastern tradition of not opening gifts immediately in the presence of the giver.

"Go ahead! Open it!" goaded Mah Step.

John was careful not to tear apart the wrapping savagely in the Western tradition. When he had carefully peeled the adhesive tape, a red folded cloth was revealed. John opened it out to discover that it was a shoulder bag made of thick cotton yarn.

"It's hand made. Woven actually, by the women of the Pangama tribe," Mah Step explained.

"Wow! This is great! It beats my leather laptop bag any day!" exulted John.

"You can carry your books and papers in the bag," suggested Mah Step.

"Right! This will come in very handy," agreed John. "Thanks! Much appreciated!"

"Don't mention it," Mah Step said embarrassed.

"I don't mean to look a gift horse in the mouth but is this from the tribe that is violent?" asked John.

"Yes, but that needn't worry us as far as this bag is concerned!" said Mah Step.

After the mandatory afternoon tea, they went out for a walk. As they walked, John wondered if he should tell Mah Step about Nora's outburst of tears but decided against it. John mentioned the country music and the posters he saw in the house of the headmaster of the middle school.

"All of us who listened to those radio programs wrote in to the stations requesting the gifts they offered on the air. From time to time they gave away posters, vinyl LP records or cassettes, mint stamps and first-day covers, T-shirts, station pennants and other mementos. In part, it was propaganda. But radio was good. It broadened our horizons and increased our knowledge. Not everybody had a radio then. We sat in groups listening to our favorite programs. I still remember when the first radio arrived in our village. It was the pastor's. That huge German radio—I remember it was a Telefunken—had many valves and could be heard almost a mile away," explained Mah Step.

"Your village is still quiet. Do you all still listen to shortwave?" asked John.

"Not like before. Not in groups, anyway. Almost everybody has a transistor radio today, but they listen mostly to our national stations on medium wave. In the Big Town people watch the TV these days for national and international news. As I told you before, radio has been a big influence in my life."

"What were the stations that you listened to on a regular basis? I know you mentioned the BBC and the Voice of America and FEBC broadcasting from the Philippines. Were there others as well?"

"In addition to the BBC and the Voice of America and FEBC, we also listened faithfully to Radio Australia, Deutsche Welle, Swiss Radio International, and Radio Nederland Wereldomroep transmitting from their relay station in Antananarivo, Madagascar, and zany shows from Radio Sweden in Stockholm and gospel programs from HCJB all the way from Quito, Ecuador."

"Wow! That's a very international line-up of radio stations!"

"Those were the good old days! I even remember an officer from the intelligence department coming to investigate my radio listening. The government must have been keeping tabs on the exotic foreign mail that I was receiving."

"What happened?"

"The investigator seemed a little disappointed that I wasn't a spy or anything. He took some mail and program-schedules as proof and left," Mah Step said.

"In the US, we have a whole slew of radio stations on FM and AM and even on satellite. You can find stations that only play a particular style of music." John paused. "There is something totally different that I wanted to ask you about. Nora had told me about marriages not being arranged here like in the plains. How much freedom do people have in marrying someone they like?" asked John.

"We have all the freedom we want. The only restriction relates to endogamy. We are exogamous. Marriage within the clan is prohibited. It is strictly taboo. In addition, each clan has a few other clans that are considered related. Marriage amongst these clans is proscribed as well. Other than that, there is complete freedom in marrying anybody one chooses."

"Even people outside the tribe?" asked John.

"That has always been frowned upon because it has been mostly our women who marry men from outside the tribe. Not so many of our men marry outsiders. The majority of the plainsmen who marry our women do not assimilate well. They hold to their own customs, language, and religion. That is a problem in a tight-knit society like ours. Most of them are not Christians."

"What about their children?" John wanted to know.

"Since we are matrilineal the children are considered part of our tribe. As I told you in our Internet chat, the offspring take the surname of the mother—not of the father," said Mah Step.

"Yes, I remember you telling me this in one of our chats. That is a unique custom. Does it cause any problems?"

"No, it is a little difficult for people from patriarchal societies to comprehend our customs. But there is actually no difference. It is just an inversion. Lineage is traced through the female line in our tribe, whereas, in other communities, it is on the father's side."

"That *is* quite unusual," remarked John thoughtfully.

"Actually, it is not. It is much like you driving on the right side of the road and we on the left."

"So, the children from mixed marriages are considered members of the tribe?"

"Yes, even if one of our women marries outside the tribe, her children still belong to the tribe. In the rare case of a Sakhi man marrying an outsider, a new clan is created as there is no pre-existing female line. Our tradition is not unusual for another reason. It may seem so in the present day but you must remember that most ancient societies started out matrilineal. In any case, as someone—was it Shaw? I could be wrong—caustically stated, when it comes to parentage one can only be certain of the mother!"

"But that was before DNA testing came along," commented John and they laughed together.

"But seriously, how strong are marriages here?" persisted John.

"In our society, young people are free to date, and they choose their own life partners. Not all unions are solemnized in church. Almost half are common-law marriages. In some cases, marriage happens after children have been born out of wedlock. But regretfully our divorce rate is very high. Some estimate it close to fifty percent."

"That's high," agreed John.

"But here is the funny part. In the plains, the parents arrange the marriages of their children. Sometimes the couple meet each other for the first time on the day of the marriage. Yet their divorce rate is low—less than ten percent. Can you believe that?"

"Why do you think that is?" asked John.

"I don't really know. Sociologists are trying to figure that out. Maybe it is because divorce is frowned upon in their society? There is a theory going around that our matrilineal system is to blame for the high divorce rate."

"Is there a move to switch to the patriarchal model that is universally accepted?"

"There is a small group of men who have started a campaign for this, but they don't have much public support. Change is not easy. This change will strike at the very root of our clan system. There would be chaos. Tracking exogamy in marriages will become a nightmare."

"What's the church's position on this? Isn't Christianity patriarchal?" asked John.

"Christianity was born in the patriarchal Judaic society. But the tenets of Christianity do not support a male-centric universe."

"Are you sure? I have heard of Bible verses being quoted in support of male supremacy."

"That's a fallacy. Jesus treated women with the same importance as men. The Bible teaches us that men and women were created equal. All are one; there is neither male nor female. I think the patriarchal bias was man-made—not God ordained. I'm glad the Welsh missionaries did not force us to change our custom. Maybe they wouldn't have succeeded even if they had tried."

"Wasn't it Korea that changed the surnames so people could get around the exogamous restrictions and marry freely?" asked John.

"Yeah, I read about it somewhere. Won't ever happen here, though."

"What about children born out of wedlock? How are they treated?" John wanted to know.

"There is no stigma at all to the children. Children are considered a gift from God. And since we are matrilineal, the mother's family is their support group."

"Ever since I got here I've admired the affection bestowed on Sakhi children," said John.

"Yes, I agree. We do pamper our children," Mah Step agreed.

"They really seem to enjoy their childhood," said John.

"Children are carefree, and they are safe. They can run around the whole village and play wherever they want. They need not be afraid of anyone molesting or harming them."

"That's really wonderful. Children are so protected in my country. They have so many restrictions."

"I heard about child molesters in your country."

"Yes, that is true. It's very sad that in an enlightened and progressive society like ours there is still such evil."

"Mercifully, we do not have that here."

After they had walked on quietly for some minutes, Mah Step stopped and turned to John slowly.

"There's something I have to tell you. It's a confession, actually," said Mah Step gravely.

John turned to look at him, surprised.

"During our chats, I had told you I was single. That is true. I am single now. But it isn't the whole truth. I was married till a year ago. It was a common-law marriage. And I have a child. He's four years old."

"That's OK! I'm not scandalized. I told you about my live-in relationship with Elaine and how we parted ways amicably about two years ago."

"I feel guilty that our marriage broke up. I feel even more culpable that I am an absentee father," said a visibly distraught Mah Step.

"Do you pay child support?"

"No, we don't have that system here. But I do buy things for my son. I love him very much. He and his mother stay with his grandparents who are well to do. He is the apple of their eyes."

"Elaine and I broke up because we were completely different people. She is an epicure and I am a stoic. She's high on aesthetics; I am a utilitarian. She collects stuff while I try to simplify and get rid of stuff. She likes to buy and I hate shopping. We parted amicably. She is beautiful and kind and I still love her," John said wistfully.

"That's too bad. Do you think you two could get together again?" asked Mah Step.

"I wish we could. But, no, I don't think that will ever happen. We would both be unhappy in the long run. If I'm not being too inquisitive, what caused your split?" John was curious.

"Very bluntly, my infidelity. I'm not proud of it and, in hindsight, I probably would never repeat my mistake. But at that time, I did not know better. The third party was a colleague at work and it just happened. It wasn't real love or anything long-term."

"That's too bad. Since you still love your wife and son didn't you try to patch things up?" asked John.

"I tried but she was adamant. She said it was the end of our relationship because I was unfaithful. There was no older person to mediate and bring us together. My parents were pretty upset with me for what happened," Mah Step said ruefully.

"It must have been painful," commiserated John.

"It still is. I was stupid. Just thinking about it makes me angry with myself."

"Some take it to heart. Others get over it," said John.

"I wish I were like my friend in the Big Town. He is an incorrigible philanderer. But his wife forgives him each time."

"He is lucky," was all John could think of saying.

"Yeah, it is funny too. He drinks a little too much at parties and always sleeps with some woman or the other that he meets there. When he gets back home he doesn't enter the house right away. He stands outside the door loudly confessing his sin and pleading for his wife's forgiveness. She shouts at him, calls him names and threatens to chase him back to his clan. But in the end, she forgives him," said Mah Step.

"And then his wife lets him enter the house?

"No, there is more. Even after his wife forgives him my friend is still in tears and in the throes of self-castigation and self-abasement. He wails loudly that he is unclean and unworthy to enter the house. His wife then brings out a bucket of hot water and soap and my friend strips down to his shorts and bathes himself in the front courtyard of his house in full public view. This usually happens in the night but the neighbors all get up to watch the drama. His bath done, my friend enters the house, and all is forgiven."

"A kind of self-absolution, huh?"

"Something like that. When his neighbors see him bathing in his front-yard they immediately know that he has committed adultery again! And practically the whole town comes to know of it the next day!"

"He has got to be careful. A hot bath doesn't wash away STD or AIDS," said John.

"True," agreed Mah Step.

"By the way is AIDS a problem here or in the Big Town?"

"The honest answer is 'I don't really know'. Nobody does. There are NGOs (by that I mean private nonprofits) and government agencies involved in this field, but my guess is that what is publicly reported is much less than the actual because of the stigma attached to the disease. Even cancer or some other serious diseases are only whispered about. Nobody talks about them publicly. Sexual diseases are even less discussed," said Mah Step.

"Isn't there some law?"

"It cannot be legislated. If someone falls seriously ill and dies, the clan quietly buries him or her. Even in accidental deaths, autopsies are not always performed. People are not comfortable about cutting up the body. In the neighboring provinces, there is a high prevalence of HIV/AIDS."

"Mostly drug users?" asked John.

"Yes, that's right. Being adjacent to the "golden triangle", drug running is a big part of the underworld economy in the neighboring provinces. The other is gun running."

"Is there a market for arms?"

"All the neighboring provinces have simmering discontent and latent independence movements that have been waging an underground war against the federal government. It is not much known in the West, but it is a serious problem. That and drugs."

"The drugs go to Europe and America?" asked John.

"That's right. I don't know their modus operandi but the main market they aim at is America. I am very scared for the children of our tribe. They are so impressionable, and the pushers deliberately target the young. I have seen young men and women in the Big Town completely broken by drugs; mere shells of their former self. In some cases, their limbs are amputated after gangrene sets in. It is tragic."

"I can imagine. You said the problem in neighboring provinces is much worse?" asked John.

"It is. I fear for those tribes and mine. When the problem explodes, it will decimate them just like it did in Africa. That will be the end of tribal innocence," Mah Step said forlornly.

"I hope it never comes to that," responded John. "If the government and the nonprofits get their act together hopefully it can still be contained?"

"I hope so. But all this talk is quite depressing. Let's change the subject," suggested Mah Step.

They talked of computers, MP3 players and e-books as they walked back to the house.

When John saw Nora, freshly bathed with the still damp dark brown hair combed neatly back, he felt a twinge of desire. Nora saw it in his eyes and blushed.

Chapter 13: A Death in the Village

After the cold of the night, John was languorously curled up enjoying the warmth of the dawn when he heard a light knock at the front door and whispered exchanges. Nora who answered the door must have gone around the house and woken everybody up because suddenly there were many of them talking in hushed tones. Something felt amiss as John jumped out of bed pulling on his corduroy trousers and headed for the kitchen. He had not seen the family like that before. They were standing in a circle with their arms around each other's shoulders. When they turned to look at him he saw that there were tears on the faces of Ma and Nora. This was the first time John had seen the family in physical contact with each other.

On seeing John, Mah Step said quietly, "We just received word that our nephew in the Big Town passed away yesterday."

John was stunned. "I'm so sorry. Was he ill?"

"No, it was an accident. He was on his way to school. He fell from the bus. He was only seventeen."

"Oh, my goodness! I'm really, really sorry. This is very sad."

"Thank you. We are all stunned. He was the only son of my elder brother. The other two are daughters."

"Is there anything I can do to help?" John could think of nothing else to say.

"Not really. But we all have to go for the funeral. Would you like to stay here on your own or would you like to come with us?"

John took only a moment to decide. "I'd prefer to come with you—if that's OK."

"Good. We will leave in an hour. Pack some clothes," Mah Step said.

"Pack some clothes? How long will we be gone?" John asked.

"Three days," Mah Step replied, "Funerals take long here."

"Will we be staying at your home in the Big Town?" asked John.

"No, I'm sorry for confusing you. My nephew died in the Big Town, but he will be buried in his village about half an hour from here."

It was closer to two hours before they left the house. The mood was somber and subdued in the dilapidated old jeep, with Pa and John sitting with the driver in the front and Ma, Nora and Mah Step sitting in the seat behind. In the back of the jeep, Mah Step had placed a sack of rice and large aluminum cooking vessels.

The ride took about forty minutes over a bumpy road pockmarked with deep potholes. When they reached the village, it wasn't difficult to spot the house of mourning. There was a small group of people in the front yard. Two jeeps were parked haphazardly by the side of the lane in front of the house. As they drove up John saw that behind the house people were already at work. There were two open wood fires from which smoke was rising. It also looked like a temporary shed was being constructed in the backyard.

As they got down from the jeep Mah Step's elder brother came out looking dazed to shake his father's hand. Pa patted his son's shoulder as he comforted him. Ma and Nora broke into sobs. Mah Step hugged his brother before introducing John. "*Hooblei!*" the brother said as he shook hands. Mah Step called out to one of the boys and three of them came to carry the sack of rice and the large cooking vessels inside.

"The body hasn't arrived yet," Mah Step explained. The front room was being rearranged. All pictures, calendars and other decorations had been taken down or turned around to face the wall. The room behind had already been prepared for the dead body. There was a wooden bed in the center of the room with white sheets hung like curtains on all four sides and a thin mattress covered with a white bed sheet.

"Come let us sit outside," Mah Step said, and they walked out again to the front yard. A group of young men were arranging backless wooden benches four feet long in neat rows on either side of the path leading to the front door.

"These benches are from the local school. These won't be enough. They will need to bring benches from the church," Mah Step said and then went over to talk to the boys. John sat down on the nearest bench and placed the red shoulder bag that he had carried down by his side. Just then three young girls came around the side of the house. The first one carrying a plastic bucket handed out cups from it to the people sitting around and the second one with the large kettle poured out milk-tea, holding the heavy kettle with both hands. The third girl carried an open white plastic tray on which thinly cut slices of cake were placed. She held out the tray to those who had already been served tea. The trio went from guest to guest offering first the cup, then the tea and lastly the cake. When they came to John they tittered nervously. The one who handed out the cup blushed deeply and the girl who carried the kettle had trouble pouring straight. The one with the cake tray was the nonchalant one; when he picked up a slice of cake she smiled conspiratorially and raised her eyebrows.

People kept going in and out of the house. It appeared to John that the people had forgotten their grief in the act of being busy. After a while, two girls came holding aluminum basins to their hips. They picked up the empty cups left under the benches. Two other girls brought *kwai* on white enamel plates. They moved around offering it to the people present and then left the two plates on empty benches for people to help themselves. One of them came to John and held out the plate smiling but John waved a polite "no".

Just then a huge roll of blue tarpaulin was carried out of a jeep along with long bamboo stakes. The workers began driving the stakes into the ground around the perimeter of the yard. Mah Step walked over and sat by John.

"They are going to put up a temporary awning," explained Mah Step.

A loud yell from the lane startled everyone and galvanized them into action. Those who were sitting, stood up. Some ran into the house where a small commotion was heard.

"The body has arrived," Mah Step explained.

A little later a white hospital ambulance drew up to the house. Mah Step's father and brother and other men came out of the house as the dead body, shrouded in white, was taken out of the ambulance. Women began to wail loudly from inside the house. Grief was back in their midst.

Mah Step's brother, the dead child's father, cried out in anguish as the stretcher was taken out of the ambulance. The whole crowd encircled the stretcher as it was carried into the house. John walked with Mah Step as the body was placed on the bed and the sheet removed for all to take a look. The women's wails rose to a heart-rending crescendo. The boy's mother was inconsolable and had to be supported by two women on either side of her. The boy's face bore no marks of external injuries and seemed serene in death. When everybody had had a look, the women sat down on reed mats near the bed and the men drifted away.

"You can either sit in the front room or outside," Mah Step suggested.

"I think I'll sit outside. It's a pleasant day," John said.

"You will have to excuse me for a while. I need to go and help with the arrangements inside," said Mah Step.

"That's OK. You go right ahead. I'll be fine," John replied.

Time seemed to hang still. For a moment, John wondered if had made a mistake coming. There was no one who spoke English. Everybody else was either busy with work or engaged in conversation. Thankfully, people did not seem to take note of him anymore, which was a blessing. He felt as if he had blended into the surroundings like a chameleon. The tea girls came around again; different girls this time. And instead of cake, it was two varieties of cookies. John helped himself to a couple of thin arrowroots and a cup of tea.

A little later he had a brilliant idea. He bent down and retrieved Ken Kesey's *Sometimes a Great Notion* from the red shoulder bag and began to read with his elbows resting on his thighs. He looked up guiltily once or twice to see if his reading a book was offending anyone but was relieved to find that nobody seemed to notice. "It's a good thing I don't have a watch on me," he thought. He would have kept checking the time far too often.

He was roused from his reading by a young boy of ten or eleven who stood in front of him. The boy spoke to him in Sakhi but John could only make out *"sahep"* and "Mah Step" and nothing else.

"I'm sorry, what did you say?" John asked as gently as he could.

The boy didn't seem to comprehend. John realized that everyone in the yard was looking at him now. He looked around but didn't see anyone whom he could ask for help.

The boy repeated what he said before and this time turned and pointed to the house when he mentioned Mah Step's name.

"I get it. Mah Step wants me to go see him," John said. Since the boy didn't speak any English, John thought this might be as good a time as any to try speaking Sakhi. Unfortunately for him, his attempts were incomprehensible to the lad, and a source of much amusement to the onlookers.

John realized he had made an error. "I must have mauled the Sakhi language real bad," he thought ruefully. He quickly shoved the book into the cloth bag and got up. The boy seemed infinitely relieved as he led John to the back of the house, where under a plastic awning were arranged three long tables with benches on either side. Some were seated while others were engaged in serving them. Further out in the backyard there were three wood fires over which men stirred large cauldrons of food.

"Ah! There you are Mah John!" Mah Step called from the middle table. "You must be hungry. Let's have some food."

"Good deal! And not a moment too soon," said John softly.

"Come, let us wash our hands first," Mah Step suggested.

They washed their hands at the green drum of water at the foot of which sat two women on their haunches washing a small mountain of plates and cups in large aluminum basins. The water dribbled down through a rubber tube hanging from the side of a green iron drum. John washed his hands drawing water from a plastic bucket with a mug and using the small bar of soap placed beside the bucket. There was a towel hanging from the back of a chair nearby, but John preferred to shake his hands dry.

No sooner had he sat down at the table than a stainless-steel plate was placed before him on which was soon heaped a small mound of steaming white rice. Then came the ubiquitous lentils, mixed vegetables, and meat. The beef was cooked with spices and only very mildly hot and the pork was fried in a paste of sesame seeds.

"Do you need a spoon or a fork?" Mah Step asked.

"No thanks," John replied, "I'm good with my hands now."

He was hungry and the food was delicious. It was a surprise to him how they cooked in such large quantities and yet achieved the perfection of a family meal. "Strange," he thought, "all the cooking is done by men and the food still tastes good."

"The beef is simply superb. I have never had this dish before," John said aloud.

"Yes, that's true. It is cooked this way only at funerals. It's a rather unique tradition that we have," Mah Step said.

It was hard to resist a second helping. When it came to the third, though, John had to protectively put both arms around his plate to prevent the insistent server.

Mah Step had to laugh. "You know how one asks for another helping?"

"That shouldn't be difficult, I should think," John said.

"But it is! Etiquette doesn't allow you to ask for a helping for yourself. So, what you do is signal a server and request him or her to serve your neighbor. The hint is taken. You are served even if the neighbor has had enough!"

"Interesting," John said as he and Mah Step rose up and carried their plates over to the washing spot.

"That was a good meal," John said as he patted his hands on a cloth towel that hung on the back of the wooden chair nearby.

"I am glad we ate now. The crowd's going to get much bigger in a little while. Shall we go outside?" Mah Step suggested.

There were more people outside than before. The men seemed to prefer the benches in the front yard while the women all went indoors.

"Looks like nobody went to the fields today," said John.

"You are right. The majority of them didn't. It is considered disrespectful not to be present at the wake. Plus, my brother and sister-in-law are held in high esteem in the village. Those who went to the fields probably had some urgent unfinished work. They will come back early from the fields today."

"Dying must be expensive here. How does the family afford to feed the whole village for three days?" John asked.

"That's the beauty of our system. Nobody has life insurance, and nobody saves up money for funeral expenses. Yet when death comes calling, all is taken care of. There are no debts, no loans."

"How do you do that? You told me the other day how poor the people are and how little they have in terms of savings. From where do they get the resources to feed the entire village? Does the government provide grants?" John asked.

"No! It's all from within ourselves. We help each other in times of trouble. The whole community chips in. Each one brings a little cash. Some will provide rice or vegetables. One might donate a pig. Others might bring a few chicken or eggs. The young men volunteer with the work. They carry water and firewood, dig the grave, and help in other ways. The girls help with the cleaning and dishwashing, serving tea and snacks. The bereaved family entertains the entire village for almost three days. Yet at the end of it, they have some money and provisions left over. It is like the loaves and fishes all over again. Debt is not an additional burden to grief. There is never any debt."

"That is amazing!" John marveled.

"I'll need to find out why the coffin is taking so long. You stay right here. I'll be back soon."

With that, Mah Step wandered away to the road and John went back to reading Kesey. From time to time, he rested the book by his side and reconnected to what was happening around him. There was a group over on the other side that might have been at a raucous wedding party and not a funeral. They were laughing and rolling about on the benches. But nobody seemed to mind their antics as other groups carried on their own quiet conversations. Tea and crackers came and went regularly and the plate of *kwai* was never allowed to run empty.

It must have been almost midafternoon when the coffin arrived, tied with ropes on top of a jeep. It was carefully lifted down and carried inside. It smelled of fresh pine and was shiny and polished. But Mah Step was nowhere to be seen. "He must have gone inside while I was reading," John thought and went back to his book.

The next time the tea came around John gladly accepted a cup and a cream cookie. Mah Step came out of the house much later with his sleeves rolled up.

"Sorry for being away so long. I had to help wash the body."

"Is that the custom?" John asked.

"Yes, it is. We have no morticians here; nor any funeral homes. The dead body is washed by family members and then dressed in the best clothes and placed in the coffin." Mah Step's voice broke and his hand went to his forehead as he continued, "I'm glad the hospital did not do a post-mortem. That would have further saddened the family. Poor thing! The wheels of the bus went over his lower abdomen. There must have been an internal hemorrhage."

John could not find adequate words. "I'm sorry," was all he could manage. But inwardly he wondered, "If this had happened in the US would the boy have died? Could his life have been saved?"

Mah Step quickly composed himself and was business-like again. "If you like you can go in and view the body now," Mah Step offered.

The boy looked tranquil in death, his face washed, and hair combed. He had on a dark coat and a white shirt. Wreaths of flowers were all around the coffin. The women who kept vigil had their shawls over their heads and talked in hushed tones as they sat on the rush mats around the bed. There was no crying or tears. Grief and sorrow appeared to have retreated into the background. Visitors who came in shook hands with the mother who sat in the center. John noticed that as they shook hands they slipped money into her hands, which she dropped into a small cloth bag hanging from her neck.

Mah Step followed his sight. "That is one of the ways we help in times of need. No accounts are kept of how much each one gave. What is important is that all give as they are able. No one flaunts their generosity. The giving is practically anonymous although it is done personally. The money is put straight into the bag and used for the funeral expenses."

"Is that enough to cover all the expenses?" John asked.

"You would be surprised. As I said earlier, there is always some left over. Don't forget, in addition to money, they also contribute in kind, with rice, meat, vegetables, etc., and also with labor."

John noticed the plate of food placed near the head of the coffin.

"Why do you keep food near the corpse?" whispered John.

"Oh, that. We would like to believe that he is still with us—at least in spirit. At every meal, a plate of food will be placed near the body. After the burial is over also a plate of food for the departed will be kept aside at every meal for the next three days."

As they walked back outside to the front yard Mah Step told John that he had changed his mind about staying on for the night. "It's going to be quite crowded in the house. People will be sleeping all over the place. On benches pushed together, and even on the floor. All the lights will be kept on the whole night and all the doors and windows will be left open. We believe that the spirit of the deceased will come visiting the home and all his favorite haunts and should not be constrained. There will also be a lot of drinking. The young men won't sleep till early morning. They will sit around the fires in the backyard drinking all night telling stories. You won't be able to sleep. You won't be comfortable here at all."

"Then it's not a bad idea to be going home for the night. I'll give anything to sleep in a proper bed tonight. Sitting on these benches with no backrest or arms has left my whole body, stiff," John said.

Soon they were off in one of the jeeps but not before they had gone around and wished everybody good night. Pa, Ma and Nora would not be coming home; they would stay the night. John had been on the lookout for Nora since they arrived, but she was not to be seen. It was in the kitchen that they found Nora. She was helping with cleaning the rice, picking stones and other foreign matter from the rice before it was washed and cooked. In the crowd of people both of them were at a loss for words. John said a quick goodbye and stepped out with Mah Step.

"I hope you weren't too bored," Mah Step said.

"No, not really. I don't want to sound like a voyeur, but it was fascinating to watch the funeral customs here. So different from ours. But I badly need to take a leak. With the big crowd of people in the house, I kind of balked at using the outhouse there," said John.

"No problem! We will stop just outside the village and you can go behind a tree."

That was soon taken care of and they were on their way again.

"The one thing that frustrated me today was the language," said John. "How I wished I could talk to everyone and understand what they say. How great it would be to communicate!"

"That's not always true," Mah Step said with a wry smile.

"What do you mean?" John asked anticipating a story with an interesting twist.

"One of my friends from the Big Town married a girl from the plains. Usually, it is the other way around; our girls marry outsiders, most of them unscrupulous. This girl did not speak one word of our language. Other than that, she seemed to be adjusting very well to our customs. The newlyweds got along well with each other and the girl got on famously with the family. They couldn't talk much to each other, but they smiled a lot and even laughed together. After about two months she wanted to learn the language to communicate better."

"And things got even better?" John asked.

"That's what she expected to happen. But when she began to learn the language, she also began to understand what they were actually talking about. And she found out that her sisters-in-law were not only making fun of her manners and her accent but also disparaging her people and their customs. She realized that unknowingly she had been laughing at herself when she had laughed with them. And she discovered that the relatives who came to see her mocked her too. The marriage barely lasted another three weeks. She couldn't take it anymore. She went back to her people in the plains."

"But didn't you say she loved him?" John asked.

"In the beginning, she did. They were both deeply in love. But when she found out that he did precious little to stop his sisters from poking jokes at her, and in fact seemed to laugh with them, she fell out of love. Her love just evaporated."

"That's a pity!" John remarked.

"I agree. Sometimes ignorance is bliss. Language can also be a barrier instead of being a bridge. During the Second World War, the national government discovered that our language was better than having a secret code. No foreigner knew our language and very few of our own countrymen outside of our tribe knew it. So, by a quirk of fate our able-bodied young men became the backbone of the army signals division. The Japanese couldn't break our code. I guess it was utter gibberish to them."

"It would have been a tough test for Turing!" John said jocularly.

"Talking about understanding languages, I was at a training in Bangkok on HIV/AIDS. The facilitators were from America, two ladies, and a man. I guess the women had contrasting teaching styles and during the coffee break, one of them complained to the man about the other. 'She sucks' was what she said. She was so furious that she didn't care that she was within earshot of the participants. Later during lunch, I heard a woman participant at my table say to her companion in Thai: 'These Americans are so shameless. They shout intimate secrets in public.' Obviously, she did not know what the word meant in slang."

"I remember, when I was in school my parents fined me a quarter each time I used that word," John said.

"At the same training, the male speaker kept using the phrase 'phone home'. During the afternoon coffee break, I overheard one participant say to the other. "I am the first one in my family to go to college. Nobody at home knows anything about AIDS. How can they help me? We don't even have a phone at home!" The American facilitator had no idea of the confusion he was creating."

"That's funny too! I guess we must be extra careful about the choice of words and phrases when speaking to people of other linguistic backgrounds."

"You know what was the worst part? The American facilitators kept throwing candy and chocolates at us for answering correctly. The participants thought candy were for children—not for grown-ups. In our culture, we don't throw things at people. We respectfully hand them over with dignity."

On reaching the house Mah Step went to the kitchen and lit a fire. He filled the biggest aluminum pot he could find with water from the drum outside and set it on the fire.

"Since we have come from a wake we must have a bath first. That's our custom," Mah Step said.

"Any particular reason for that?" John asked.

"It is just a custom. Dead bodies are considered unclean. And I guess during the time of infectious diseases bathing made for better hygiene."

"That makes perfect sense!" John agreed. "But do you have such outbreaks often?"

"Not anymore. Inoculations and the modern medicine that the British brought have taken care of that. But the older generation tells stories of a virulent cholera epidemic that decimated a quarter of our tribe's population. My great grandfather and his wife saved themselves and many others by using potassium permanganate. My uncle would tell us stories of those days and how my great grandfather would go bravely from house to house, with no fear of death, handing out vials of potassium permanganate to the villagers. People died like flies around him."

"It must have been terrible," said John.

"It was. Only the great earthquake of 1897 was more terrifying. We have frequent tremors here and we live in fear of the next 'big one'. I just remembered something."

"What is it?" asked John curious.

"Remember our discussions about the existence of God? How some people miss the obvious?"

"Yes, I do recall our conversation."

"Animals—dogs, farm animals, birds—can sense an impending earthquake before it hits."

"So?"

"The sound of an earthquake must be outside the frequency range of the human ear," said Mah Step gravely.

"I still don't see what you are getting at," said John puzzled.

"Just as dogs can hear fifteen kilohertz above the upper range of the human ear, likewise, I think it is the level of spirituality that causes a person to see or not see the Creator. Just because you and I cannot hear a dog whistle does not mean it's not there."

"Are you suggesting that the declining spirituality of the West is the cause of the atheistic movement?"

"I wonder if you have heard of Gabriel Vahanian and the 'Death of God' theology?" asked Mah Step.

"No? That sounds like an oxymoron—theology and the death of God together."

"In a way, it is. Several atheistic thinkers misunderstood Vahanian's statement about the death of God. What he was actually stating was that modern man did not feel a need for God. But that does not imply that God himself did not exist. He held the position that God was inevitable even if not necessary for modern man. He was stating the case for a transcendent God in place of the pagan god that man had turned God into. I think Vahanian has been much misunderstood. He was not an atheist as some people seem to think. At least that is my interpretation. I could be wrong."

"I haven't heard of this guy. Must look him up at the library after I get back."

"Please do. And let me know if you agree with my perception. Anyway, to get back to what we were discussing, our hearing deteriorates with age. I've read that there is a marked decline after fifty. My theory is that, in a similar fashion, the distractions of modern life cause the waning of spiritual consciousness. For us who live close to nature, it is still there but it is not as strong as it was in our ancestors."

"You're saying a man who says there is no God is lacking in spiritual perception?"

"That's right. He or she is probably honest. It's just that they cannot hear the "whistle" or call of God."

"Very profound!" John said.

"You go first," John offered when the water was ready, remembering that Mah Step had washed the dead body.

Mah Step poured the hot water into a plastic bucket and carried it to the bathroom. John went to his room to get his towel and soap. He was tired and just wanted to sleep but Mah Step didn't take long and soon it was his turn.

When he came back to the kitchen with the empty bucket he saw that Mah Step had set a steaming meal on the table.

"Now how did you do that?" John asked surprised.

"My mother packed some rice and meat for the two of us. I just heated it while you were having your bath."

"The bath made me realize how hungry I was," John said and sitting down and waiting for Mah Step to say the customary grace.

"Food never tastes better than when you are hungry!"

The meal, not uncharacteristically, was a quiet affair and was soon over.

"I am not going to keep you up much longer tonight. Tomorrow's the funeral. Since it was an accident we are not going to wait the customary three days. I need to be there really early tomorrow. Among other things, I need to check if the grave has been dug properly by the boys. But you can sleep late. I will send the jeep for you around ten o'clock so you can have an early lunch before the funeral. The funeral is going to be at two-thirty in the afternoon." Mah Step said.

"All right! Sounds good to me!" John said.

Sleep came easy and quick to John. It must have been the open air and the warm outdoors.

When he woke up it was bright daylight outside. Mah Step must have slipped away quietly in the dawn. The livestock wasn't as noisy as usual. "He must have fed the chickens and the pigs before he left," thought John. He tried his hand at lighting a fire without much success and even got some ash and soot on his face while trying to blow with the iron pipe. Then he noticed the kerosene stove and quickly boiled water in a shining aluminum kettle for making tea. The bottle of sugar and the biscuit tin were easy to find. He carried a *lora* out to the verandah and sipped the tea there sitting by the open door watching the chickens in the distance.

Time seemed to have come to a standstill. Life had been stripped away of all its artificial accouterments and embellishments leaving behind only the pure kernel of creation. In a flash of intuition, he suddenly comprehended with never-before-clarity the vision of Thoreau, the American he most admired. The welling joy transported him to another world.

When the spell broke, he arose from the *lora* humming "Morning has broken". He washed the cup, put it back on the rack and then he went back to his bed. "I've never felt this contented before," he thought as he drifted off to sleep.

He awoke to the knocking on the front door. It was the jeep driver with a note from Mah Step. It was close to 10:30 as he quickly got ready for the ride back to Mah Step's brother's house for the funeral.

After an uneventful ride, John arrived to find the house bustling with activity. The benches outside were neatly lined up and the blue plastic awning had been pulled tight. Everyone seemed to be hurrying about. Mah Step met him at the front door.

"Good morning, Mah John! Did you get a good night's sleep? You must be hungry!"

"*Hooblei*, Mah Step!" John responded. "I slept like a log. Overslept, actually. I made a cup of tea on the kerosene stove and raided the biscuit tin."

"I'm glad you managed without a microwave and a coffee machine," laughed Mah Step. "We had better have lunch straightaway."

They passed through the room where the body was laid out. There were more women sitting on mats on the floor. Nora came up to them in the next room.

"Good morning, Mah John," she said self-consciously.

"*Hooblei*, Ni Nora!" John responded and Nora blushed.

"Come," she said leading them to the first table.

Lunch was as good as it had been the previous day. There was the special beef, curried pork, and lentils. Nora waited on John and Mah Step while they ate. After lunch, they moved to the front yard again. But the respite was brief as more people started arriving from the Big Town and from neighboring villages. The benches were slowly filling up and the girls with the tea and biscuits were busy flitting to and fro locating the new arrivals who hadn't been served yet. Several people came over to shake John's hand. But sadly, none of them spoke any English.

The pastor from the Big Town arrived a little late. He was ushered into the front room by Mah Step and his brother. A little later Mah Step came out to call John inside.

"The pastor wants to meet you," Mah Step said.

The pastor wore a dark suit and had on a blue old-fashioned striped tie. His hair, neatly combed to the side, was graying at the temples. He had studied theology in Singapore and Wales and spoke very good English. He evinced interest in John's desire to live in the village.

After the initial exchanges, the pastor said, "While I was in Singapore I was offered a chance to go study in the US. But I did not go."

John could not resist the question, "Why did you turn it down?

"Almost everyone in my class wanted to go to America! Nobody who went to America ever came back. I think they were all after the good life," the pastor said evenly without any trace of disapproval. "I was the first one offered a scholarship to a fundamental Bible college in the mid-west. My American professor told me that if my theology was correct and if I could speak English well, I would be a big success because of the pigment of my skin. I did not show it then but I was deeply hurt. I thought that went against the oneness that is at the heart of Christianity. It also sounded racial, though I'm sure the professor did not mean it that way. Anyway, my call was to serve my own people. I turned the offer down, much to the surprise of my classmates, and came back to the Sakhi Hills."

"Your principles are admirable," John said quietly. Inwardly he pictured the pastor as a successful television evangelist or the pastor of one of those mega churches in California or Texas. 'Would that be success?' John asked himself. 'Or was serving a small impoverished indigenous population the superior accomplishment?'

The funeral service began a little later. From somewhere they had arranged a microphone and large box speakers. The pastor from the town and the village pastor stepped jointly out of the house and were led to chairs placed a little outside the front door. Just then the sound of weeping and wailing emanated from inside the house as the family said their last goodbyes before the coffin was finally nailed shut. It was then carried out with the weeping family trailing behind. The mother was especially distraught as she wept under the black shawl pulled over her head. The closed coffin was gently deposited on two bare benches placed together in the center of the yard. The service began as soon as the family sat down on benches on either side of the coffin. The hymns were all in the Sakhi language, but John easily recognized most of them. 'Nearer my God to Thee' was the first, followed by 'Safe in the Arms of Jesus'. Then the pastor from the Big Town spoke gently and softly in Sakhi. The village pastor led the prayer and then they sang again the hymn that the dead boy had loved best, 'Amazing Grace'. The pastor from the town spoke again before they moved to the cemetery. Heart-rending cries rent the air as the coffin was carried to the rusty trolley near the road. A young boy holding a large wooden cross led the procession. John walked with the crowd that followed on behind. It was downhill initially and then they turned to the left and began to climb the path that rose uphill. It took about half an hour to reach the cemetery. It wasn't on level land but was on the side of a fairly steep hill. As the trolley could not go up any further, the coffin was carried up the hillside to the freshly dug grave. John saw that the graves had been dug haphazardly. The scattered wooden crosses at the heads of the mud-covered graves seemed to reflect the randomness of death. Some no longer had a cross but only a rough stone planted at the head of the grave.

For them no more the blazing hearth shall burn,
Or busy housewife ply her evening care:
No children run to lisp their sire's return,
Or climb his knees the envied kiss to share.

The graveside service was brief. After the final prayer by the pastor two ropes were passed under the coffin and four men, two on either side, slowly lowered the coffin into the grave. 'Dust thou art and unto dust thou returnest,' intoned the pastor in Sakhi and English (ostensibly for John's benefit) before throwing a fistful of dirt into the grave and everyone followed suit. John trailed the crowd downhill wiping his mud-stained hand on his trouser leg.

Back at the home, the benches had been neatly rearranged for a prayer meeting that commenced after all had been served tea and *kwai*. There wasn't any outpouring of grief anymore, just a pervading sense of closure and the finality of a dearly beloved family member's irreversible absence. Mah Step's whispered translation of the pastor's sermon was illuminating. The pastor spoke of the need to comfort the bereaved family; of death being an inseparable part of life; of resurrection and eternal life; of Lazarus; and of hope, the assurance of things not seen. At the end of the service, Mah Step's brother stood up self-consciously to thank (Mah Step again translated) the pastor, the church and the village for their assistance and love during the time of grief and requested everyone to stay for dinner in honor of his departed son. After that, it was controlled chaos as batch after batch moved to the back of the house for dinner. The servers managed to come up with an inexhaustible supply of food while the scullions ensured an unending procession of clean plates.

By the time Mah Step and John climbed into the jeep it was well past ten o'clock. Mah Step's Ma and Pa decided to return home, but Nora stayed back to help. Nora came over to the jeep to bid him good night.

As she held out her hand Nora said, "I will come tomorrow. *Phiah sook!*" In the dark he could not see her blush, but her hand was soft and gentle in his.

"Good night, Nora! *Phiah sook!* Take care!" John responded.

The ride home in the back of the jeep (Mah Step's parents had to be persuaded to take the more comfortable front seats) wasn't pleasant at all but John didn't care. He felt a strange combination of emptiness and assurance as they drove back home; sadness for a life snatched in its youth and acceptance of the death as a link in the chain of life. John found the quiet celebration of the young life and the unreserved support that the whole community lent to the grieving family heartening.

Chapter 14: Back in the Big Town

When Nora returned home the next evening she explained how she had helped with the remaining work at her brother's home that day. The whole house was washed clean. The youth helped in hauling the benches back to the school and the church and in taking down the awnings. The women carried all the clothes and furnishings—a gigantic pile—to the nearest stream for washing. In the afternoon, all the personal effects of the dead youth that would not be of any use to anyone else was burned in a bonfire in the backyard.

It took a few days for life to come back to normal in the house, though Mah Step left for the Big Town two days later. Pa and Ma appeared to be the hardest hit. They spoke in hushed tones and rarely smiled. Nora busied herself with the household chores.

Time sped on. John updated his journal on the IBM laptop and read. He saw Tess in an entirely different light as he read Hardy again. But Conrad became his favorite. In some convoluted way, he saw a parallel with Lord Jim in his predicament, though he hoped his end would not be nearly as tragic. He wondered idly what, in his case, was the abandoned ship *Patna* that did not sink.

It was amazing how quickly the days passed even without all the rushing about that he was accustomed to in America. He knew the passing of a week with certainty only when Sunday came around. The last Sunday he had, much to his embarrassment, dozed off in the middle of the sermon. It was Mah Step who nudged him awake. "Good thing you didn't snore," Mah Step chided him gently later.

When on Monday Mah Step renewed the offer of a trip to the Big Town, John gladly accepted not because he was overcome by ennui in the village but as he was curious to see how his friends—and the world—had been faring in the interregnum. When the village taxi finally rumbled to a stop near the main market, John felt guiltily elated to be back in the Big Town. Whether he would have been as happy to be back in Washington, DC, was, however, debatable. The mere anticipation of the bewitching sirens of the indoor toilet, the warm bath, the daily newspaper, CNN and BBC on TV, and, most of all, the Internet had all seduced him long before the taxi rolled into town.

"Let's go straight home!" John shouted with undisguised glee as they got out of the taxi.

The market was the usual morning rush with villagers and porters carrying their produce in bamboo cones (called a *phoh*, John learned) and the haggling middlemen trying to con them even before they got to the market.

The "share taxi" had only two passengers and they would have to wait until there was a total of seven. But John could not wait that long.

"You know what, I will pay for the three empty seats. I just want to get home. I don't want to wait here the whole day in this taxi," John said with uncharacteristic insistence, and the faintest trace of impatience, and they were soon rolling along.

As Mah Step opened the house, John announced he wanted to take a long bath.

"Hold on a sec, let me take a leak first," Mah Step said.

What a pleasure it was to sit on a proper toilet bowl instead of having to squat in the outhouse precariously perched on wooden beams and bamboo matting over a fly-buzzing open hole!

"Maybe there was something in what that American lady said after all," mused John.

"I can even read in the toilet!" rejoiced John as he picked up an old issue of *Time* from the table by the sink.

The shower was pure luxury. No more bending and pouring and misdirecting half of the precious hot water. The shower stayed hot unlike the fast-cooling water in the bucket in the village. And, best of all, no carrying hot water from the kitchen! He promised to pamper himself with a bath in the bathtub later in the evening.

By the time John had got out of the shower, Mah Step had breakfast all laid out on the table: toast, butter and jam, bacon and eggs, and coffee.

"This is great!" John said with happiness. "Thanks for fixing the eggs sunny-side up. That's the way I like them."

"Yes, I don't forget easily," Mah Step laughed.

"Do you have a class to teach this morning?" asked John.

"Yes. And I have classes this afternoon as well. I can meet you only in the evening."

"That's okay. I have plenty of things to do till then. Email is first!" John said.

When John switched the computer on after breakfast he discovered that he could not connect to the Internet. The dial-up would not work. It was a reminder that nothing could be taken for granted here except the good will of the people. John could not hide his intense disappointment.

"Don't worry. I will take you to a cybercafé," offered Mah Step.

So, they left the house together, Mah Step going to his college and John, following Mah Step's directions, to the nearest Internet booth or 'cyber' as they were popularly referred to in common parlance. The broadband connection was faster than the home dial-up but still nothing compared to the blazing speed at his Greenbelt home.

He wasn't prepared for the deluge of emails in his inbox. There were well over two thousand. It took him a long while to sift through and delete all the spam and unwanted email. There were bank and credit card statements and updates from his stagnant 401(k) account, which was headed south, but he could not care less. When he had finished deleting all the unwelcome emails, he went back over the ones that needed replying. It would have taken him hours to answer each one separately. Ultimately, John wrote a short general update on his situation and emailed it to everyone, assuring the recipients that he was alive and kicking. After much thought, he left out the reference to having discovered Utopia. "They would not understand. They would think I was hallucinating or on drugs," reasoned. He wrote a long email to Elaine, though, describing as best as he could the affection and hospitality of the Sakhi people. "And, yes, Mah Step is every bit what I expected him to be," he could not help adding with a trace of smugness. Considering how much she loved horses, John wondered if Elaine would be upset by the fact that he had eaten horsemeat, but he mentioned it anyway.

By the time he was done with emails it was past one o'clock. He was hungry. While climbing down the narrow stairs to the road, the Chinese restaurant on the opposite side of the road caught his eye. John always liked Chinese food. It was never spicy and was easy on the palate as well. As he stepped into the restaurant, his eyes dilating after the bright sunshine outside, he realized this was no upscale eatery but was probably at the other end of the spectrum. He was about to step back out and look for another restaurant when he recalled what Mah Step had told him about the cleanliness of the Sakhis. There were three customers there clustered together on a small wooden bench. John chose the bench opposite and squeezed into the narrow gap with some difficulty, his back scraping the wooden planks that formed the wall. The woman smiled at him over her plate, but the two men just looked at him poker face. The owner-waitress came over wiping her hands on the checked *sainjyrshah*. John soon realized she didn't speak any English. "Noodles," he said but she didn't seem to get it. "*Pokshau*," she replied. Puzzled, John tried "Noodles" a second time. The response was "*Pokshau*" again. The three diners found this exchange hilarious and were practically guffawing much to the discomfiture of the owner. Finally, on the fourth try, it all became crystal clear. "Pork chow" was what she was trying to convey. "Pork chow!" said John with finality slapping his palm face down on the table. The woman smiled in relief and John joined in the general merriment with the three customers. The pork chow turned out to be fried noodles with lots of small pieces of blubbery pork. John was famished and as he dug into the food the pangs of hunger were obvious. John asked for a second serving and had a cup of prepared tea to round off a very satisfying meal. When he paid, he realized that the whole meal had cost him all of thirty-five cents—and she wouldn't accept a tip.

After getting home John felt sated and languid. "Ah, for a life like this without a care! What luxury!" John thought as he fell asleep on the settee.

When he awoke, it was past three. He made himself a cup of coffee and watched the BBC news on TV. The names and places may have changed but not the substance of the stories. The same bloodshed and mayhem in the Middle East; the same poverty and disease in Africa; the same news of large numbers being killed in calamities or accidents in Asia. The stories on CNN were much the same but with a different accent and a slightly different slant. But mercifully there was no "local news" with instances of random violence and accidents involving just a few, incessant weather reports and drab traffic updates taking precedence over large-scale misery and destitution in the rest of the world.

Suddenly John had had enough.

He wanted to be back in the village. *The world is too much with us*, he murmured quoting

Wordsworth. He realized also that he did not want to wait till Mah Step got back. He would find his way back on his own, he decided. Hastily scribbling a note to Mah Step, John rushed to the main market and quickly found the line of taxis from the village. The taxi drivers recognized him also and nodded and smiled. He was deferentially given a front seat next to the driver. He didn't have to wait very long as the afternoon traffic was outbound from the city to the villages with farmers and villagers returning home after buying and selling in the big market in the city.

When he reached home Nora and Ma were in the kitchen. They were surprised to find that he had come back early and alone.

"What happened?" asked Nora anxiously.

"No, nothing's the matter. I came back on my own. Mah Step has to teach a class all afternoon. I couldn't wait to get back," said John.

Nora gave him a puzzled look as she translated for the benefit of Ma. By the time John had changed into comfortable home clothes, Nora had a cup of tea and biscuits ready for him.

"You must be hungry. Would you like to have some rice instead?" asked Nora.

"No thanks. I had lunch at a small Chinese stall. A cup of tea would be good, though!" said John.

"If you want to have a bath I'll heat the water for you," offered Nora.

After sitting for nearly two hours in the taxi squashed against the grimy and sweaty driver, a bath sounded like a fabulous idea.

John didn't have to wait long. The water was scalding hot as he carried the plastic bucket to the bathroom. After the cleansing bath, John felt drowsy. 'Must be the higher altitude of the Big Town,' he thought. He wanted to read a book but felt more lethargic than Tennyson's 'lotos-eaters'. In the end, he just lay down on the bed and drifted off into a pleasant nap.

When he woke up it was already dark. The rest of the house appeared dark too. Wondering if there was a power outage John got gingerly out of bed and headed for the door next to which the light switch was. It took some finding in the dark and, sleepy-headed as he was, he forgot for a moment that switches worked in the opposite direction here. He was turning away in disappointment when realization hit him, and he flicked the switch down. The sudden brightness of the naked bulb caused him to squint his eyes. Thinking it was already too late in the night, he was surprised, on opening the bedside traveler's clock, to find that it was only a little after seven in the evening. After a bit of yawning and indolent stretching, John made his way to the kitchen to look for Mah Step. There was no one in the kitchen but the fire was still burning and there was a large aluminum pot with water over it. "Hmm, they must have stepped out somewhere," thought John as he headed back to his room. On the way, he switched on the lights in the sitting room. John thought he would do a bit of shortwave listening but remembered that he had lent the radio to Mah Step. As he lay down and looked at the cloth ceiling the thought of painting it with a long brush returned. He pondered over how frantic ordinary life was back in Washington, DC. "There is probably no Type A person in this whole village. Maybe not in the whole Sakhi tribe!" John thought amusedly. His musing was broken by the lightest of taps on his door. Scrambling up he found Nora standing in the doorway looking like an angelic apparition with a halo around her head from the light of the sitting room behind her.

"Nora!" blurted out John.

"Mah John, you were sleeping?" asked Nora.

"No, not really. I woke up a short while ago. It's good to see you. I didn't see anyone in the kitchen," said John.

"I was having a bath. Ma has gone to a friend's house. Pa has been out since morning. He didn't say where he was going."

As she walked into the room and under the overhead light, John realized how radiant and fecund she looked after a bath. He remembered a previous time he had seen her emerging fresh after a bath looking pristine and naturally sensuous. The fact that Nora wore no make-up and did not use any creams or lotions or perfume, only added to her allure. "She looks far more beautiful and fetching than a fashionable high-society heiress. A real natural, if ever there was one," said John to himself.

"Ma Step should be coming soon," said John rising to get the chair for Nora to sit down. He had just picked up the clothes he had carelessly thrown on the chair and was turning to drop them on his bed when, without any warning at all, the lights went out.

Looking back, he never could explain how it happened.

One moment he had his clothes in his arms, the next he was holding Nora, and both were clinging to each other for dear life. All the passion and ardor that he thought he had banished were back with a vengeance. John ran his hands through her hair as she clung to him, kissing first her forehead and then her cheeks. A shiver went through Nora as his lips touched hers and her arms held him in a fierce grip as John's hands caressed the softness of her body.

Just when it looked like crossing the Rubicon was an inevitable and a foregone conclusion, the power came back as abruptly as it had gone off. Startled by the blinding light, they looked like stunned deer caught in the headlights. The harsh glare of the naked bulb brought them crashing back to reality. Nora's hands that were holding him in a desperate clinch a moment earlier, fell to her sides and then flew to cover her face. John stepped back and smacked his forehead with his open palm. In an instant shame, had replaced ardor.

"I'm sorry. Truly, truly sorry. I apologize. Didn't mean to. Don't know what came over me," John said contritely.

Nora didn't say a word. She stood like a stricken doe, tears streaming down from under her hands that covered her face. John moved towards Nora as if to touch her, but Nora cringed back and then fled from the room crying.

John felt crushed in body and spirit. He felt utterly defeated. For a brief moment, he stood confused in the midst of the clothes he had dropped on the floor. Then he rushed out of the room calling, "Nora! Nora!" But Nora wasn't in the kitchen; John found the bedroom door locked. He knocked a couple of times on the door and called her name repeatedly.

But there was no reply.

Resignedly he trudged back to his room, gathered the strewn clothes from the floor and tossed them unceremoniously on the chair before collapsing on the bed.

"I've blown it. Darn it ... just two and a half weeks left and I had to go and spoil it all," he castigated himself remorsefully.

He didn't know what he would say to Mah Step when he returned from the Big Town. "Would he not think that I came back early with the intention of seducing Nora?" he wondered.

"Why did you do it, you stupid idiot?" he chided himself.

He decided to make a clean breast of it when Mah Step returned from the Big Town. But soon he had second thoughts. He wasn't alone in this. There was Nora to be considered. What if she didn't want anyone else to know what had happened?

John felt that he had not only broken the trust of Mah Step and his parents but also, by extension, that of the entire Sakhi tribe. Surely his actions were contrary to their traditions and culture. The only saving grace was that the contretemps had ended before it had started. But the credit for that, he admitted, went to the return of electricity (not a moment too soon) and not to his sense of honor or propriety. John was disgusted with himself for having fallen so abjectly from the high standards he had set for himself.

He lay on his bed unmindful of time till he heard voices. Ma had returned and was talking to Nora in the kitchen. A little later there was a soft knock on the open door of his room. He raised himself on his elbows to find Nora framed in the doorway.

"Mah John, come and have dinner," she said, without any trace of the recent emotional roller-coaster.

"Thanks, Nora. I'll be with you in a minute." John said hastily getting up from the bed.

He made a quick dash to the outhouse and then washed up before going into the kitchen. Ma smiled at him graciously as she always did, and he made a valiant attempt at beaming back as usual. Dinner was the usual silent event, but John could not help stealing sidelong glances at Nora to see if there were any signs of the upheaval earlier in the evening. There was none. Looking prim and proper, Nora studiously avoided direct eye contact with John even when he held out his plate to her for second helpings. Only once did he catch her looking at him and as their eyes locked for the briefest of moments it seemed to him that she was gauging the impact the earlier incident had on him.

"Mah Step is late today," remarked John, sipping red tea after dinner.

"Sorry, I forgot to tell you. Mah Step is not coming today. He had an additional class to teach late in the evening," explained Nora.

"How did you find that out?" John asked.

"Mah Step sent a note through one of the bus drivers. The driver gave it to Ma as she was coming back from her friend's house."

"Your communications network is amazing!"

Ordinarily, Nora would have smiled but today she looked away expressionless and said, "Pa is also staying in the Big Town tonight."

John sat around till his cup was empty. Then he wished them both a good night and slowly dragged himself away to his room.

As he lay in his bed, sleep did not come easy. Another "Lucy poem" came to his mind and the words made John smile wryly.

Strange fits of passion have I known:
And I dare to tell,
But in the Lover's ear alone,
What once to me befell

Quite incongruously *I'm a Believer* by The Monkees popped into his head as well. "At least I'm *some* kind of a believer now!" he thought wryly. The shame he had felt earlier was replaced by a deep longing to hold Nora in his arms and never let go. The yearning was so sharp it seemed to tear him apart as he tossed and turned till sleep came and put him out of his misery.

Chapter 15: The Proclamation of Love

The next day John thought he had found the perfect opportunity to make up with Nora. It was after brunch and Nora had just started on the laundry after having washed the dishes and utensils. John watched from the window as she scrubbed the clothes stretching them on the cemented patch on the ground and then rinsing them first in one bucket and then the other. He went back to his computer and continued updating his journal. When he came to the window again Nora had finished the washing and was pouring the soapy water down the open drain. As she carried the wrung clothes in the aluminum basin towards the clotheslines, John grabbed a book and went out.

"Good morning, Nora!" he called out in a guardedly cheerful fashion with a hint of what he hoped was 'I-hope-all-is-forgiven' charm.

"Good morning, Mah John," Nora responded but it didn't need a psychiatrist to figure out that her guard was still up.

"Nora ... I'm sorry about yesterday ... I don't know how to say this ... I'm truly sorry. I didn't mean to upset you," John said softly.

If she heard what he said, she gave no indication. She carried on intently with her work, hanging the clothes up on the iron wire and attaching plastic clips to hold them in place in the breeze.

John was stumped. It was clear as daylight that Nora did not want to talk about it. He thought of taking a different tack but decided against it.

"I'll go for a walk then. Bye for now," he said as he trudged away with obvious disappointment.

"Come back soon," he heard her say and turned around surprised. But Nora had already turned away, bending down to pick up the next garment from the aluminum pan.

The shady grove on the grassy knoll did not cause to diminish the self-recrimination as he had hoped it would. "I wouldn't have given a hoot if this had happened at Cambridge or Greenbelt. Anywhere but here in the Sakhi Hills. And anyone but Nora," he thought reproachfully. He spent the rest of the morning debating how best he should break the news to Mah Step.

At last, he got tired of thinking about it and tried to read but his heart was not in it. Instead, he yielded himself to the languid somnolence induced by the warmth of the sun. When he woke up an hour or so later he felt a strange sense of relief—the burden had mysteriously lifted.

"I did not try to seduce Nora or outrage her modesty. Nor did I harbor any dishonorable intentions. What happened was instinctive and mutual, though totally unexpected; not planned with malice aforethought," he reasoned. "And what's more, it was more affection than lust." John decided finally that what happened was Nora's and his business alone. He would tell Mah Step of it only if a situation arose that required him to do so or if Nora, for whatever reason, wanted him to. If it came to that he would gladly take all the blame. "But I am not going to jeopardize Nora by a hasty admission of guilt without her concurrence," he decided.

It was a much-becalmed John who returned to the house in time for a cup of hot milk-tea and sticky rice in a small ceramic bowl.

John was tapping on the ThinkPad updating his journal when he heard Mah Step come in. He walked into the room in his bare feet with his trademark cloth shoulder bag still slung over his shoulder. For a moment, John felt a twinge of disquiet.

"Had Nora told the family about what had happened?" he wondered.

"Mah John, *Hooblei!* So, how are you?" asked Mah Step cheerily.

"Great! Couldn't be better!" John replied. "How did your lectures go?"

"Good but very tiring. Sometimes I feel like throwing in the towel. This is one such moment."

"Why, what's the matter?" asked John.

"The students won't read on their own or think independently. They still expect the teacher to dictate notes for them. They then learn the answers by rote."

"Their answers must all look the same at the exam?"

"Yes, unfortunately so. It all boils down to a test of memory rather than a test of knowledge or learning."

"That's sad."

"Yes, it is. But I don't want to bore you with my work woes. How was your day? Did you have any problems getting back yesterday?"

"No, none at all. Returning on my own was a breeze. A piece of cake, really. The taxi drivers from the village recognized me instantly and I didn't even have to ask around."

"That's good. Remember what I told you? You are safe here in our midst. I dare say Americans are safer here than in their own country," Mah Step said smiling.

"That's not very complimentary! But yes, I don't expect to get mugged or shot here," John agreed. "Are you tired or do you want to go out for a walk?"

"No, I'm not tired. Give a few minutes to change my clothes. I'm dying for a cup of tea."

It took a little longer than that but finally they were out of the house. With the sun way down the horizon, the warmth was ebbing.

"It's really beautiful, isn't it?" Mah Step asked.

"It sure is!" John replied.

"I don't see how any man can look at nature and doubt the existence of God. It seems so myopic."

"I think it may be the technology that insulates modern man and also the 'Invictus' way of thinking," John ventured.

"You mean the *'I am the master of my fate: / I am the captain of my soul'* stuff of Henley?" Mah Step asked.

"Why am I not surprised!" exclaimed John.

"I think his estrangement with Stevenson was truly sad."

"I think it was the death of his daughter, an only child, that broke his spirit," said John.

"I'm sure he realized later how misleading his brave-sounding verses were. By the way, were you able to check your email?" asked Mah Step.

"Yes, I sent out a general note to everyone. I wrote a separate email to my friend, Elaine. I mentioned the horsemeat. She will be mad. She loves horses."

"What horsemeat?" asked Mah Step.

"Remember the horsemeat that Nora cooked the other day?"

Mah Step appeared puzzled for a moment. Then his face relaxed and he began to laugh.

"What's the joke?" asked John. "You and Nora laughed that day too."

"That wasn't horsemeat! That was beef!"

"But she said it was horsemeat," said John slightly peeved.

"She was joking. That was her way of saying she wasn't impressed you couldn't tell it was beef," explained Mah Step.

"Neither of you told me the truth even later."

"We thought you realized it wasn't really horsemeat. We thought you knew it was actually beef," Mah Step said apologetically.

"At least Elaine will be pleased I did not eat horsemeat. Not that it matters."

"I eat anything and everything. My faith gives me that liberty. I find it difficult to understand Christians who have religious sanctions against certain types of food. I think it goes against the freedom that my faith offers. Anyway, when it comes to unfamiliar food of other tribes, my policy is to ask what I ate only after it is down the hatch and well and truly settled in my stomach. Never, before or during."

"That sounds like a good policy!" conceded John.

"It has won me acceptance with alien tribes and saved me a lot of trouble. I have eaten wild birds, snakes, wild cats, monkeys and even elephant meat."

"What did the elephant taste like?" John could not resist asking.

"It tasted more like pork than anything else. It had a lot of fat. It was while eating the monkey stew that this embarrassing incident happened."

"What incident?" asked John.

"It was with the Tsomi tribe. A colleague from the plains was with me on that research trip. At the end of the day, we were invited to dinner with the tribal chief. According to the Tsomi custom, rice and meat were placed in large pots in the center of the table and each diner helped himself using the large spoon (almost a ladle, actually) on their own plate. Things were going well. My friend and I were enjoying the meal after a long, hard day. My friend especially enjoyed the stewed meat. In fact, he liked it so much that he swirled his spoon around in the bowl searching for a big piece. When he thought he had found one, he lifted it slowly out of the gravy.

The piece turned out to be the head of the monkey and it looked so remarkably human that my friend was stunned. He stared at it for a moment before dropping his spoon into the pot and running out of the room retching and screaming."

"I can imagine the shock of your friend. I wouldn't eat monkey's meat."

"Given a choice, I wouldn't either. But when you are with an alien tribe you cannot decline their food without distancing yourself. Needless to add, the Tsomis were not as cooperative with the research after that. My philosophy has been: if they can eat it—whatever *it* is—and survive, so can I."

"Very admirable!" said John.

"Anyway, what happened to my friend was not half as bad as what happened to the American missionary with the Harley Davidson."

"Was he a missionary to the same tribe?" asked John.

"No, he was a missionary to the Pangama tribe for whom dog meat is a delicacy."

"I think I can guess. He had a dog?" asked John.

"Yes," replied Mah Step.

"The villagers stole his dog and ate it?"

"No, it was far worse. The missionary's servant ran out of meat one afternoon. Try as he might there was no beef or pork or chicken to be found that day. The servant was determined that the missionary should have meat at dinner. Sure enough, when the missionary came home for dinner there was a plate of fried meat to go with the rice and the vegetables. It was only after the missionary had finished his meal and looked around for his dog that he discovered the horrible truth. He was completely devastated. The servant couldn't understand what the fuss was all about."

"That's a sad and terrible story," John said shaking his head.

"You are absolutely right. It is a very depressing story. Let's talk about something else," suggested Mah Step.

"OK. You told me you read the Bible every day. Is that right?" asked John.

"Yes, I do. Or at least, try to. I think it gives me spiritual nourishment the same way food nourishes my physical body."

"I know the Bible comes in a myriad of different versions. Which version do you use?" asked John.

"This might seem a little strange, but my favorite version is the King James Version. I do not take the position, as some do, that only the King James Version is inspired by God. But I do think the KJV has a certain elegance, majesty, and stateliness that the others lack. I do not have a problem understanding the language because I studied it and have got used to it."

"I read somewhere that many of the words have changed meaning since it was written," said John.

"That's very true. 'Prevent' actually means 'precede' and 'leasing' means 'falsehood'. But 'mortgage' in Nehemiah has the same meaning as we know it today."

"I have heard of Bibles that had various kinds of typos—the 'adultery' Bible, the 'breeches' Bible, the 'wife-hater' Bible, and the 'Judas' Bible."

"True they all had comical errors in them. Here's something that I'm fairly certain you haven't heard of. I have read that there is a lot of discord in your country between Republicans and Democrats, between conservatives and liberals."

"That's true. I would call it disagreement or difference of opinion, though."

"OK, call it what you will! But I have the perfect unifying verse for both factions. This is from the Book of Isaiah. I think this will satisfy both sides of the fence. *The vile person shall no more be called liberal.*"

"What? Would you care to repeat that?"

"*The vile person shall no more be called liberal.* Isn't that great!"

"You are not making this up, are you?" John asked suspiciously.

"No, I am not. I was surprised too when I stumbled on this verse in chapter thirty-two, if I remember right."

"I'll have to look that one up when we get back," said John.

"It holds great promise for the liberals," Mah Step said smiling.

"Yes, I know. I'm a Democrat!" laughed John. "What about the Revised Version?"

"It is funny that many mistakenly think the Revised Version is recent. It was actually revised in the late nineteenth century."

"Is that so? I thought it was more recent. Maybe the 1950s?" John said.

"No, it is much older than that. I think you are confusing it with the Revised Standard Version."

"That's easily possible," conceded John.

"Talking about Democrats. One of the men I admire most is Kennedy. He was head and shoulders above anyone else of his time."

"He had his faults too, you know," John said.

"Like any other human being. The killing of Kennedy and King made me lose hope in my youth. It took a long time for me to recover," said Mah Step.

"They say people can recollect vividly what they were doing when they heard the news of Kennedy's assassination."

"I can still see that day clearly. My father heard it on the radio and he had tears in his eyes as he told us about it. I remember running to my mother and throwing my arms around her neck. I was a small boy then," Mah Step said broodingly.

"I am surprised Kennedy's assassination had that impact even here in the Sakhi Hills, so far away from America."

"Martin Luther King's killing five years later was equally painful. It made me lose faith in justice for a period of time," Mah Step said pensively.

"I can understand that. King was a great man. He had the courage to stand up for justice. I never cease to be roused by his 'I Have a Dream' speech. Each time I see it on TV it gives me goose bumps."

"I saw it for the first time only fifteen years ago, after the advent of TV to the Big Town."

"I think it's time we turned back. It's beginning to get dark."

They walked in silence for a while, each lost in his own thoughts.

Suddenly John stopped and turned to Mah Step.

"There is something I must tell you."

From the look on Mah Step's face John realized that the seriousness in his tone had confused, if not alarmed, Mah Step.

"My time here is nearly gone. My visa lapses in two weeks' time and I will fly back to America. I have been happier here than I have ever been in my life."

"I am happy to hear that," Mah Step said with guarded happiness.

"This place is indeed the Shangri-La that you told me it was during our online chats. It is, without doubt, an idyllic Utopia. But there's something else that I need to tell you."

"What is it, John? What happened? What is the matter?" asked Mah Step, suddenly anxious.

John took a deep breath. "I have fallen in love with Nora," John said softly.

Mah Step stood rooted to the spot as if he had been struck by lightning, his arms frozen in mid-gesture.

"I want to marry Nora if she will have me," John added.

Mah Step clutched his jaw and his forehead creased in thought but did not utter a word. With his left forefinger, he pushed back the frame of his glasses as he stared hard at the ground.

"I'm sorry if this has upset you. What do you want me to do? Leave town?" John asked.

"No, no, no, I'm not upset. Nor offended. Just surprised. I didn't see it coming," said Mah Step at last with an effort.

"I have come to realize that I love Nora deeply. But as much as I love her I do not want to cause any pain to you or to your parents and, least of all, to Nora."

"Mah John, it is Nora's decision," said Mah Step gently. "If she is willing, I doubt if my parents will have any objection. I certainly don't!"

"That is such a relief. A huge weight off my chest," John said, a smile of relief lighting up his face.

"I never thought we would end up as brothers-in-law!" Mah Step said recovering his composure.

"Neither did I. I just hope Nora is willing and it all works out," John said fervently.

"I think Barkis will be willing. I know she likes you a lot. But as per our custom you need to talk to my parents and formally ask for Nora's hand in marriage. I will be more than happy to be the translator or mediator!"

"Thanks! That would be a big help. Doing this in English is difficult enough. To do it in Sakhi would be insurmountably difficult!"

Mah Step laughed. "This calls for a celebration!"

As they walked back to the house, Mah Step said, "We will not tell anyone about this today. Not even Nora. I will let you know when it would be best to talk to Ma and Pa."

Try as he might, John could not hide his happiness and Nora was quick to notice it at dinnertime. She looked questioningly at Mah Step and then again at John searching for clues. As she handed back John's plate with a second helping of rice and beef curry their eyes met and they smiled at each other. Mah Step's poker face gave nothing away as they completed the meal, as was wont, in silence.

As he lay sleepless in bed, John was practically euphoric as he contemplated his future. If all went well, he would have as his spouse a beautiful, unspoilt, down-to-earth, authentic woman with no trace of artifice. And he would also be a privileged member of the Sakhi tribe.

"What more could I wish for! What bliss it would be to divide my time between Greenbelt and the Sakhi Hills or, even better, to settle down here for good." thought John.

The thought of swapping the rat race and the senseless pace of modern life for the quiet and affection-filled tribal life was certainly appealing. But Nora's companionship was more devoutly to be wished for than any treasures on earth.

"How lucky can one man get!" he mused.

John hummed the lines of '*Let It Be Me*' as he turned out the light.

Chapter 16: The Tie is Cast

Some days passed with no further discussions about the betrothal and John began to wonder if Mah Step had surreptitiously talked to his parents and they had not consented to the marriage. He thought Sunday might be the auspicious day for this sort of thing, but they walked together to church the same way they had done on previous occasions and the subject did not come up for discussion. After the service, Pa and Ma went visiting and did not come home till late in the evening.

In his heart of hearts, John wanted to get it over with as soon as possible. The waiting was nerve-wracking. He told himself that this wasn't America and that he must be patient. But this did not make the grating uncertainty any the more bearable.

What was most trying was the fact that Mah Step had suggested that he not propose to Nora before talking to Pa and Ma. He would have preferred going about this the other way around: that he propose to Nora first, and then go to her parents for approval.

"This is likely the most momentous decision of my life. It is not a mere question of marriage. It is a whole paradigm change of life, work and values. It is almost like moving into a different dimension. I need to know where I stand," he thought impatiently.

He was a little surprised, therefore, as they were sitting outside on *lora*s sipping milk-tea in the warmth of the morning sun, when Mah Step said, "We will talk to Pa and Ma today at 11 o'clock."

"Today? At eleven a.m.?" asked John surprised and startled.

"Yes, today," said Mah Step.

"That's not enough notice!" John wanted to say but he bit his tongue.

This was what he had been anxiously waiting for. He could not contain his excitement. Adrenaline pumping, he rushed off for a shave and a bath before the meeting. He wanted to look sufficiently presentable for the big occasion. He remembered what a difference a bath and a shave had made to his appearance on the first day.

When Nora heard that John was going to bathe earlier than usual she was quick to take a pot off the fire and replace it with a tall aluminum vessel filled to the brim with water. John suspected from her behavior that she hadn't so far been told of the meeting.

After the shave and the shower, John chose the only "smart casual" attire he had—a white half-sleeve shirt with pale blue stripes and a pair of khaki LL Bean corduroy trousers. Though the meeting was going to be indoors he slipped on a pair of fresh black socks and put on his slip-on leather traveling shoes.

When he walked into the sitting room two minutes before eleven, he realized immediately that he looked somewhat overdressed when compared to the others who were in their daily house garb. But he didn't care; to him, this event was supremely important, and he did not mind demonstrating how significant it was to him.

Pa and Ma sat together on one of the two rattan settees in the room. One end of the other settee had been pulled to the center of the room so that it was at an angle to the first and Mah Step sat on the end closest to his parents. When John entered the room Mah Step rose and offered him the vacant seat to his right. This placed John approximately in the middle of the room facing Pa and Ma but, because the settee was obliquely placed, he had to turn slightly to be facing them. Pa and Ma returned John's smile, but it was not difficult to see that they were not their usual relaxed selves.

Mah Step set the ball rolling by talking to the parents in the Sakhi language. John did not understand any of it but trusted him to plead his case. Pa interrupted Mah Step a few times with questions, but Ma busied herself with deftly peeling *kwai* while listening intently to the conversation.

Finally, Mah Step turned to John and said, "I have told Pa and Ma of our discussion. You can now seek their permission."

In the past five days, John had thought many times about this moment and what he should be saying but now that the time had actually come, he felt his throat tighten, his palms sweat, and his mind turn blank.

"You can speak in English," Mah Step said. "I will translate after you have finished."

Clearing his throat nervously, John began. "Respected Pa and Ma. Mah Step was very kind to invite me to the Sakhi Hills to be your guest. I came here to see for myself and to experience the Sakhi way of life. You all have been very good to me, treating me like a part of the family. In the past seven weeks, I have come to respect and appreciate your tribal customs and traditions and most of all your attitude to life." John paused. It was very difficult to continue looking at the uncomprehending faces of Pa and Ma. Mah Step stepped in quickly translating what John had just said.

"I am truly grateful for all that you have done for me. You all have been most kind. The past few weeks have changed me in so many ways I cannot even begin to explain. I came here hoping to carry back with me to America the principles of the Sakhi way of life. I am much indebted to you all. In some small way, I thought I would reciprocate by arranging for Mah Step to come visit me in the US. About a week ago, my attachment to all of you was raised to a whole new level. That was when I admitted to myself that I had fallen deeply in love with your daughter Nora."

"And with your permission, I would like to marry Nora," he added after a brief pause.

Mah Step translated again, and Pa grunted a few times towards the end. When he had finished Mah Step adjusted his glasses pushing it back with his left forefinger against the bridge of his nose.

There was silence as Pa seemed to be lost in thought. Ma discreetly broke the spell by handing out *kwai* to Pa and Mah Step.

Finally, after what seemed an eternity Pa turned to Ma and they talked in hushed tones though Ma's answers were mostly monosyllabic. Finally, Pa turned to Mah Step and spoke at length. John thought he made his pronouncement with sagely deliberation.

"We have to ask Nora what she thinks," explained Mah Step translating. John was disappointed with the laconic translation. He would have preferred a word-for-word literal rendition of all that was said. Ma called out for Nora. She must have been waiting just behind the door because she came in demurely pulling the blue and white checked *sainjyrshah* tight with her left hand. She had freshened up and changed into clean clothes. Nora avoided John's eyes as she moved to the vacant space between Pa and Mah Step, deferentially bowing as she did so and sat down on the *lora* that she had brought in with her.

It was Pa who spoke. He seemed to be struggling for words as he fidgeted, straightening his shirt and brushing off imaginary dust from his trousers. John felt humbled when he realized how much more difficult all this was for Pa and Ma than it was for him. They could be losing the daughter whom they loved dearly and who was to have cared for them in their old age.

When Pa had finished speaking and all three were intently looking at Nora, John realized that the question had been posed and they were waiting for her answer. Nora appeared to constrict herself as she bent further down on the low stool and covered her mouth and lower face with the blue-checked *sainjyrshah*. Pa spoke again, gently and soothingly. When he had finished talking Nora nodded her head, still staring at her bare toes sticking out from under the apron that touched the ground. Pa and Ma looked at each other and Pa spoke to Mah Step.

John was relieved when Mah Step, at last, turned to him and conveyed what had just transpired.

"My parents wanted to know if Nora was willing to marry you. She has, in her own shy way, indicated that she is willing. My father then asked her if she considered all the pros and cons carefully. Whether she was willing to go to America or anywhere else in the world with you. She has agreed to this also. He also told her not to worry about not being there to take care of them. He is certain that the Lord will provide. Finally, my father has asked me to tell you that you have my father's and my mother's approval to marry Nora."

Mah Step beamed broadly as he got up to stand in the arc between the two settees. As John wondered what he was supposed to do next, Mah Step gestured towards Pa and Ma. John quickly rose and went up to them, respectfully holding out his hand. "*Hooblei!* Thank you!" John said as he shook hands with Pa. In a gesture of endearment, Pa patted John's shoulder with his left hand. It was Ma's turn next to stand up and shake John's hand. She spoke as gently as she smiled. When John turned to Mah Step he translated what Ma, who had been mostly silent through the entire proceedings, had said. "She blessed you and Nora. She wished you both and your children good health, prosperity, and peace."

Finally, he turned to Nora who had risen to her feet, still looking down demurely. John was tongue-tied as he held Nora's soft hand. In his heart, he wanted to say, "I love you," but he knew that public display of affection, even in words, was not the Sakhi custom. He didn't know what to say but words hardly mattered. Nora looked up, her left hand still holding the *sainjyrshah* over her mouth, and their eyes met. In that instant time seemed to hang still and they exchanged unspoken promises of love.

Mah Step broke the trance by announcing, "Congratulations!" and holding out both arms. Nora disengaged her hand from John's and moved towards Mah Step, who kissed her formally on both cheeks. Then it was John's turn. Never a hugger when it came to men, he wasn't sure what to do. In the end, they ended up shaking hands and Mah Step said, "We definitely are going to be brothers-in-law now!"

Pa suggested tea and Ma headed for the kitchen, with Nora in tow. He then patted the seat beside him beckoning John and Mah Step to sit down. Soon Pa and Mah Step were engaged in an earnest conversation, totally oblivious of John who did not follow a word they were saying. On his previous foreign jaunts when confronted with similar situations, John had overcome the feelings of being excluded by returning the compliment, in a manner of speaking. He would be there physically, but his mind would tune out and he would be many miles away. It was almost as if he slipped on a pair of noise-canceling headphones to shut out the incomprehensible alien tongue or got into a soundless time machine that whisked him to another world. This coping mechanism had fallen into disuse in the Sakhi Hills because he had never really felt excluded here. The Sakhis had a marvelous way of causing their affection to transcend the language barrier. But today it was

John who was oblivious of what was happening around him as pictured in his mind an adaptive Nora being the toast of Washington's high society as a sort of modern-day Pocahontas. The thought of it brought a smile to his lips but the entrance of Ma carrying the tea tray with Nora trailing behind bearing another tray of bowls and saucers brought him quickly back to earth.

"We will have lunch a little later than usual today if it's OK with you," Mah Step said.

"Not a problem. This looks like lunch enough!"

The bowls contained rice with curried beef and pork dumplings. Pa said a longish grace (John guessed, on account of the matrimonial decision just taken) and then Ma handed him his cup of tea and a salad plate piled with dumplings.

"I love these dumplings," John said as he took a bite before sipping the tea. The sweetness of the milk-tea was a delicate counterpoise to the bland taste of the dumpling. "Reminds me of bacon and grits."

"What are grits?" asked Mah Step.

"Hominy grits are coarsely ground corn with the germ removed. It's a popular southern breakfast food. I like it with butter and bits of bacon or boiled egg."

"Sounds like the equivalent of our rice gruel!"

"Some more tea?" interposed Nora softly.

Holding out his cup John looked up and was dazzled by the radiance she emanated.

"Thank you," John said fervently, and Nora smiled as she drew away the aluminum kettle.

"How about a walk after tea?" suggested Mah Step and John was quick to agree. The happiness bursting out inside him wanted to escape the claustrophobic indoors for the wide-open spaces and the sunlight outside.

They walked quickly to the familiar grassy spot. It wasn't as sunny outside as John had hoped. Gray clouds blanked out the sun, reducing its warmth.

"Sorry, we almost cut you off in the conversation there. Pa was asking me about the details before tea," said Mah Step.

"What sort of details?"

"He wanted to know when you wanted the marriage to be solemnized. Would there be an engagement before that? And would you settle down here or would you take my sister with you to America? Things like that."

"Oh, I see. I haven't really thought about it. I have to talk to Nora too before we decide. I will be happy to stay here in the Sakhi Hills in the Big Town, but it might be a better idea to divide our time between the US and the Sakhi Hills. As for the marriage, I'd marry Nora today if I could. What are the Sakhi customs?" asked John.

"Well ... we normally have the banns published for three consecutive weeks in the church. More importantly, we have to arrange a huge marriage feast for the whole village."

"There's not much time left before I go back, is there?" said John.

"No, unfortunately not. Were you planning to marry before you left?"

"Only if I could take Nora with me to the US."

"She doesn't even have a passport, let alone a visa!"

"Yeah, I knew it was impractical. Just wishful thinking, I suppose. But seriously, I will come back in about six months. After the wedding, Nora and I will travel back to the US together."

"That sounds like a good plan. I will start working on getting Nora a passport right away. I will also apply for one myself. We will apply together for our passports, Nora and I."

"Yes, you must. We will have to figure out the best time for your visit. Whether you should come before Nora and I get married or whether you should come visit us after."

"I am in no hurry, Mah John. Tickets are expensive and you need to think of Nora first. I can wait. The Lord knows the best time for me," said Mah Step.

"I just thought of something. I hope people don't see Nora as a trophy wife when we are back in America. That's my only fear. I really don't care for the opinions of others. But if they sneer at Nora and make her feel bad it would be painful," said John pensively.

"She's my sister and I may be a trifle partial in saying this. Nora is too smart to be just a trophy wife. I think she will assimilate well. Though, frankly, I cannot picture her right now speeding down an American highway at breakneck speed!"

John laughed. "I don't expect driving to pose any problems. I have seen immigrant women from Asia and Africa in their fifties take to driving like a duck takes to water. I am more concerned about Nora being hurt by insensitive people in social situations. I remember being disgusted by all those old white men at Bangkok airport with young Thai girls in tow."

"The two of you will not look anything like that. And Mah John, you don't look like a cradle-snatcher!"

"Thanks, Mah Step. If Nora doesn't like it in the States, I will be happy to come live here in the Sakhi Hills."

"Mah John, even after living two months with us I see that you still have a very high opinion of our tribal way of life. This is very flattering. At the same time, I must tell you that we Sakhis are not perfect. We have our own faults. We are far from being politically correct. And that's putting it mildly. Frankly, we are incredibly racist. For us it is still 'us vs. them'," said Mah Step.

"'Them' being the rest of the world?" asked John.

"Yes. We lump all the non-Sakhi people together and call them *wakhais*. It is a derisive term much like *tassantassas*."

"*Tassantassas*? What's *that*?" asked John.

"You haven't heard of that term before? I'm surprised. It's from your country. That's what the Powhatan Indians called the English settlers and everyone else outside of their tribe," explained Mah Step.

"Ah!"

"For us Sakhis, the *wakhais* are the most despicable dregs of the world. Especially if they are malnourished, idol-worshippers from the plains."

"Does the term include us Americans as well?"

"No! The white man falls under a different group, the *phirang*. The *phirang*s (by that I mean *sahep*s and *mem*s) are respected but they are outsiders too."

"I think every social group has the same attitude deep down, but they don't articulate it. Has there been any communal conflict here?" asked John.

"There always has been an undercurrent of tension and the dislike is usually not well camouflaged. It has broken out into an open conflict only twice in recent memory. When the trouble erupted fifteen years ago, plumes of black smoke could be seen rising from different localities of the Big Town. Some Sakhis died too but more *wakhais* were killed. Many of them had to sell off their houses and possessions at a throwaway price and leave."

"We have had some incidents like that. The Los Angeles and the Washington, DC riots."

"Anyway, some of my colleagues at the college were gloating about the cows they had purchased cheaply from the fleeing *wakhais*. I told them they were wrong. They would never prosper from ill-gotten wealth, I told them. I said the tears shed and the blood spilled by the *wakhais* will come back to haunt them for many years. My outspokenness did not enhance my popularity."

"The sins of fathers being visited on their children and their children's children?" asked John.

"Yes, it is the same with injustice anywhere. Whether it is the Armenian genocide or the Holocaust or the ruthless acts of a plundering army. The perpetrators of violence are heaping untold miseries on themselves individually and on their nation collectively," stated Mah Step emphatically.

"You really believe that?" asked John skeptically.

"I do. I think every country has to ultimately pay a high price for the pain and suffering it causes, even if it is unintended and part of a military operation. Luckily for us our conflict lasted only a few days. There has been an uneasy truce since then. Geographically the turfs have been redrawn and each group is wary of the other. I was relieved when the conflagration was quickly put out."

"Has there been similar conflicts between the people of the plains and the other hill tribes?" John wanted to know.

"Oh, yes! Ours was nothing compared to what happened in their territories. In the case of the Duhongi tribe, they killed many plainsmen traders Balkan-style. The traders from the plains are generally unscrupulous, cunning, vicious and extremely greedy. They will do anything for money. And they are all cow-worshipping vegetarians. The beef-eating Duhongi tribe obviously do not hold them in any high esteem. They make life miserable for the traders from the plains. The traders get even by charging exorbitantly high prices with impunity. They have an absolute monopoly and control the supply of almost everything from foodstuff to clothes. In spite of the high risk, they continue to stay and do business with the Duhongi tribe because of the unreasonable profits they make."

"Are more highlanders getting into business now?"

"Yes, more than before. But it is still a closed supply chain. The plains traders have contacts with their fellowmen from distant provinces. It's like the mafia. It's difficult to break into and compete. The playing field is far from level."

"It sounds similar to the Jews who controlled business and finance in Europe," remarked John.

"Yes, there's a resemblance there. There is another thing I haven't told you about my tribe. Traditionally we practiced divination. The present followers of the indigenous faith continue the custom."

"I don't think that's anything unique. All societies had that—and still have. The modern society has tarot card readers, soothsayers, and fortune-tellers. At the very minimum, there's the horoscope section in the daily paper!"

"Christian Sakhis don't practice divination but the traditional believers do. They have animal sacrifices—only chicken now, used to be goats and cows before—and the shaman foretells the future by breaking an egg."

"By breaking an *egg*?" John said amusedly.

"Yes, the diviner looks at the yolk and the egg white and makes a prediction. The voodoo and superstition don't bother me much because generally Christians don't go in for that stuff. It is the mistrust of the rest of the world that's more worrying."

"I stayed here eight weeks with you and I didn't feel any of that."

"That's because you have adjusted so well to our life. And you feel a stronger sense of acceptance because the Western society is fragmented while ours is still a tight-knit tribal culture."

"In spite of all your real or imagined shortcomings, the Sakhi tribe is still at the top of the list for me. And it'll always stay up there," said John with a smile.

"I can give you an example of the close bonds of our social structure. When I took up a certificate course in German at the local university in the Big Town, my pastor asked me to think of the benefit this will bring to others in the community. I hadn't looked at it that way when I joined the course. I had selfishly been thinking only of the benefits that would accrue to me personally if I learned German. Now I see it as raising the collective consciousness or the collective knowledge of my people."

"I cannot see that perspective becoming very popular in the United States. What one accomplishes by way of higher learning goes to embellish one's own résumé and hopefully lead to career advancement."

Mah Step and John took the long round way back home, strolling down first to the village market. They were just in time for lunch.

"There is one issue that we did not discuss," said John.

"What is it, Mah John?" asked Mah Step.

"The problem of pain and suffering," said John quietly.

"That *is* a difficult subject. I have thought about it a lot. I don't have any conclusive answers," admitted Mah Step.

"I have wondered why 'good' people are afflicted by incurable ailments like cancer or Alzheimer's, while the dissolute and the incorrigible live a charmed life. I see stories on local TV all the time of innocent people killed in traffic accidents or senseless shootings. I have asked myself many times why there's no justice in this world?"

"I will say this again. It is a very, very difficult question. I don't have all the answers. If I did I shouldn't be here talking to you now! I have struggled with the same thoughts when I see the wicked thrive. The Book of Psalms helped me a lot in clarifying my thinking."

"And what conclusions did you reach?" John asked.

"It rains on the just and the unjust alike. Just as rain cannot fall only on good and fertile fields, ignoring rocky and fallow grounds, likewise troubles, mishaps, and diseases do not happen selectively," pondered Mah Step.

"Are you suggesting that these are random acts without rhyme or reason?" challenged John.

"I must concede that to the human understanding these occurrences do appear accidental and arbitrary. But it may not really be so."

"How do you explain the pointless murder of an innocent bystander or the rape of a pious woman?" John asked a trifle testily.

"I cannot. I cannot because I do not have all the facts. Without implying that their predicaments are retribution or just desserts for secret sins, let me say that our judgment of the goodness or innocence of a person is extremely superficial. Only God can see the innermost core of a person's being. How often have we been surprised by the secret sins of upstanding leaders, be they religious or political? Countless paragons of virtue have turned out to be the most despicable scoundrels. If they had died in unfortunate circumstances before their sins came to light and they fell into disgrace, who would have thought that they really deserved what they got? That said, let me also add that we often fail to perceive the impact such incidents have on others."

"Isn't that too high a price to pay? How is it fair to the victim?" countered John.

"Again, only the Divine can answer that. But you and I know how straitened circumstances and misfortunes have produced diamonds of radiant beauty—be it music, literature, art or even a life par excellence that is an inspiration to countless others."

"I cannot deny that. But it is still not a completely satisfying answer," John said unconvinced.

"Mah John, I cannot give you an entirely satisfactory answer to this vexed question. To what I said earlier about the rain falling on the just and the unjust, I will add this. Calamities apparently do not distinguish between good and bad people. I say apparently because our human understanding has severe limitations. Yet, there is a difference. The difference is the *response* to the tragedy; it is the response that separates the spiritual from the carnal. We like to see immediate cause and effect. But justice, in the long run, is beyond human comprehension."

"Whoa! That's too deep for me! I wish these things were more easily understood by the common man."

"Then there would not be any mystery to this life, would there? Nor would there be any personal privacy. Just think! Let me tell you a true story. I mentioned how the people of the plains were not receptive to missionaries and how they clung to their belief in a multitude of gods and in the divinity of animals like the cow and the elephant and reptiles like the snake. In spite of their implacable intransigence, missionaries from England, Scotland, Wales and the United States continued to serve them bringing health and education. I have often wondered what motivated them to persist when they did not have the success their counterparts in the hills were enjoying."

"They must have really believed in what they were doing," opined John.

"They did. They must have also believed that the results of their work are not measured in human terms. If that were not the case, they would have moved to more fertile areas where they would have had stunning results to declare. Anyway, I am straying from the story. Several years ago, I had occasion to travel to a remote village in the plains. When I visited the local school—it consisted of only two dilapidated rooms—I was surprised to find an inscription on the wall of the inner room. It was a dedication by the missionary from England to the memory of his teenaged daughter. This is tragic in itself, but what truly wrenched my heart was the fact that it was the daughter who persuaded her widowed father to forsake the comfort of their home in England and travel together as missionaries halfway around the world to this remote and desolate region. She endured that long journey only to die of malaria within three months of their arrival. I was deeply moved by what I read. I was troubled too. I kept asking myself 'Why did it happen that way?' and 'Why did she have to die so soon after traveling many months by sea to get here?' I did not find easy answers. To be honest it depressed me. Only months later did I think: 'What did those three months of the life of this idealistic young woman mean to the people of that village?' 'What effect did her passing have on the lives of the people she came to serve?' 'How many lives did she touch?' I had to admit I did not know the answers to those questions. What I do know is that the father stayed on ministering to the people and teaching the children until his death. He did not go back to England. I can only surmise that he would not have stayed on if he thought his daughter had died in vain."

"That is a deeply moving story. I am touched," John said thoughtfully.

"I'd like to believe that her death was not in vain," said Mah Step quietly.

They walked the rest of the way home in silence. Ma and Nora had cooked up some special items in addition to the staple dishes. There were deep fried sardines, devilled eggs and sautéed spinach.

It was dusk when people started dropping in. They were all still in the kitchen just having finished dinner. Pastor Highborn and Mah Listrin, the schoolteacher, were among the first to arrive. Mah Jo, the village headman, came with his wife and children. Soon others started trickling in. Everyone seemed genuinely happy as they congratulated John. They also shook hands with Pa, Ma, Mah Step and Nora. Ma and Nora worked overtime on the *kwai* and tea. The neighbors moved unfettered from room to room talking excitedly. Looking around John said to himself, "The Sakhi equivalent of a cocktail party!" John marveled again at the speed and efficiency of the village grapevine and the conviviality of the Sakhis.

It was well past ten thirty at night when the last guest departed. The five of them were alone again. Ma offered tea but there were no takers. Looking back John was not sure how it happened. One moment they were all there chatting and smiling. The next, or so it seemed, only Nora and he remained. Mah Step was the first to slink away. When Pa and Ma unobtrusively left, John thought they would soon be back. It took a while for John to realize that they had all retired for the night allowing Nora and him some personal time together.

They smiled at each other as John said, "*Hooblei*, Nora! I can't tell you how happy I am!"

"Thank you," Nora responded.

"Today is the happiest day in my life," said John.

"I am happy too, Mah John," said Nora shyly.

They were silent for a while. Then, on an impulse, John held out his right-hand palm facing up. Without any hesitation, Nora placed her right hand in his. John lightly placed his left hand over hers. They sat that way for a while till Nora gently disengaged her hand.

"I think it is time for us to sleep," Nora said.

John could have sat there forever but he knew he had to be patient. As he stood up from the low stool he felt pins and needles in both legs that had gone numb from sitting stationary for so long on the low *lora*. He had to hold onto the wall to keep from losing his balance.

"Are you OK, Mah John?" asked Nora anxiously

"I'll be fine. My legs are a little stiff. But I'll be fine. Good night, Nora! See you in the morning!"

"Good night, Mah John!"

As John limped to his room, Nora extinguished the fire in the brazier and kept a pot of water over it for good measure.

Chapter 17: Such Sweet Sorrow

What would, in different circumstances, have been the hoped for, eagerly awaited, day of deliverance, after eight weeks of isolated living in a "primitive" third-world village, turned out, instead, to be the day of dread and despondency for John.

Tomorrow John would leave the village and go, via the Big Town, to the airport in the plains to catch the flight to Bangkok and from there on to Frankfurt and Washington Dulles.

The usual silence at meals seemed to hang even heavier that morning as the family sat around on *lora*s for brunch. Everybody seemed to be avoiding eye contact as empty plates were passed to Nora for second helpings of rice, stir-fried vegetables, and curried chicken.

When John caught Ma looking at him wistfully, she sighed softly and turned her head away, resignedly brushing her hair with her right hand. She turned away to rearrange the firewood and sift the ashes.

Nora's face was inscrutable as she pulled the *sainjyrshah* shawl tight over mouth as she sat staring intently at the floor of the kitchen. Only when John declined the third helping did their eyes meet over the empty plate. Her limpid eyes seemed to be asking, "Why do you have to go?" and he had no answer.

Afterward, Mah Step and John carried their *lora*s to the verandah to bask together in the warmth of the morning sun one last time.

It was Mah Step who broke the silence. "Everyone is sad because you will be leaving tomorrow."

"I wish I could stay and not have to go," John responded. After a brief pause, he added, "You've all been very good to me. It's equally difficult for me."

There seemed to be nothing left to say. The uneasy silence was broken by the arrival of Mah Listrin, the school teacher. After the customary greeting, Mah Step and Mah Listrin engaged in a discussion that John guessed, from references to Bangkok and Frankfurt and Dulles, was regarding his travel.

Mah Step tried to lighten the atmosphere by telling a funny story.

"John, have you heard this one on Sakhi names?"

"The gear joke?"

"No, this one is about laughing names."

"Laughing names? No, I don't think so. How does it go?"

"A Sakhi student seeking admission to a university in Bangkok was asked his father's name. 'My father is Laughing,' the boy replied. 'What is he laughing about?' the university official asked. 'His name is Laughing,' the boy replied. 'Hmm ... what is your mother's name then?' 'She is Smiling,' he replied with a straight face. 'You must be kidding!' the professor exclaimed. 'No, that's my brother. I am Joking."

"That's a good one!" John said laughing.

"That didn't go too well. This is not the best time for jokes, is it?" asked Mah Step sheepishly.

"I guess not," said John. As an afterthought, he added, "But there's no cause for sadness. This is not going to be a long parting. I will come back as soon as I can."

"Let's go for one last walk, Mah John," said Mah Step rising.

They walked down the same path they had walked so many times before. When they reached the grassy knoll, John dropped to the ground and lay spread-eagled in utter abandonment looking up at the fleecy white clouds drifting lazily against the blue sky ringed by the dark green of the tree tops.

For a long minute, John savored the serene silence.

"I'm going to miss this place almost as much as I will miss the Sakhi people," thought John.

Mah Step was subdued as he broke off a blade of grass and chewed it meditatively.

Suddenly everything fell into place.

Smiling, he turned to John and said, "I don't feel sad anymore."

John turned to look at Mah Step raising his eyebrows quizzically.

"You know, I realized something. Our tribal custom doesn't allow us to be sad at partings. That's a bad omen. But the insight I got now was something else. I should be happy—not sad—for the last two months. You traveled twelve thousand kilometers to come to my village and you lived like one of us. You made my family and tribe happy. You decided to marry Nora and be one of us. What have I got to be unhappy about? Even if—God forbid—we were not to meet again due to some cataclysmic event, I will still have the memories of the past two months to cherish."

John sat up. "Mah Step, you are a philosopher!"

Mah Step only smiled.

"Mah Step, I have seen you being patient and forbearing all the time. Have you ever lost your temper or been unkind?"

"Mah John, I wish what you say is true! I am not always kind or gentle. In recent years, I have mellowed down a bit. But even then, I am not close to where I want to be," said Mah Step.

"Can you give one example of your harshness?" teased John.

"I will have to think. OK ... this happened at a small group session in Bangkok. We were being completely open and transparent with each other, sharing intimate details and providing direct feedback. One of the participants was being excessively obnoxious. He seemed to have a blind spot the size of an elephant. The facilitator asked him, 'Do you suffer fools?' Before the chap could reply, I chipped in with, 'He seems to be perfectly at peace with himself.' It took a moment for what I said to register," said Mah Step.

"You have an acerbic wit! That reminded me of the famous 'There, but for the grace of God, goes God' quip of Churchill!" John laughed heartily.

"We were told to be brutally honest. That's why I did not hold back," explained Mah Step.

As they walked back home the gray cloud of parting had lifted.

John's packing was easy. As promised he gifted the ThinkPad to Mah Step. All his data had been transferred and burned onto two CDs using a CD-writer that Mah Step had borrowed from the Big Town for this purpose. Mah Step was absolutely thrilled with the laptop. He lovingly cleaned the screen and the outside first with a damp cloth. Then he formatted the hard disk erasing all data before reinstalling the operating system and software. John was impressed with the methodical way in which Mah Step personalized the laptop and gratified that he had given it to someone who would possibly make better use of it than he himself had.

Following Mah Step's suit John wiped clean the Sony *ICF 77* radio till it looked shiny and new. He then carefully wrapped it up in brown paper (in lieu of gift-wrapping) before taking it to the kitchen. Nora did not see the package he was holding behind him and thought he had come for a cup of tea. When he held the packet out and presented it to Nora, she was all agog. She was so excited she was literally shaking as she received the brown-paper package.

"This is for you, Nora," John said. "Go ahead and open it."

Nora placed the package gently on the low dining table and carefully slit the adhesive tape with a kitchen knife. When she saw the radio, her hand flew to her mouth.

"No, no, Mah John. This is too expensive. I might spoil it," she said.

"It is for you Nora. I'd like you to keep it. Mah Step can show you how to use it. He knows more about it than I do anyway!"

"Thank you very much, Mah John! I don't have anything to give you in return. I will use it carefully. I will listen to the Voice of America and the BBC and improve my English," Nora said excitedly, making no effort to hide her joy.

John marveled at the gratitude and honor with which gifts were received in the Sakhi Hills. He received the same tribute when he presented the travel clock to Pa and the LED flashlight to Ma. All his books went to Mah Step.

That evening turned out to be the best farewell party John had ever attended. It was all unstructured and unplanned; yet, everything seemed to be intricately choreographed. It felt as if the whole village had come to bid him good-bye. They dropped in one or two at a time, talked to Pa and Ma, chewed *kwai*, had a cup of tea and left after shaking John's hand and wishing him God's bountiful blessings and a safe journey back. Some, like Mah Aks and Mah Zan, had even brought their children along. The children giggled as they shook John's hand. Mah Jo, the village headman, presented him with a red coral. Mah Listrin's present was an old edition of the English-Sakhi dictionary published by a Welsh missionary over fifty years ago, and surely out of print.

By the time the last guest left it was close to midnight. Pa, Ma, Mah Step, Nora, and John were alone in the kitchen. Pa muttered something softly looking at the ground. He seemed almost as vulnerable as he had been at the death of his beloved grandson.

"He said you are leaving tomorrow," Mah Step translated.

The silence was heavy and awkward. Nobody had anything to say. Pa and Nora looked down at the floor; Ma busied herself scraping *kwai*; Mah Step and John sat with their arms around their knees. After a little while, Pa stood up.

"We have to be leaving very early tomorrow. It's time to sleep," said Mah Step.

"Right. I'll turn in then. Be sure to wake me up. I don't have a travel clock anymore."

John repaired to his room. Sleep did not come easy. It was only after an hour of turning and tossing that he was able to sleep, and that too fitfully.

Mah Step shook him awake at four thirty in the morning. The rest of the family were already up. Ma and Nora were busy packing lunch and preparing breakfast. Pa sat in the front room reading the Bible. John settled for a plain cup of tea. It was too early for breakfast. The others had a normal full meal by the time the taxi came.

John initially insisted on sitting in the back seat but was persuaded to take the front seat with Mah Step in the middle, wedged between John and the driver. Pa, Ma, and Nora sat in the rear with Ma ensconced in the middle. They were able to beat the morning traffic and reached the Big Town in under an hour.

"Do you want to stop at our house and do email?" asked Mah Step.

"No, let's keep going. I can do email at Bangkok airport."

At Dongpoh, the tiny hamlet half-way to the airport from the Big Town, they stopped for a restroom break and lunch. Ma and Nora took out the lunch packets from the cloth bag and handed them around. They ate sitting cramped together in the car and then went into the restaurant for tea. The return journey seemed much shorter than the drive up from the airport to the Big Town on his arrival, not all because it was downhill all the way to the plains. Everyone was subdued because of the imminent parting.

"There's something I have been meaning to tell you. Somehow, I have kept putting it off. It's a book recommendation," said Mah Step.

"*The Lost Horizon* by James Hilton?" asked John wryly.

"No, this one's by the Irishman, Bernard Shaw. The book is titled *The Adventures of the Black Girl in Her Search for God*," said Mah Step.

"Never heard of it!"

"It's not as well-known as his plays. Probably out of print now. I found a dusty, worn-out copy at the public library," explained Mah Step.

"Thanks. I'll try to locate that book after I get back. I have a reading suggestion for you as well. It's called *The God-Seeker*, the story of a missionary from Minnesota. Want to guess who wrote it?"

"Thurber?"

"No. Sinclair Lewis. The book's not as well-known as *Babbitt* or *Main Street*. Nonetheless, it is a good read."

They reached the airport a little before ten o'clock. Much to John's chagrin, the airport allowed entry only to passengers because of heightened security. That meant they had to bid their goodbyes sooner than they had planned. The unexpectedly sudden parting under the awning in front of the airport was clumsy and awkward.

"I am not good at farewells," John said clearing his throat nervously.

"Since they won't let us in, you go on in. We will go back to the Big Town. Your flight is not until a quarter to one o'clock and it is too hot out here in the sun."

"All right, then. Thank you again for everything. It has been an amazing experience. I will miss you all. *Hooblei!*"

"It was our pleasure, Mah John! *Hooblei!*" responded Mah Step.

Pa and Ma shook hands with John first and then it was Mah Step's turn.

"Good-bye!" said Mah Step choking.

Finally, it was Nora's turn. Try as she might she could not prevent the pearly tears from rolling down her cheeks. John wanted to hold her in his arms and kiss her good-bye but propriety would not have allowed that.

All he could say was, "I'll be back soon. Take care! Good-bye!"

Then gently releasing her hand, John picked up his bag, turned and walked briskly into the terminal. When he had reached the counter, he looked back to see them walking in the blazing sun towards the taxi. He saw Nora turn around to look, but he knew that she could not see him through the glass walls because of the brightness outside.

The flight to Bangkok was over in a daze. Back in the ambience of the developed world, John wondered if the past eight weeks had been a dream. He trudged to the Internet corner and paid for a two-hour connection to send emails announcing his impending return. He sent an email to Mah Step as well for good measure. He did not write a separate email to Elaine.

The wait seemed interminable. Starbucks and McDonald's were sorely tempting, but John had a curious sense of self-actualization that held him from succumbing.

Once inside the plane, he sank back in his seat overwhelmed by the sheer elation of the life-altering experience he had just been through and the heart-wrenching sadness of leaving behind Nora and her family and the loving Sakhi people.

As the lumbering Jumbo lugubriously climbed to cruising altitude, it was almost a disembodied John that was headed back home, leaving his heart and soul behind.

The epiphany had indeed come to pass.

The author welcomes comments at:
aa-books@outlook.com

For more information about the author's books:
www.abiealexander.com

www.ingramcontent.com/pod-product-compliance
Lightning Source LLC
Chambersburg PA
CBHW032146190626
46814CB00005BA/1857

* 9 7 8 1 9 4 6 5 9 3 3 8 2 *